MAR

THE BURMA OFFENSIVE

MARINE H: SBS

THE BURMA OFFENSIVE

Ian Blake

First published in Great Britain 1996
22 Books, Invicta House, Sir Thomas Longley Road,
Rochester, Kent

Copyright © 1996 by 22 Books

The moral right of the author has been asserted

A CIP catalogue record for this book is available
from the British Library

ISBN 1 898125 64 3

10 9 8 7 6 5 4 3 2 1

Typeset by Hewer Text Composition Services, Edinburgh
Printed in Great Britain by Cox and Wyman Limited, Reading

1

'Name and rank.'

'Tiller. Sergeant Tiller.'

The captain's pen stayed poised over the form in front of him, a frown of anger wrinkling his forehead. It was so deep that the bald patch, which gleamed an unattractive pink through his thinning hair, puckered too. The three pips on his epaulettes twinkled under the glare of the bare bulb which dangled from the ceiling. His batman, Tiller decided, must have spent hours buffing them to such perfection.

'Tiller, *sir*,' the captain grated, not raising his eyes. 'It's normal to address officers as "sir".'

Sergeant Colin 'Tiger' Tiller, Royal Marines, watched the furrows ripple up the officer's bald pate, and noticed the scrawny neck poking out from his collar, an odd contrast to the pudginess of the fingers holding the pen. He stiffened instinctively. 'Tiller, *sir*,' he snapped.

In his mind's eye he was back again on the parade ground at Eastney Barracks, facing the drill sergeant, his scarlet sash across his tunic, his metre stick tucked under his arm, his barrel chest gleaming with medals.

'Seventeen years old and never been kissed, eh, Tiller?' The accent was Scottish, the tone as abrasive as a cheese grater. 'Well, stand up straight, laddie, straighten your arms and feel the seams of your

1

trousers with your thumbs, and one day you may be lucky. In the meantime you are on parade, you poor wee sod, not slouching around in a brothel. Are we ever going to make a proper Marine out of you, you miserable, spotty-faced schoolboy? Well, are we?'

Tiller could still remember the smell of the sergeant-major as the man stuck his face within inches of his own. It wasn't a smell of sweat or tobacco or rum; it was the smell of absolute, total, crushing authority – but, curiously, also of someone who cared. Not for him, of course, but for the 250-year-old traditions of the Royal Marines and the ineradicable belief that they were the best fighting force in the world.

The pudgy fingers moved. 'That's better,' said the captain silkily, pushing the pen with deliberate sweeps. 'Some of you people seem to think that just because there's a war on, Army Regulations don't apply to you.'

The officer picked up a blotter and rocked it across Tiller's name with a force which made Tiller wonder if he was hoping to obliterate it. He then added the date, 1 December 1943, and blotted that. He still hadn't looked up. 'Well, let me tell you, Sergeant, they bloody well do.'

'Yessir.'

There was something in the way Tiller spoke that made the captain raise his eyes. For the first time they took in the height and breadth of the man in front of him, the leather-brown face, the blue gimlet eyes – now fixed on some indeterminate point behind the captain's head – and the sand-coloured beret with its curious winged cloth badge.

The captain's look had meant to be a withering

2

one. But it changed to bafflement when he saw the cap badge. What on earth did it signify? Then his gaze fell on the red and blue Combined Operations badge – a montage of the RAF eagle, a tommy-gun and an anchor – that adorned the upper sleeves of the sergeant's uniform. The captain knew that meant the man was commando-trained, and almost certainly serving with special forces of some kind.

He didn't like being reminded that while he pushed a pen others were actually fighting. He averted his eyes downwards but this only made matters worse, for they next encountered the parachute wings displayed above the sergeant's left breast pocket. And below the wings was sewn, not very neatly, a ribbon of vertical black and red stripes which showed that the wearer had been awarded the Distinguished Conduct Medal for bravery in the field.

The captain's prominent Adam's apple bobbed up and down. He passed a hand nervously over his nicotine-stained moustache. His bald patch glowed with a thin veneer of sweat. The silence was palpable. So palpable that the clerk clicking away at his typewriter at the back of the office stopped and discreetly watched.

If the captain had just wished the sergeant good luck on his next assignment and hoped he would be comfortable during his short time in the transit depot, that would have been that. The sergeant would have saluted and left the office and the clerk, who seemed afflicted by a hacking cough, would have had to go back to hitting his typewriter with his forefingers, and would not have been able to delight the corporals' mess that evening with the humiliation of his superior.

But the captain was not a pen-pusher for nothing; he had not spent nearly four years in the north of England in the meticulous administration of supply dumps, base camps and transport maintenance workshops, for nothing either. He always felt he had had another job to do too, and that was to uphold discipline and enforce the King's Regulations wherever they might be flouted.

What was more, he had just caught the end of a flicker of a smile on Tiller's face as he had remembered that drill sergeant at Eastney and the part he had played in making him an efficient, dedicated fighting machine.

'Is that a regulation cap badge, Sergeant?'

'Yes, sir.'

'What is it?'

'Special Air Service, sir.'

The captain hesitated, shuffled the papers in front of him, found Tiller's movement order, and then looked up in triumph. 'But this says you are a member of a unit called the Special Boat Squadron.'

'Yes, sir.'

'Well?'

The clerk coughed and smiled encouragement at Tiller. He could see that the captain was walking into a trap of his own making.

'My commanding officer never got round to having a cap badge designed, sir. And as the Special Boat Squadron was part of the SAS before the SAS was split up at the beginning of the year, we continued to wear the SAS badge. When we were in uniform, that is, sir.'

The enormity of Tiller's last sentence percolated

4

slowly into the captain's mind. From being a flabby white, his face became suffused with a reddish hue. His colourless eyes, surrounded by puffy flesh, bulged in disbelief.

'When you were in uniform?' he queried. 'You mean that on occasion you were on active service in His Majesty's forces out of uniform?'

Tiller remembered that the last time he had seen his commanding officer the major had been wearing corduroy trousers, brothel-creepers and a trilby hat. He remembered too the disgracefully dirty fisherman's trousers his squadron commander, Captain Magnus Larssen, had worn. They had been supported by a wide leather belt to which was always attached Larssen's commando knife, a 9mm Colt pistol and two 36 grenades. He wore the trousers week in week out until they had practically walked off him.

Tiller liked the way the captain had emphasized 'His Majesty' as it made the hole Tiller hoped the officer was digging for himself that much deeper.

'Yes, sir.'

The Dodecanese campaign, waged for the possession of a scattering of Greek islands in the Aegean Sea, had been a bitterly contested one, in which the SBS, with their motorized caiques, had played a prominent part, although no one could say it had been an orthodox affair.

'And your commanding officer knew this?'

'Yes, sir.'

The clerk's grin broadened. He forgot to cough. He didn't know what the end of this conversation was going to be but he knew now it was going to be one worth repeating.

The captain leant forward. At first he seemed dumb-struck. Then he spoke very slowly. 'You're quite sure you know what you are saying, Sergeant? Are you telling me your commanding officer allowed his men to wear civilian clothes while on active service?'

'Yes, sir.'

The captain became suddenly jocular. 'And I suppose he wore them himself, too?'

'Yes, sir.' Tiller hesitated, but couldn't resist it. 'He was particularly fond of wearing a trilby, sir.'

It was too much for the captain. He opened a drawer and drew out a notepad. 'And what is the full name and rank of your commanding officer, Sergeant?'

The decorations awarded most officers and men were not commented on by the press. There was a lot of bravery, but not enough space to describe it: the paper shortage was acute. The names of those officers decorated appeared in the court page of *The Times* and that was about it.

Very occasionally, however, the army's public relations wallahs made sure that the press splashed the story of the award of some particular decoration across their pages. Often, as with the Dodecanese campaign, it was a deliberate ploy to divert the public's attention from an ignominious defeat. The army's PR machinery had lit upon Tiller's commanding officer, who had just received a well-merited bar to his DSO for his unit's work in the Aegean. As a result, just days previously, the story had hit the headlines, though there had been no mention of the special forces unit he had commanded – the censors had seen to that.

'Jarrett, sir.'

Filled with righteous anger as he was, the penny

did not drop with the captain. It did with his clerk, who had difficulty stopping his coughing turning into laughter.

'Come on, Sergeant,' the captain snapped. 'I said I wanted his full name and rank.'

Accompanying the newspaper plaudits there had been photographs of Tiller's CO receiving his award from King George VI. That, of course, had been more than half the point of publishing the story in the first place. Tiller himself had not known until he had read the caption underneath one of the pictures: 'The King decorating his cousin at Buckingham Palace during his weekly investiture yesterday.'

'Major the Earl Jarrett, sir.'

The captain's jaw dropped. He quickly extracted his handkerchief.

'We called him George, sir,' Tiller added helpfully.

A lorry rumbled by outside. The clerk's cough threatened to become uncontrollable. The captain wiped his mouth and then blew his nose.

'I see,' he said, though he didn't at all. Life had never seemed to treat him fairly. Perhaps because he was always trying to avoid it.

It was the tea lady who saved the captain, or so the corporal told his mates later. At that moment she came through the door without knocking, her trolley clanking and clattering across the floor, and the captain was able to tear her off such a strip that by the time she had gone he had regained his composure sufficiently to shuffle the notebook back into the drawer and to ask Tiller his eventual destination.

'Kingairloch, western Scotland, sir.'

The captain wished Tiller luck with his forthcoming

assignment and hoped he would be comfortable during his short stay in the transit camp. Tiller thanked him, saluted and left. As he closed the door behind him he could hear the captain berating his clerk for not reporting sick.

2

To port the clouds hung low over the mountains of Kingairloch, and the north-east wind, funnelled by the narrow confines of Loch Linnhe, was bitterly cold and carried with it more than a hint of snow. The naval barge which had picked up the five-man party from Oban bobbed and swayed as it punched its way into the short, steep waves. Occasionally a spume of spray thrown up the bows was caught by the wind and whipped across the barge and into the faces of those aboard. It was like being hit by icicles fired from a crossbow.

'You should see it when it's really blowing,' the petty officer in charge shouted. 'I'd prefer the Atlantic convoys any day.'

He had undone the strap above the peak of his naval cap and had tightened it under his chin to keep the cap from flying into the loch. Tiller had never seen that before. Well, there was a first time for everything, he supposed. As he had now officially become a member of one of the Special Boat Sections of the Commandos, he was wearing the coveted green beret. But as all Commandos were volunteers they were just seconded from their regiments and retained their regimental badges. So Tiller wore the burnished badge of the Royal Marines: the Globe and Laurel.

'Where are we heading?' one of the party asked.

'Loch a'Choire. It's an inlet further up on the port side. Leads to Kingairloch House.'

'Is that where we're being billeted, Kingairloch House?'

'Some hope. That's been requisitioned for a jiggery-pokery unit no one knows the name of. They spend most of their time blowing things up. Night and day they do it. Bloody nuisance if you're trying to have a kip, but you get used to it.'

Tiller's interest was awakened. As a demolitions expert, blowing things up was just his line. However, he doubted whether the real reason he had come to Kingairloch was his line at all. But his old CO, Major Henry 'Blondie' Tasler, had urged him over the telephone to undertake the course on Welman miniature submarines – 'It's where the action is, Tiger' – so he had put his name down. Anything to avoid a routine posting.

Tiller hadn't earned the DCM and a mention in Dispatches by doing what he was told. But Blondie was different. Blondie didn't officially request, or order, or demand. He'd simply said: 'You're just the man, Tiger. Why not have a go?'

Tiller called Tasler 'sir' when the occasion demanded it because the Taslers of this world – and there were bloody few of them – commanded his respect. The two men had fought together in the 1940 Norwegian campaign and as a very junior corporal, still learning the ropes of leadership, Tiller had noticed that Hasler never ever asked anyone to do anything that he had not himself done first. He made sure everyone had their grub before he started eating his own; and if there was anything dangerous that needed only one man to do it, Tasler did it himself. If it needed two or more then there wasn't a man who stood back when Tasler asked for help. If Tiller had learnt discipline from the drill sergeant he had learnt leadership from Blondie. He had also learnt that the best leaders didn't mind being led, so long as they followed someone they respected.

'We're not under canvas, are we?' another member of the party asked in alarm.

'You'll wish you were by the time you've finished,' said the petty officer cheerfully. 'No, you'll be aboard the depot ship. HMS *Titania* she's called.'

'*Titania* or *Titanic*?' asked the wit of the party.

'Aye, I've heard that one often enough,' said the petty officer. 'But she don't move and I've not seen icebergs in Loch Linnhe yet.'

'You surprise me,' said Tiller wryly, pulling his greatcoat more tightly about him.

'The wind's cold enough and so's the temperature sometimes,' said the petty officer, 'but the water's too warm – the Gulf Stream sees to that. You'll be glad it does.'

The first hint of what they would be doing renewed Tiller's doubts. Well, it was too late now and Tasler had hinted that if Tiller didn't get himself fixed up quick he might be posted to a training depot, for his operational record had come to the notice of the RMO. Officially he was due to be 'rested'. Tiller knew what that meant: he had seen too many good fighting men languish in some ghastly backwater. It might come to him eventually but he was going to avoid such a fate as long as possible.

A veil of rain swept down the loch, obliterating the land on both sides and churning the water ahead. When it had passed, the party saw the dim outline of a ship anchored close inshore in front of them.

'Is that the *Titania*?'

The petty officer shook his head. 'That's the *Bonaventure*. The HQ for the X-craft boys.'

'The lot that got the *Tirpitz*?'

'That's them.'

The launch quite suddenly turned sharply to port and made for the shore. Now broadside on to the waves and wind, she took on an awkward wallowing motion. Tiller cursed under his breath as a wave slopped over the side right by him. One good thing about operating under the water he remembered from the one time he had been a passenger in a submarine: there were no waves and no frigging wind that cut you in two.

Just when it looked, in the dim late afternoon light, like the launch was being run ashore, Loch a'Choire opened up ahead of them. As they approached it, darkness and another veil of rain began to swallow up the surrounding land and then pinpoints of light appeared at the far end of the loch. The mysterious Kingairloch House, Tiller supposed. He was surprised that whoever was stationed there did not obey the blackout regulations. But then Kingairloch was a long way from anywhere, certainly well beyond the range of the nearest Luftwaffe base in Norway.

The launch's wallowing motion lessened and then ceased, and the land closed in on either side of them. They were in the loch. Then around a bend the party saw their home for the next few weeks: a long, low slab of riveted steel almost indistinguishable in the dying light from the land behind her.

'What is she?' Tiller asked the petty officer. 'Or rather,' he corrected himself as he peered through the gathering gloom at the ship's antiquated outline, 'what was she?'

'In Edwardian times the pride and joy of Lord Dunleaven and his family,' the petty officer replied. 'Monte Carlo every summer until 1914, but she's been going downhill ever since then.'

'A steam yacht?' Tiller asked incredulously.

'Too right, Sergeant. Requisitioned by the Admiralty in 1939, did her bit at Dunkirk, and then served as a harbour defence vessel at Greenock. That is, until even their lordships could see she was a danger to navigation, not to mention her crew. Now she's called an accommodation ship. That's a laugh, too.'

The launch came alongside a companionway which led up to the quarterdeck. They climbed aboard, saluted the quarterdeck as naval custom demanded, and were met by the officer of the day with the traditional telescope tucked under his arm. He sent them forward to the Regulating Office, where they were assigned to cabins the size of coffins. The wizened-faced ordinary seaman who showed Tiller to his cabin chuckled as he did so and said: 'You wait till you get in a Welman, Sarge. It'll make this seem as roomy as a suite at the Ritz. Don't suffer from that claustrophobia, do you?'

Tiller shook his head. The nearest he had ever come to feeling claustrophobic was when hiding in a French farmer's cupboard while Gestapo men in long raincoats searched the farm. That had been when

MARINE H: SBS

he was on the run after the canoe raid on German shipping at Bordeaux. Come to think of it, it hadn't been claustrophobia he'd suffered from – just sheer paralysing fright. In action he found there'd rarely been time to be frightened, but just waiting in that cupboard for the worst to happen had been something else. He shuddered inside at the memory.

'Good thing, too,' said the seaman. 'One of the last lot we trained, he got it, panicked, pushed the joystick the wrong way, and nosedived into the mud. Took us twelve hours to get the poor sod up to the surface. Not much help to him as the oxygen supply only lasts ten hours.'

Claustrophobia was one of the first things the chief petty officer instructor asked them about the next morning.

'It's not something some people like to admit to,' he said, surveying their faces closely. 'Some silly buggers even think can overcome it by volunteering for a course like this. But now's the time to say if you do suffer from it. No disgrace. You sure?'

The group of five SBS men shifted uncomfortably in their seats, but all nodded with sufficient confidence for the CPO to say: 'That's all right then. Let me just give you a bit of background. This ship's the training depot for Charioteers as well as yourselves. A chariot – or Jeep as they're also called – is different from a Welman. It's powered by compressed air and has a crew of two who ride on top of it. They wear special suits and have individual oxygen equipment. We call them Jeepmen; they call us Sardine Men. Any of you ever seen a Welman?'

Everyone shook their head.

'Well, you'll see one in a few minutes, and when you do you'll see why they talk about Sardine Men. The Welman's a one-man submersible, nearly seventeen feet long unarmed, and just over twenty with its warhead. It weighs, with the warhead, 4600lb. It's battery-powered and has a range of thirty miles.'

Sketched on a blackboard beside the instructor was the electrical layout of the craft with its twenty-four batteries. When he had finished explaining how the batteries were connected to the starter motor, which came from a London Transport bus, and worked the prop shaft, he took them on deck.

Under a small crane amidships lay, side by side, several large, cigar-shaped steel objects. Their propellers and hydroplanes were plainly visible and each had a tiny conning tower amidships.

'What nut came up with this gimmick?' Tiller asked as the group approached the strange-looking objects.

'Officially, that's hush-hush,' said the CPO. 'Unofficially, it was the idea of a boffin at a secret weapons establishment at Welwyn Garden City which belongs to the same mob who have taken over Kingairloch House. Something to do with the Ministry of Economic Warfare. Don't ask me who they are because I don't know. Even if I did I wouldn't tell you.'

When the group had gathered round one of the Welmans, the instructor started pointing out its main external features. 'You can see that the warhead is attached to the bows and fits very snugly on to it. The warhead has two very powerful magnets on top of it – here and here. The idea is for the Welman to come alongside its target and once the warhead has become locked on to the target with the magnets, the driver releases the charge by turning a small wheel situated directly in front of his seat. Then he puts the Welman into reverse and scarpers. Quite easy, really.'

'How is the charge detonated?' Tiller asked. 'A time fuse of some sort?'

The instructor nodded. 'The fuse, normally a five-hour one, is automatically activated when the warhead is detached.'

'But supposing the target gets underway, won't the pressure of the water knock the warhead off the hull?' one of the group asked.

'Or the Welman's seen and divers are sent down to detach the charge?' another queried.

'There must be a sympathetic fuse as well,' Tiller said instantly.

The instructor looked at him quizzically. 'You know your explosives then, Sergeant.'

Tiller grinned awkwardly. He did, but he knew he should learn to keep his trap shut when under training. However, the instructor smiled at him in a friendly way and said to the group: 'Sergeant Tiller's quite right. There's a sympathetic fuse as well which reacts to vibration or any movement.'

'What's the explosive charge, chief?' Tiller asked.

'Torpex – 560lb of it.'

Tiller whistled. He knew they'd just started using Torpex in depth-charges with devastating effect.

'What's that?' one of the group piped up. 'I thought all explosives were TNT.'

Tiller looked at the instructor, who nodded.

'It's a mixture of amatol and aluminium which can be up to eighty per cent more destructive than TNT,'

Tiller explained. 'That Welman charge could blow the bottom off a bloody battleship, no trouble at all.'

'Which,' the instructor interjected quietly, 'is exactly what it's designed to do.'

Silence settled on the group. They were all volunteers and volunteers rarely, if ever, had a clue what they were volunteering for – except they knew it was hazardous. Now that was confirmed. For it was no secret that the *Tirpitz*, Germany's most powerful battleship, still lay in the fiords of Trondheim, a constant threat to the Arctic convoys supplying the Russians. The X-craft had damaged her, and she would be non-operational for some time yet, but their explosives had not been powerful enough to sink her.

A gust of wind blew a light dusting of snow in their faces and Tiller tugged at his greatcoat collar to close it. Norwegian waters would be a lot colder than Loch Linnhe, so he'd better get used to it.

No one asked if the *Tirpitz* was their eventual target because the only answer would have been a frigid stare from the instructor. But they knew two and two made four.

'Right, gentlemen,' the instructor said briskly. 'Let me give you a guided tour of one of these little beauties.'

He opened the access hatch on the top of the conning tower of the nearest Welman and pointed to the bucket-type seat positioned immediately below. 'If that seat looks familiar to any of you, then you drive an Austin Seven. That's where it comes from. And in the unlikely event of anyone recognizing the joystick in front of it, then you must be a one-time fighter pilot, as it comes from a Spitfire. The luminous direction

17

indicator on the instrument panel here is also from a Spit. All made up from odds and sods is the Welman. Very ingenious.'

The instructor pointed out what the different gauges were on the instrument panel in front of the bucket seat – an ammeter, inclinometer, depth gauge and so on – and described the miniature submarine bit by bit, working from bow to stern. He showed them the wheel of the trim weight control – which the pilot turned to bring the Welman on to an even keel after diving or surfacing, and which compensated for the loss of weight after the charge had been placed – and the wheel which released the charge.

He then showed them the hydroplane and rudder controls, the bilge pump, the ballast tanks, the banks of batteries and the oxygen bottles. He explained that the ballast tanks, one on either side, were filled with water by operating the main vent lever, which he pointed out to them. Once the ballast tanks began to fill, and the Welman began to submerge, the motor was switched on and the hydroplane, manipulated by the joystick, manoeuvred the craft vertically. When the craft was surfacing, the ballast tanks were emptied by compressed air and it was guided up by the hydroplane. It could also rise vertically to the surface if the motor was switched off and the tanks were 'blown', emptied of water, with the hydroplane set in a horizontal position.

'The pilot wears an oxygen mask and is fed oxygen through a rubber lung strapped to his chest,' said the instructor. 'It's a Yank invention called a Munsem lung. It's inflated before the operator enters and is then fed from the bottles. The pilot has enough oxygen to last him about ten hours.'

It hadn't been enough for that poor sod stuck in the mud, Tiller thought.

'See the keel here,' the instructor said, pointing with the toe of his boot. 'Lead – 630lb of it. But if you get stuck on the bottom it can be detached from the hull. Without the keel the Welman has enough positive buoyancy to rise to the surface even if the ballast tanks are fully flooded.'

'What happened to the bloke who got stuck on the bottom last week, then?' Tiller asked.

The instructor glanced at him and shrugged. 'He landed upside down in the mud. Christ only knows how he managed it. The keel just pushed him further into it. Releasing it didn't do any good, of course. He must have gone through one hundred and eighty degrees while submerged. Or hit the bottom vertically and toppled over. It's not meant to be possible.'

Sod's Law, Tiller thought, and pushed the image from his mind.

They spent the rest of the morning climbing in and out of the Welman and familiarizing themselves with how it worked. Then came two days of lectures before one of the tiny subs was cranked over the side by the crane and lowered into the cold water of the loch alongside a small wooden raft. The Welman was then connected to the instructor by a telephone wire which was plugged into the hull via a waterproof connection. The instructor wore headphones and a microphone.

The first student climbed into the Welman while it was still attached to the crane and was ordered by the instructor through the intercom to flood the ballast tanks. Tiller watched the craft sink and then rise again as the water was expelled from the ballast tanks. It was, he found when his turn came, surprisingly easy to work, but it was horribly cramped and visibility was very restricted.

By the end of the week they were allowed to manoeuvre the Welmans on their own, though the instructor had taken the precaution of attaching a red buoy on a long line to each of the miniature submarines.

The instructor, whom everyone by now called Tammy, was interested in Tiller's expertise in explosives, and would often talk to him about it. One evening he asked Tiller if he would like a run ashore, if only to get out of uniform for a few hours.

'Is there anywhere to go?' said Tiller, surprised.

'Lochuisge. There's a pub in the village run by an ex-navy chap. We can sometimes get a bit more than our ration of beer off him. Have you been drinking your tots?'

Tiller shook his head. He'd never fancied rum. The sweet, sickly smell of it when it was being dished out below decks always made his stomach turn. As attached personnel he wasn't entitled to the threepence a day that a member of the crew could receive in lieu of his tot. But he knew enough about naval customs to draw what was due to him and to preserve it in a bottle. The precious liquid could be bartered for just about anything.

'Take it with you, then. Mac enjoys his rum. He'll give you several pints for it.'

The liberty boat, empty apart from themselves and its two-man crew, chugged its way up the loch towards Kingairloch House and then pulled alongside a wooden pier. The wind sawed eerily in the pines clustered around the edge of the loch.

Tammy wrenched two old bikes out of some nearby bushes and they set off along the narrow road that meandered towards the house, which, though largely shrouded in darkness, showed a number of lights in its windows. Tiller had hoped to get a close look at it but as they approached, it was obscured from view by a high brick wall which ran alongside the road.

They cycled up over the brow and down a gentle incline for three or four miles before coming to a small cluster of houses, one of which turned out to be the pub. It was called The Ship and Compass and its sign, showing a black-hulled barque sailing across an old-fashioned compass rose, creaked gently in the wind. They propped their bikes against the wall and went inside.

The place was surprisingly full. A few elderly men, obviously local, sat silently by a large open fire or played dominoes in one corner, but the room was dominated by several groups of young men and women who were talking and laughing loudly. Tiller knew at once that they were from Kingairloch House. One or two of them glanced across at the instructor and raised a hand or beer mug in greeting as the two men walked towards the bar.

'Evening, Tammy. How's tricks?'

'Hello, Mac. This is a friend of mine, Colin Tiller. Tiger we call him. Joined us at the start of the week.'

Mac, like many athletes past their best, had run to fat, but he was big and powerful and the tattoos on his arms rippled as he wiped the glasses with a cloth. Behind him was a large wooden badge consisting of crossed clubs, the naval insignia for a physical training instructor, which was why they were always

nicknamed 'clubs'. Either side of it were photographs
of teams: boxing teams, football teams, hockey teams,
running reams. Mac seemed to be in all of them, arms
akimbo, his muscles bulging out of whatever kit he was
wearing.

He stretched out his hand and shook Tiller's.
'Welcome to Kingairloch,' he said, and then added
shrewdly: 'You're no brown job, are you?'

'Course he's not, he's a Bootneck,' Tammy said,
using the naval slang for a Royal Marine. To an outsider, it didn't sound too complimentary a description.
But the Marines were part of the Royal Navy and
on the whole the two got along well enough, bound,
if by nothing else, by their contempt for anyone
even remotely connected with the Army. The senior
service was the senior service, and no one had better
forget it.

The rum was exchanged for two pints of beer and
four more were put on the slate to Tiller's credit.

Tiller glanced around him as they moved away from
the bar. 'Seems full.'

'Yeah. Knowing your professional interests, I
thought you might like to meet some of them. I'm
a married man, but I thought you might be interested
personally as well.'

He could say that again, Tiller thought. There were
several ATS – women from the Auxiliary Territorial
Service – among the crowd, and one or two girls in civ-
vies, but most were wearing a uniform he did not recog-
nize. When he asked Tammy about them, the instructor
replied: 'They're FANYs. Never heard of the FANYs?'

Tiller shook his head. Looking at their curves it
seemed an appropriate word.

'Stands for First Aid Nursing Yeomanry.'

'Kingairloch House is partly a hospital then?'

The instructor chuckled. 'The name's a bit of a misnomer really. It started off that way the last time we gave the Krauts a beating, but this time round they mostly work as cipher clerks, confidential work, that kind of thing, or as drivers for the top brass. All strictly volunteers.'

'Is that right?' But Tiller was more interested in what filled the uniforms than in what their contents did.

But then the instructor said quietly: 'You've worked in Special Operations, haven't you? I've seen your records. So you know how to keep your mouth shut, don't you?'

Tiller nodded. What was Tammy on about?

'And you know Kingairloch House is a training ground for some hush-hush mob?'

'So I heard.'

'Those girls. They're here to be trained. Just like the men.'

'For what?'

The instructor shrugged. 'How would I know. But I got friendly with one of them once. We even spent a leave together in Glasgow. But she never, ever said what she was up to and shut up like a clam if I even got close to asking. Then one day she was gone. Just a note: "Goodbye. Wish me luck." That was all. Never seen her since.'

Tammy still seemed astonished by the memory. And aggrieved.

One of the men, dressed in civilian clothes, strolled over to them and said: 'Come and join us, Tammy.

Some of our newcomers want to know what fish you can catch in the loch. Who's your pal?'

He was an older man with a bristly military moustache, and Tammy introduced him to Tiller as Sergeant Rod Winant, an instructor at the house. 'Tiger's well up on your line of work, Rod. If you like we might be able to spare him for an afternoon. He could give your pupils a talk on the practical application of some of the stuff they're learning to handle.'

'Good idea. I'll fix it.'

Introductions were made all round. The only thing Tiller knew about fish was how to eat them and after a while his eyes fell on a dark-haired girl in a FANY uniform who looked as bored with the conversation as he felt with it. They smiled at each other and two beers were cancelled from Mac's credit slate.

She introduced herself as Susan and spoke with just a trace of a foreign accent.

'Are you French?' Tiller asked.

She just smiled. It was a slow, sad smile. She had the most beautiful wide, deep-set eyes. 'Partly. Are you here for long?'

Tiller spun her some yarn which she interrupted by laying her hand on his arm.

'I'm sorry,' she said. 'I shouldn't have asked. I think you're awfully brave. I'd get claustrophobia and panic if I had to do what you do.'

It was a stock remark but she seemed to mean it. Tiller grinned awkwardly and, without thinking, asked her what she did.

'Just a typist,' she said vaguely. 'Nothing interesting, I'm afraid.'

They spent the rest of the evening together, but

when the pub closed Tiller didn't ask if they could meet again, partly because he didn't want to go through what Tammy had, but mostly because he knew she would find a way of saying no in the nicest possible way.

It wasn't until after the war that he learnt who she was from a photograph in the newspapers. He would have known those eyes anywhere. He read the caption beneath the photograph and felt himself fill with anger at her terrible fate. As a member of the British sabotage and subversion organization known as Special Operations Executive, she had been parachuted into France at the end of 1943 as a wireless operator. But she had been betrayed to the Germans, who had shot her in Ravensbrück concentration camp the following year. She had, the newspaper reported, been awarded a posthumous George Cross for her bravery. A lot of frigging good that would do her now, Tiller had thought bitterly. It was then September 1945 and it seemed to him that all the best people were dead.

3

'Shit,' Tiller muttered under his breath as he strained to see out of the tiny front windows of the Welman. Between the two buoys he could see bobbing on the water ahead was, he knew, the first anti-submarine net. It stretched from just below the surface down to fifty feet. As if that was not bad enough, there would be a second net half a mile further on that stretched from fifty feet down to one hundred feet, the theoretical maximum depth at which the Welman could operate. Then beyond that again was a third net which was laid like the first.

'Well, here goes,' Tiller said to himself. He opened the main vent lever and heard the air in the ballast tanks on either side of the craft being released and the gurgle as it was replaced by water. Slowly, the water rose up the front window and then he was submerged. Carefully, he eased forward the joystick which was between his knees and felt the Welman tilt downwards.

There was so little room in the craft that its sides touched his shoulders and his legs were bent at an awkward angle as his feet worked the bars that controlled the rudder.

The first net was a filthy-looking contraption, its heavy steel mesh draped with green slime and coated in barnacles. It moved with the current like a flag flapping lazily in the breeze.

Tiller stopped the Welman and allowed it to sink vertically. The needle of the depth gauge swung steadily round. The glimmer of sunlight disappeared and the visibility began to deteriorate. The needle reached fifty feet, but still the netting barred his way. Tiller swore. Despite the cold his hands felt clammy and sweat pricked his eyes.

Then suddenly the net was above him and he eased the Welman under it. Then hastily, too hastily, he brought the joystick towards him, instinctively aiming for light and, eventually, fresh air, and it took him a few moments to bring the craft under control. He forced himself to move the joystick forward and once more the Welman dipped down. At fifty feet he saw the second net ahead of him, alarmingly close. He put the motor in neutral and again allowed the Welman to sink. Sixty feet . . . seventy-five . . . eighty . . . The needle swung inexorably around. His heart began to pound. Being so deep seemed unnatural, defying nature. Ninety feet . . . one hundred, and the net was above him. Below him, he thought he glimpsed the bottom: mud and rock and waving fronds. He passed at full speed under the net.

A spume of water suddenly erupted in his face. It was like being hit with a high-pressure hose and he heard himself shouting as he gasped for breath. He struggled to maintain control of himself and the lurching Welman.

He saw that the water, icy cold, was spurting from a crack in the front window with terrifying strength, and soon it had soaked him from head to foot. Somewhere behind him a fuse blew and the tiny cockpit filled with fumes.

He turned off the engine, set the hydroplane horizontally and groped desperately for the valve which would operate the compressed air to expel the water from the ballast tanks. He found it and twisted it, then heard the reassuring sound of the hissing air.

The water continued to pour in. He could feel it around his ankles now. He watched the depth indicator. The Welman was rising but the water coming through the cracked glass was offsetting the loss from the ballast tanks. The craft rose to forty feet and the needle hovered there. He knew there was only one thing left to do. As he pulled the lever that released the keel, the Welman shot to the surface like a cork.

He could see the sun on the water and hear the approaching launch. The Welman lurched unevenly on the surface, its stability gone with the lead keel. The water slopped around his calves and the fumes made him take great gulps of oxygen from the mask. He could hear someone clambering aboard and working to release the clips on the conning tower hatch, and at last a blast of fresh air swept the fumes away. He clambered out and was violently sick into the loch.

Two weeks later, after the commanding officer aboard HMS *Titania* had submitted a report of the incident, he was informed by Combined Operations Headquarters that there might be a fault in the Welmans and that they were not to be taken below fifty feet. But training was to continue.

January became February, and February turned into March, but still no word reached Kingairloch. Once the

SBS men were packed and ready to move to Scapa Flow to mount the attack, but then the op was cancelled. The group at Kingairloch House was replaced by another. The days got longer and gradually less cold, and still they practised manoeuvring the Welmans under the submarine nets without taking them below fifty feet. An admiral came to see them in action, and two weeks later a general. At the end of March Tiller was given the additional training necessary for him to become an instructor in Welmans, but still there was no sign of any action.

Then, one bright morning in mid-April, Tiller was called before the CO, a lieutenant commander in the Royal Navy.

'You must know the Welman like the back of your hand by now, Sergeant.'

'Yes, sir.'

'Inside out.'

'Yes, sir.'

The officer's hands lay on a mound of paper. He flicked at it as if not knowing what to do with it. He probably didn't, Tiller decided.

'Nothing seems to be happening, does it?'

'No, sir.'

Tiller had long ago been told that most wars consisted of hanging around waiting for something to happen. Certainly this one did. He'd learned to be patient, to conserve his energies, so that when it did happen the surge of adrenalin in him carried him through. He'd seen others – brave, experienced men – fall to bits from waiting. They hadn't been able to handle it. He had learned to cope by going into a kind of mental limbo, a sort of hibernation. But this had been a very long winter, and spring must surely be around the corner. He wanted action, and he wanted it now.

'I'll be frank with you. I'm in a bit of a dilemma, Sergeant,' said the CO.

A new course of Jeepmen was being run round the upper deck by the resident PT instructor. They could both hear the thudding of feet above them and the voice of the clubs roaring at one of the laggers.

'I consider you one of my best men, Sergeant. I expect that from the Corps, of course. You handled that emergency very well. If any op's going to be mounted I'm going to need you.'

'I'm glad to hear that, sir. I'm looking forward to removing the bottom of the world's biggest battleship.'

'But yesterday I received a request for your transfer.'

Tiller's heart sank. Was his luck about to run out?

'An old chum of mine wants you.'

Oh, Jesus. Instructing Wrens in the art of saluting, perhaps. Tiller felt the rebellion welling up in him.

'And because he's an old chum I'm inclined to let you go.'

Bloody navy, bloody old boy network, bloody papershifters! Why hadn't he joined the bloody army? He knew why he hadn't joined the bloody army.

'But, sir, I . . .'

'No buts, Sergeant,' the CO said briskly. 'We've all got a job to do. Of course, it's up to you, but if you refuse I'd really have no option but to return you whence you came.'

Tiller remembered the captain and his polished pate and pips, and the clerk with the hacking cough.

'Yes, sir.'

'The fact is, I have been told there is no hope of any operation in the near future. The nights are getting too short. The RAF is claiming it can do the job. With these new blockbuster bombs I dare say it can. The Russkis want to have a go, too. So you Sardine Men are some way down the pecking order.'

Tiller said nothing. He wasn't running the war. They could have removed the bottom of the Kraut battleship weeks ago – he knew that and he knew his CO knew that too. But his CO wasn't running the war either.

'So I'd advise you to think carefully before coming to any decision.'

'Thank you, sir. I will.'

Why the fuck doesn't he get on with it? Tiller wondered as he watched the officer rummaging in a pile of paper in his pending tray.

'Ah, here we are. The post is as a Welman instructor.'

It could be worse, Tiller decided. Filing paper in Whitehall and teaching Wrens to salute would be worse. He couldn't think of much else, though, that could be. He knew he'd never make a good instructor: he was too impatient. He waited but when the CO seemed disinclined to enlighten him further, he asked: 'Who's requested me, sir?'

'A very old chum of mine,' said the CO enthusiastically. 'Passed out of the course at Greenwich together in '35, and then we both served in the *Hood*. Major Tasler. You know him?'

Blondie, the old bastard. Why hadn't he let him know direct?

'Yes, sir.'

The grin that split Tiller's face did not go unnoticed. 'You seem happier now, Sergeant, at your prospects. You'll accept the job?'

Instructor, hell. Blondie wouldn't make him an instructor. He was up to something.

'Yes, sir.'

'Even when you don't know where the post is?'

'Yes, sir.'

The CO's eyebrows were raised. 'Well, I must say such loyalty is most commendable.'

'May I ask where it is, sir?' Tiller didn't much care where it was. Tasler was always where the action was and that was what mattered.

The lieutenant commander glanced at the paper. 'Somewhere I've never heard of, I'm afraid. Hyatt's Ferry. Mean anything to you?'

'No, sir.'

The CO bit his lip. 'Ah, yes, here we are. Northern Ceylon. Know Ceylon, do you?'

Christ almighty, what was Blondie up to?

'No, sir.'

'Nor do I. Pretty place, I believe. But my guess is you won't be there for long. You know where most people end up when they go to fight the Japs?'

'Where's that, sir?'

'Burma, Sergeant. Burma.'

Jesus.

'I went there when Singapore fell in '42. A stinking rotten place full of flies and mosquitoes. It's hell on earth during the monsoon. The land's mostly impenetrable jungle, the coastline's nothing but mangrove, mud and crocodiles. Sure you still want to go?'

'Yes, sir.'

'Want to think about it for five minutes?'

'No, sir.'

'Good man. I know that Major Tasler is keen for you to go.'

'Is he already out there, sir?'

'Good heavens no. He's a staff officer at Combined Operations HQ in London. Richmond Terrace. You're to be there on Friday at 1400 sharp. He wants a word with you before you depart for the Orient. A number of Welmans, incidentally, are earmarked to go to Ceylon by ship. Here's your travel warrant. A boat's leaving for Oban in an hour. My orders are for you to be on it. Good luck.'

He leant across the desk and shook Tiller's hand. Tiller saluted and turned.

'Oh, Sergeant . . .'

'Sir?'

'What do you think of the Welman? You can be honest.'

'A death-trap, sir.'

The CO grinned broadly. 'You're right, of course. Oh, just one other thing. It's the Japs who have the biggest battleship in the world.'

Richmond Terrace was a narrow street almost opposite the Cenotaph which connected Whitehall with the Victoria Embankment. Tiller always found the Cenotaph a depressing monument with its permanent collection of withered wreaths. One year he had attended the annual

ceremony of honouring the dead of the Great War
when the Marines had provided the guard of honour.
'We shall remember them,' the padre had intoned and
everyone present had reverently repeated the words.
He recalled the ceremony now as he turned into
Richmond Terrace. He didn't seriously expect anyone
to remember him if he copped it. Why should they?

There were sentries outside the headquarters of
Combined Operations, a large, ugly, red-brick Victo-
rian building part of which overlooked the Thames.
But Tiller was in uniform and they didn't look at him
twice. As he went through the swing doors a large
limousine with a flag on its bonnet drew up. Tiller went
up to a glass enclosure where a commissionaire sat
with an appointments book. The man was thumbing
through this when there was a stir in the large hall.
Tiller looked round. Down the sweep of the stairs
came a tall, slim figure whose naval cap glistened
with a double band of gold braid – irreverently called
'scrambled eggs' by everyone in the navy – and sat at
a jaunty angle on his head. Beneath the cap the long,
handsome face of the ex-chief of Combined Operations
was set in a slight smile, for he was fully aware of the
stir he was causing. He raised his hand to his cap to
acknowledge the salutes of those he passed in the hall,
making the one broad gold and three thin stripes of a
full admiral on his sleeve glitter and reflect the light.

Near the door he stopped so abruptly in front of a
chief petty officer who had just entered the building
that his large entourage tagging along behind him
almost collided with one another. Tiller could hear
him clearly.

'Bainbridge, isn't it?'

'Yes, sir.'

'*Javelin*, November 1940. Am I right?'

'Yes, sir.'

'You were just a leading seaman, then chief. Torpedoes.'

'Yes, sir.'

'We had bad luck, didn't we, Bainbridge? I thought we had those Jerry destroyers. Instead, they had us. We've got Jerry on the run now, though.'

'That's right, sir. We have.'

'Good luck, Bainbridge.'

'And you, sir.'

The mercurial figure swept through the door and was gone.

Tiller looked at the commissionaire, whose eyes seemed to have misted over. 'You know who that was, don't you?' the man said.

Tiller nodded. He knew. Nineteen thirty-eight in Malta it had been. Once met, never forgotten.

'What a man!' said the commissionaire. 'If we had more like him we'd have won the war years ago. Here's your pass, Sergeant. Room 431 on the fourth floor. The lifts are over there.'

Room 431 was in fact two rooms. The inner one, next to the corridor, housed a blonde Wren, a desk and a typewriter, the outer one, with a view over the Thames, housed Major Henry Tasler DSO, Royal Marines, his red-gold moustache even droopier than Tiller had remembered it. They shook hands like old friends, which indeed they were. With Hasler was a naval commander – a sharp-eyed, ruthless sort of cove, was Tiller's first reaction to him – and a mild-looking civilian in tweeds who was sucking on an empty pipe.

The commander had propped himself on the corner of a table, the civilian was seated, legs crossed, in the only comfortable chair in the room. It looked as if he had been there some time.

In the presence of these two strangers Tasler's greeting was restrained, though he explained to the two men that he knew Tiller well.

'Tiller was with me on the Bordeaux raid,' Tasler said.

The commander's face softened slightly in admiration. 'Is that so?'

The civilian nodded his approval. He obviously knew all about the raid by Marine canoeists which had been mounted at the end of 1942 to sink Axis shipping in the River Gironde. Tiller and Tasler had been the only survivors and had taken several months to return to England via neutral – but very unfriendly – Spain.

'The major tells me your escape line worked well on the whole, Sergeant,' the civilian said after inspecting the bowl of his pipe. Tiller remembered the farmer's cupboard again, and felt queasy at the thought.

'It got us out,' Tiller said, and then felt ungrateful. The French farmer's hiding them had been a far braver act that anything he, Tiller, had done during the whole operation.

'Rather more sophisticated nowadays, of course,' said the civilian, bowed over his pipe bowl, 'but we were pleased how well it functioned.'

Then he glanced up sharply and looked Tiller straight in the face. He had a very penetrating gaze quite at odds with his quiet demeanour. 'The major tells me you worked with him in his Boom Patrol Detachment for some time. You were his first choice to test the Sleeping Beauty, but you left just before the prototype arrived. How long were you with him?'

Tiller glanced at Tasler. The Royal Marine Boom Patrol Detachment was just the cover name for Tasler's unit which had been formed to develop a British explosive motor boat and various other methods of attacking enemy shipping. It was a top-security unit. Tiller had never heard its true function mentioned by any outsider before. But Tasler nodded at him encouragingly and said: 'This gentleman knows all about what we were up to.'

'For six months,' said Tiller.

'And then you were seconded to the Special Boat Squadron as an explosives expert?'

'That's right. In the Aegean.'

'Clandestine operations in caiques mostly,' the commander said. It wasn't a question, but Tiller nodded his agreement. These frigging officers – for the man in tweeds was obviously an officer too – seemed to know more about him than he did about himself.

'An immediate DCM,' said Tasler proudly as if he had been awarded the decoration himself. 'Tried to sink two Jerry destroyers by turning a speedboat into an explosive one. Didn't succeed, but he then sank them with limpets.'

The civilian's eyebrows rose slightly. 'Good man. Congratulations.' He sucked at his empty pipe as if trying to clear its stem of some obstruction, but his eyes were still fixed on Tiller.

'You like that sort of work, Sergeant, obviously.'

Tiller hesitated. 'What sort is that, sir?'

'Well, ah,' the civilian seemed at a loss as to how exactly to describe it. 'Let's say secret work.'

Had it been secret work? Pirates, more like it.

'As long as there's action, sir.'

'I think we can promise you that. And you can keep your mouth shut, I'm sure.'

The commander seemed to have made up his mind. He unhitched himself from the table and said abruptly: 'I'll leave you to it. Good luck, Sergeant.'

'Thank you, sir.'

'I'll come with you, Charles,' the civilian said. 'I don't think we need bother Sergeant Tiller any further.'

He tucked his pipe into his pocket and both men left the room. When the outer door had closed and the typist had resumed her typing, Tasler got up and closed the inner door.

'We're in slight confusion,' he said when he had returned to his desk. 'Supremo decided to drop in unannounced. Bloody typical. I thought he was in Delhi and he suddenly turns up here demanding to know what's happening about the Special Operations Group he wants formed. Been in meetings all morning.'

'I saw him,' said Tiller. 'He seemed in a hurry,' though not, he nearly added, in such a hurry that he did not have time to greet an old shipmate.

'He's always in a hurry,' said Hasler with a laugh. 'There are a lot of people around this building who want things done yesterday. Mountbatten always wanted them done the day before yesterday.'

Tasler lit a cigarette, offered one to Tiller, who refused, and waved the sergeant to a seat. 'First things first. I expect you were wondering who those two bods were?'

'Part of your new set-up, sir?'

Tasler shook his head. 'Commander Grant is NID.'

'NID?'

'Naval Intelligence Division. He wanted to have a look at you. This Special Operations Group Mountbatten is keen to form in South-East Asia might be required to do some clandestine work as well as special operations.'

'And the civilian?'

Hasler ran a hand through thinning blond hair. 'Yes, well, let's just say he's a civil servant. Part of the Ministry of Economic Warfare.'

'I've heard of that, sir.'

Tasler looked at him sharply. 'You have? Where?'

'In Scotland. I was told Kingairloch House was part of the Ministry's set-up. They had hush-hush groups training there in demolitions. It seemed more like uneconomic warfare to me, as they were blowing things up at all times of the day and night. I thought plastic explosive was meant to be in short supply.'

Tasler laughed. 'Uneconomic warfare. I like that, Tiger. Anyway, this gentleman you met here, he's in the same racket. Everyone's beginning to get interested in the Far East, in anticipation that we can shift more of our resources to fight the Japs if Jerry collapses when we invade Europe. Also, the Yanks are beginning to weigh in with a lot more *matériel*. So actually PE isn't in short supply any more. What is in short supply is the right people to use it. You get my drift?'

Tiller nodded. 'You mean we won't have to use 808 any more?'

Nobel 808 was the subject of a joke that Tiller and Tasler shared. It was an earlier form of plastic explosive which came in rubbery brown sticks wrapped in waterproof paper. Tiller couldn't abide the stuff. Its smell – of bitter almonds – still lingered nauseously in his memory, as did the blinding headache it had invariably given him.

'It was quite effective against that railway track,' said Tasler. 'Remember?'

'Do I ever, sir.'

It was a very powerful explosive. Provided a sawing motion was not employed, it could be cut and the flat surface was then taped directly on to the target.

Tasler chuckled. 'I'll not forget you trying to soften the 808 before we laid it.'

Nor had Tiller. Unlike PE, 808 had to be softened first if it was to be moulded around its target. The instruction pamphlet recommended this be done by holding it under the armpit for at least a quarter of an hour or by placing it in boiling water. Tiller had never found boiling water available on the occasions he and 808 had found themselves together behind enemy lines and he had discovered from that raid with Tasler that the suggested alternative had been equally impracticable. He had not found it easy to move quickly and silently to avoid an alert sentry while holding a lump of 808 in his armpit. It wouldn't have helped the accuracy of his shooting with his silenced pistol either. Luckily, he had not had to use the weapon, as the major had disposed of the sentry.

'Well, no time to reminisce now,' Tasler said with a tinge of regret. He took a last deep puff from his cigarette, stubbed it out in an ashtray already filled with dog-ends, and pulled a brown folder in front of him. 'Let's get down to business.'

He opened the folder and Tiller said: 'Do you really want me as an instructor, sir?'

Tasler grinned at him. 'What do you think, Tiger?'

'I was hoping for something more . . . active.'

'Well, you heard what our civil servant friend said. 'Don't you believe him?'

Tiller didn't, but he didn't like to say so. He waited.

'Strictly between ourselves, Tiger, and not to be mentioned outside this room, I can promise you action. All right?'

Tiller smiled in relief. 'All right, sir. Where, sir?'

Hasler looked surprised. 'Burma, of course. Where else? As I told you, Lord Louis is very keen to form a Special Operations Group within South-East Asia Command. For a start, it will have a number of Combined Operations Pilotage Parties.'

Tiller nodded, and felt the adrenalin begin to pump. Wherever there were COPP teams major Allied landings were being planned, for they were the boys who reconnoitred likely beaches, checking on gradients and the consistency of the ground.

'It's also going to include a new force of Royal Marines – Detachment 385 – who are going to need training up. They'll be employed in deception raids but will sometimes work with cockles or inflatable craft launched from flying boats. And it's planned to have four Sea Reconnaissance Units, too.'

'What are they, sir?'

'God knows. They do something exotic with paddle-boards apparently.'

41

'*Paddleboards*, sir?'

Tasler looked at the paper in front of him. 'That's what it says. Supremo is all for innovation, and fighting in Burma is not like fighting anywhere else on earth. It's going to need a new set of ground rules and we're going to need a new way of thinking.'

'We, sir?'

'Yes, Tiger, we. I've been appointed second in command of SOG.'

'And where do I fit in, sir?'

'The last element of this new outfit are three SBS groups which worked in the Med until the Eyeties threw their hand in. One's already out in Burma, and in action. It's one of Major Pountney's units, so it's basically army-controlled, but there are a number of Marines in it. Initially, I just want one of my own men on the ground, as it were, who will get a quick grasp of what the group is doing and can report to me when I arrive in Ceylon. As you know, Major Pountney isn't exactly a fan of the Corps, but he's heard of your exploits with the SBS and is quite willing – well, he grudgingly consented – to you joining the group in Burma.'

Tiller smiled. He had heard of the legendary Roger Pountney, of course, the man who had started the SBS back in the grim, dark days of 1941. He had heard, too, of the major's belief that the Marines had been constipated with tradition ever since the Battle of Trafalgar.

'What's the SBS doing in Burma, sir?'

Tasler got up and walked over to a wall map of South-East Asia. Tiller followed him.

'The Fourteenth Army have been trying to recapture

Burma ever since we were driven out of the country in 1942 and it's had to try and do it all on its own. Small wonder it's come to be called the "Forgotten Army". Well now, at last, it looks as if the Japs are in retreat throughout Burma and are being pushed southwards. But in this area of western Burma here, known as the Arakan, they keep managing to supply their troops up these rivers here: the Kaladan and so on. As you can see, these rivers run north–south and are all connected by a maze of smaller rivers. It's a hide-and-seek kind of war as the Japs use native boats to take their supplies up river and our patrols find them very elusive. Fifteenth Corps, which is part of the Fourteenth Army, is pushing the Japs back in the Arakan. This is where A Group, SBS, is working, helping to sever the Jap supply lines, among other tasks.'

Tiller looked puzzled. 'But how are COPP, and these blokes with the paddleboards, going to help?'

'The British and Indian Divisions are all west of the Irrawaddy,' said Tasler, indicating the area. 'They're going to have to cross it – and the River Chindwin – to get at the Japs in eastern Burma. The Irrawaddy's almost a mile wide in some places, so they'll need all the help they can get to cross it.'

Tasler went back to his desk, and Tiller said: 'And where do the Welman's come in, sir?'

Usually Tiller could read Tasler's face like a book. But now it suddenly became quite expressionless.

'That I can't tell you, Tiger. Not yet. But you're officially on the roll of HQ South-East Asia Command as a Welman instructor at Hyatt's Ferry, Ceylon, as of 15 April. Hyatt's Ferry is where the Group is being based. You may actually have to help train some of Detachment 385 in their use. But, to be honest, I don't think you'd make a good instructor, would you, Tiger?'

Tiller grinned. 'No, sir.'

Tasler glanced down at the dosier in front of him, and then back at Tiller.

'What are they like, Tiger?'

'What, sir?'

'The Welmans, of course.'

A tug hooted on the Thames below them.

'Death-traps, sir.'

Tasler laughed. 'That's what I heard too. Well, here are your travel documents. Air to Calcutta, then a train to Chittagong for the usual introductory course on Japanese firearms and jungle warfare, then on to Cox's Bazar, on the Indian side of the border with Burma. That's where A Group is based. You report to a Major Jim Danforth.'

4

Like everything else in Burma the deck of His Majesty's Motor Launch No. 586 was damp and sticky with heat. Tiller pressed his face against it as he felt the craft surge forward.

Already his clothes were soaked with sweat, for with the onset of monsoon weather the air had become humid and oppressive. He wanted to raise his head but they had strict orders to stay prone until past the grassy point on the starboard side that guarded the entrance to the River Mayu. The skipper, a South African RNVR lieutenant called Mick Wright, had said there should not have been any Japs within miles of it, but, he had added, the Japs were never where you thought they would be. Indeed, they always popped up where you least expected them. So keep your heads down, he'd said. And your arses, too. Someone had been shot through both buttocks a couple of months back.

Directly overhead the night sky was crystal clear, but on the horizon astern of the ML Tiller had seen the towering cumulonimbus that had begun to build. These clouds were an early precursor to the monsoon, one of the crew had told him. They looked as if some monster genie had been released in a gigantic puff of smoke which rolled and swirled 30–40,000 feet into the air. Get into a cloud pattern like that in an aircraft, the crewman had said casually, and its wings would be torn off by the storms that raged within it. Such accidents were common, he had added; aircraft simply disappeared without trace.

One of the crew walked half crouched among the prone bodies on the ML's deck to pass on the word that they were past the point and were in the river. Tiller sat up, propped himself against the mounting of the vessel's three-pounder, and placed his M2 automatic carbine across his lap. The three-pounder, which had just been cranked round by its two-man crew so that it was now trained straight ahead instead of on the point, smelt of oil and stale sweat. Silently, one of the figures on the deck got up, moved across to Tiller and sat next to him.

'It's certainly a different sort of war,' said Sergeant Dave Welsh quietly.

'You can say that again, Taffy,' Tiller answered.

'I thought you Marines were as at home at sea as you were on land? That's your motto, isn't it?'

'Yeah, that's right. *Per Mare Per Terram*. But it depends on the sea, doesn't it?' Tiller said sourly. 'And it depends what's happening on it. Fuck all on this one, from what I can tell.'

'A routine patrol is a routine patrol is a routine patrol,' said Taffy. 'Don't worry, you'll see more action than you want by the time we've finished. Mick has a nose for trouble.'

Taffy was a small, wiry character, and very reserved. He came from Devon – he was nicknamed Taffy because of his surname – and never talked much, not to anyone. Just didn't feel the need to. He found Tiller rather the same, which was why they got on. Taffy had long ago learnt that the chatterers of this world did just that and not much else. For the umpteenth time he slid out the curved thirty-round magazine from under his carbine to check that it was correctly loaded, and then clipped it back on. Automatic weapons of any kind were lethally efficient – so long as they didn't jam.

'You used one of these?' he asked.

Tiller shook his head. 'A Sten's always done me.'

'They've got a faster rate of fire than a Sten,' said Taffy. 'And they're a lot more accurate at a longer range. You've got to give it to the Yanks: they make some first-rate equipment. Mind you, their ammunition doesn't seem to have the stopping power of ours. If anyone gets hit with a .303 bullet they stay hit.'

Tiller grunted. He hadn't had the opportunity to use the carbine in anger yet. He wondered if he ever would. He had been with the SBS patrol two weeks now and the nightly excursions had all drawn a blank. It wasn't his idea of action.

The two men sat in companionable silence for the next half-hour, automatically scanning the bank as it unwound on the ML's port side, though it was much too dark to see anything except the tops of the trees silhouetted against the night sky. Tiller was just thinking that it was going to be another blank night when he heard Mick Wright on the bridge a few feet away snap: 'Starboard thirty, full speed ahead.'

The ML swung away from the left bank of the river and the swell of the diesel engines thrummed in their ears.

'Just a drifting log, I expect,' said Taffy. 'In the dark they look exactly like native canoes. No, I'm wrong. Native canoes *are* logs. Dug-out ones.'

Although Taffy didn't say all that much, he made sure that anything he did say was correct.

The two men stood up and peered into the darkness. Behind them the sky was quite light, despite the huge, ominous clouds on the horizon, but ahead the river and its jungle banks merged into an impenetrable black gloom. It was only when they strained their eyes at a long, low object on the starboard bow, pointed out to them by one of the gun crew, that they understood the reason for the ML deviating from its course.

'Bigger than a native canoe,' Taffy murmured. 'A lot bigger. And higher in the water than a sampan.'

'Stand by to board,' Wright called over his windscreen at the two sergeants. 'Taffy, don't let your men bunch together too much. I don't trust any of these bastards.'

'What is it, skip?' Taffy asked.

'It's got two masts. Could be a *tavoy* coaster. Or possibly a *mergui*. Whatever it is, I don't like it. Slow ahead now.'

The ML lurched back into the water as its speed was reduced. The native craft could be seen more clearly now. It was still making way upstream, with both its lateen bamboo sails set, but it was impossible to tell whether it was ghosting with the breeze and tide, or was under power. It maintained its course as the ML approached and then ran parallel with it. Two figures were crouched in the stern, holding on to the long, curved tiller. They were looking straight ahead as if pretending they had not seen or heard the ML. Then the Arakanese interpreter the ML always carried aboard hailed the crew through a loudspeaker and received an acknowledging wave. Slowly, the craft

began to swing away from the bank towards the middle
of the river.

The skipper called down the voice pipe for the
engines to be put in neutral, and the freed clutch set
up an eerie rhythmical whine. Wright watched the craft
carefully as it swung broadside on to the ML. The ML
was still moving forward.

'Slow astern.'

A pulse of sound came from the ML's funnel and
white smoke belched from it for a moment. Then
the ML dropped back as the craft crossed its bows.
The muzzle of the three-pounder followed the craft's
progress foot by foot.

The clutch whined as Wright ordered the engines
into neutral again.

Tiller could see that one of the figures on the craft
was running forward, and one after another the sails
came down as the craft swung round until its bows
were pointing downstream. For a moment it kept
creeping forward before its progress was stemmed by
the incoming tide. As it hung motionless in the water
an anchor dropped with a splash.

'That's not a *tavoy* or a *mergui*,' said Sandy Bright-
man, an Australian corporal who was one of the ML's
SBS patrol. 'Look where its foremast is stepped. Right
in its bows.'

The interpreter had come down from the open bridge
to join them; he always went along with the boarding
party. '*Kattu*,' he said pointing at the craft. '*Kattu*.'

'He says it's a *sandoway*,' Taffy pronounced.

'Does it matter?' Tiller asked.

'You bet your sweet Jesus it does,' said the fourth
member of the SBS team, Dopey Douglas. 'Get a

laung-zat up this way, for instance, and you'll know it's almost sure to be on Jap business. Normally, you only get them on the Irrawaddy or the Chindwin.'

Tiller shrugged. Aircraft spotting was one thing – he'd been through a course on that – but Burmese boat spotting seemed a trifle obscure. Yet the SBS team were all equally knowledgeable on the subject.

'I thought the locals were on our side,' he said. 'Isn't Burma a British colony?'

'So was my country at one time, mate,' said Sandy. 'That doesn't make us any fonder of you Poms. Rather the contrary as a matter of fact.'

'Oh, belt up, you bloody kangaroo,' Taffy said good-naturedly. 'The Burmese are on their own side, that's the truth of it.'

'The *sandoway* is a local rice-carrying craft, so it could be genuine,' Dopey remarked. 'Not that genuine is a word you could use about the Burmese,' he added wryly. Dopey was one of those Englishmen who thought everything south of Dover was nasty and foreign.

'Let's go and look anyway,' said Taffy. He called up to the bridge: 'Are you going alongside, skip?'

Wright had his night glasses trained on the *sandoway*. 'Looks all right,' he said grudgingly. 'But there's something about its behaviour that's fishy. It appeared too abruptly. From nowhere.'

'Probably came out of one of the *chaungs*.'

'You could be right, Taffy. That could be it. I'll go alongside and drop two of you off, but I want the other two to ready the cockles. You're going to have a look-see to check if there is a *chaung* over there.'

'Fair enough. You come with me, Tiger. Sandy and Dopey can get the cockles launched.'

The ML lurched forward and slowly circled the *sandoway*. More crew spilled on to its deck from the bamboo deck house and there was a lot of pointing and high-pitched excitable talk which floated across clearly to the ML as it manoeuvred to come alongside the anchored vessel.

'What are they saying?' Taffy asked the interpreter.

'They think we sink them,' said the interpreter cautiously.

'Why should we do that?'

'Oh, no, sir. Not deliberate. By accident.'

'They obviously don't think much of our seamanship,' Taffy remarked.

'Simple people,' the interpreter said humbly.

'Jeez, I've heard that before, too,' said Sandy. 'If you ask me I think they're as smart as a wagonload of monkeys.'

The ML eased its way alongside the *sandoway*. Covered by the two twin Lewis guns which were mounted either side of the bridge, Taffy and Tiller jumped aboard. The interpreter followed and the ML backed off, but the Lewis guns remained trained on the other vessel's crew.

'Who's the captain here?' Taffy asked. He held his M2 in the crook of his arm as if out shooting rabbits, but Tiller, less sure of the situation, kept his at the ready. The interpreter repeated Taffy's question in Arakanese and a tall, but bent man stepped forward. He wore at his waist a large *dah*, a native sword, from the hilt of which flowed a long tassel of horsehair dyed blood red.

'Ask him for his papers and where he's come from and where he's going.'

The captain handed over the papers and launched into a long and involved explanation. The interpreter handed the papers to Taffy, who looked at the Japanese stamp and handed them back.

'Have a look around, Tiger.'

Tiller pushed between the crew and ducked into the crude bamboo-mat-covered deck house. A curious acrid smell hung in the air and the floor was littered with the crew's clothing. In one corner a pot boiled on a Primus stove; otherwise, the deck house was empty. He went out, found the hatch into the hold and shone his torch into it. It, too, was empty. Then he shone his torch around the deck, up the masts and under the folded sails. The crew watched him in stoic silence.

'Anything?'

Tiller shook his head. 'The hold has obviously had rice in it recently. That's all. No engine.'

Taffy scratched his head. The crew of the *sandoway* continued to watch him silently. 'Ask them what they were doing up that *chaung*?' he told the interpreter, pointing towards the river bank.

The interpreter's question threw the crew into confusion. They all began gabbling at once, gesticulating at Taffy, at the bank, at themselves. The interpreter waited patiently for the hubbub to die down. Then he said: 'They no go up *chaung*. *Kattu* too big for any *chaung*. They stay on Mayu, they say. They deliver rice to Rathedaung. Now they go home.'

'And where's home?'

Even this seemed a matter of dispute, but eventually the interpreter. 'Up river, they say. Htizwe.'

'Tell them to stay where they are until you tell them they can go,' Taffy said, then gestured for the ML to come alongside. The interpreter climbed back on to the ML, and the two canoes, which had been circling nearby, moved silently alongside the *sandoway*.

Tiller had already inspected the canoes closely and knew them to be the normal eighteen-foot Mk II types used by the SBS – more advanced models of the one Tiller had used on the Bordeaux raid. They were made of rubberized canvas stretched over a wooden frame and took a crew of two, who sat in watertight man-holes. These more advanced types had a rigid frame with collapsible crossbars which allowed the canoe's beam to be reduced by two inches so that it could be passed through the torpedo hatch of a submarine. Inside each canoe every inch of space was used to stow the buoyancy bags, and the rations, weapons, water, spare ammunition, medical box, repair kit and infrared signalling equipment which made each craft and its crew an independent fighting unit.

Taffy lowered himself into one of the canoes and Tiller slipped into the other. As Tiller adjusted his weight to trim the craft, he retained hold of the side of the *sandoway* to stay balanced. His hand slid briefly down the rough wooden planks of the native craft and under his palm he momentarily felt something soft. He ran his hand back up the planking until his fingers encountered a scrap of cloth which had become snared in a splinter of wood. He tugged at it and it came away.

'Hang on a moment,' he said to Sandy, who was in the front manhole. He took his torch out of his pocket and shone it on the scrap of cloth.

'What colour are Jap uniforms?' he asked the Australian.

'Drab olive green, most of them,' said Sandy. 'Why?'

'Like this?'

Tiller thrust his hand in front of Sandy and shone the torch on the cloth.

Sandy whistled under his breath. 'Strewth. Where did you find that?'

Tiller heard a sound above him and glanced up. The captain of the *sandoway*, his hand resting on the hilt of his *dah*, was looking down on the canoe with an expressionless face. When Tiller looked up he moved away.

The second canoe circled towards them and rafted up alongside.

'What's the problem, Tiger?' Taffy called out softly.

Tiller passed the scrap of cloth over to Taffy and shone his torch on it. 'Found this snagged on the side of the *sandoway*.'

Taffy turned the fabric over carefully under the torch beam.

'Seems brand new to me,' he said, feeling it between thumb and forefinger. 'Couldn't have been there long. Everything rots in this climate.'

'Including my fucking soul,' murmured Dopey, who was holding on to the bows of Sandy's canoe with one hand as he cocked the carbine he held in front of him with the other.

'Well, let's go and see if we can find the owner,' said Taffy.

Tiller gestured up to the deck of the *sandoway*. 'The captain knows we've found it.'

'He also knows that if he moves he'll get blown

54

out of the water,' Taffy replied. 'Don't worry about him.'

The two canoes moved away from the side of the *sandoway*, the crews using double-ended paddles to drive them through the dark, turgid water towards the bank.

The darkness and sweet humidity of the night enfolded them and the *sandoway* soon blended into the shadows of the opposite bank, though they could still hear the reassuring grumbling sound of the ML's engines as it slowly circled the vessel.

The exertion of paddling, even though they moved deliberately slowly, made Tiller sweat profusely. They were dressed in long-sleeved shirts and long trousers to protect themselves from mosquitoes. These were no problem aboard the ML, but ashore it was essential to protect oneself as much as possible. Everyone took a Mepacrine tablet daily to prevent malaria. But the sickness rate in Burma was still five times higher than the casualty rate in battle.

Near to the bank the two canoes rafted up momentarily.

'We'll rendezvous here, by this fallen tree,' Taffy said to Tiller in a low voice. 'We'll go upstream for ten minutes; you go downstream for the same time. If you don't find the entrance to a *chaung* in that time, come back. If you do, signal a series of Rs with your torch and wait for me. If I signal first you come back to me. Got it?'

'Supposing there's a bend in the river?' said Tiller.

'Then come back.'

Taffy's canoe slipped away and was soon swallowed up in the dark. Tiller and Sandy swivelled theirs and, after Sandy had set a course on the compass grid which would run them parallel with the bank, began cautiously paddling downstream.

Every so often Tiller looked over his shoulder and then at the luminous dial of his watch. There was no signal from the other canoe and after ten minutes he tapped Sandy on the shoulder.

'Time to turn back,' he said.

'But do you see what I see?' said Sandy. He stopped paddling and pointed.

At first Tiller could not, but then he realized the bank was beginning to curve away from them.

'A bend?' he said.

'No, that's the start of a *chaung*,' said Sandy.

He swung the canoe so that it followed the line of the bank. When the canoe had followed it through nearly a right angle Tiller could see that it was indeed the mouth of a much smaller river, an outflow for the monsoon rains.

Once they were sure it was a *chaung* they swung back into the main river and signalled with the torch. Dot dash dot . . . dot dash dot. After a moment there was an answering flash in acknowledgement, a pinprick of light.

Tiller put the torch away and made sure he could draw his M2 from the canoe quickly, then settled down to wait.

It was surprising how quickly the tide was coming in now, forcing them to circle several times to prevent the canoe being driven upstream. The tide's speed delayed the other canoe's joining them but it eventually arrived, and after a whispered conference Taffy led the way into the *chaung*.

At its mouth the *chaung* was easily big enough for the *sandoway*, but after half a mile it began to narrow quite quickly. Taffy waved Tiller alongside and the two canoes rafted up.

'If the *sandoway* came into here,' Taffy said, 'it would not have gone much further up than this. We'll land and have a look around. You take the port bank. I'll take the starboard one.'

Tiller didn't know how he was expected to find any clues in the dark, but he just nodded and they made for the left-hand bank. Sandy steered towards a small, sandy spit and the canoe grounded gently. Tiller was out of the craft in an instant, his M2 in his hand. The muddy sand sucked at his boots but he moved quickly on to firmer ground, the weapon cocked and ready.

'Go right first,' advised Sandy from the canoe. 'Then I can cover you from here.'

Tiller moved a little way upstream and then stopped and listened. The silence was eerie and oppressive, unbroken except for the occasional throaty chuckle of what might have been a frog or even some kind of bird. He could not tell whether it was coming from the water or the tangled undergrowth of bushes, mangrove and bamboo thickets which fringed the *chaung*.

He crouched on his haunches and flashed his torch on the mud, well aware that doing so might draw the fire of a trigger-happy Japanese. But nothing broke the silence and he played the beam around him, hoping to find footprints or some other sign of life.

Instead, the light caught two prominent eyes staring at him from the black, glutinous mud and as he jerked back in surprise the creature, whatever it was, leapt into the water.

He moved on upstream until a tangle of mangrove prevented him going further and forced him to retrace his steps.

'See anything?' Sandy asked.

'Only something weird that leapt into the water from the bank.'

'A mud skipper, I expect. If you swing the cockle round I'll be able to cover you going to the left.'

Walking downstream, Tiller found that the mangrove petered out temporarily. The undergrowth away from the bank of the *chaung* was thinner and was replaced by tall grass and the occasional clump of bamboo. He looked for footprints along the bank or any disturbance of the ground, but found nothing. He was about to turn round when he came across a narrow path that meandered inland. Where it ended by the bank of the *chaung* there was a wide circle of trampled mud. He shone his torch on it and then returned to the canoe.

'About a hundred yards down, there's a path and footprints.'

'Are you sure?' Sandy said doubtfully. 'It could be an elephant trail.'

'I might be a new boy round here,' Tiller retorted, 'but I know elephants don't wear size ten boots. Not even in London Zoo, they don't.'

As he spoke the other cockle loomed out of the dark and grounded beside them. Tiller told Taffy what he had seen and the four of them, having extracted their weapons from the cockles, including a Bren gun, made they way downstream.

'They obviously unloaded something here and took it inland,' Taffy said, looking at the area of mud.

'The rice?'

'Must have been. Crew of six from the *sandoway* plus half a dozen Japs, say. Between them they could have shifted a lot of rice in a short time, provided it was properly bagged.'

'It looked as if it had been stored loose in the hold,' said Tiller. 'There were a lot of loose grains.'

Taffy shook his head. 'They wouldn't ship rice loose. It would be bagged. I expect one of the bags burst.'

'What now?' Dopey asked. 'Report back and get reinforcements?'

'You must be joking, Dopey,' Taffy retorted. 'By the time the ML signals Cox's Bazar to tell them what we've found and they dispatch reinforcements, the Japs will have picked up the rice, taken it into the mountains, cooked it and eaten it. No, we follow the path, find the cache and set up a nice little reception committee.'

Tiller nodded his agreement. He liked Taffy's style, but asked if the ML wouldn't wonder what had happened to them. Taffy swung his knapsack off his back and produced a small radio from it. 'The Yanks officially call it the SCR-256, unofficially the handie-talkie. We call it a walkie-talkie. Weighs just 5lb. See what I mean about Yank equipment, Tiger. Usually, they're not much use in the *chaungs* and mangroves, but we're close enough to make contact, I think.'

He pulled out the aerial, pressed a button and began talking to the ML. When he'd finished he collapsed the aerial and returned the walkie-talkie to the knapsack. 'They'll take the *sandoway* back to Cox's Bazar and will be in position to pick us up at dawn the day after tomorrow.'

'Any spare magazines for the Bren?' Tiller asked. He was glad they were taking along a Bren gun. In his experience it was the most reliable and efficient light machine-gun in the business, any Yank invention notwithstanding.

'Plenty,' Sandy said. 'And a sack of grenades. There's also plenty of water but bugger-all food.'

'By this evening you'll have had enough rice to last you a year,' Taffy promised him. 'In the meantime let's collect that extra ammunition and the water bottles. We may have a long trek ahead of us.'

They dragged the canoes out of the water and into the mangrove, and put camouflage nets over them. Then they walked back to the path and began to follow it. Immediately they hit swamp and mud and thick, choking mangrove that snagged their feet. The smell of rotting wood and vegetation made Tiller gasp in disgust. At times they had to wade almost waist high through the fetid water. By the time they had reached higher, more solid ground, dawn was breaking. Taffy signalled a halt and he and Sandy each lit a cigarette. This surprised Tiller almost as much as the number of matches it took to light them. No one ever smoked on patrol.

'Leeches,' Taffy explained. 'Now's the time to get rid of them.'

Tiller looked down and saw something black clinging to his forearm where his sleeve had come loose. He was about to flick it off when Sandy stopped him. 'You'll bleed like a stuck pig,' he warned him. 'The only way is to burn the bugger off.'

He came up with his cigarette and applied the lighted tip to the bloated leech, which dropped from Tiller's arm. Instinctively Tiller stamped on it and the ground became stained with blood.

'They get everywhere during the rainy season,' said Taffy. 'You'll go on bleeding for hours if you pull them off, as the head remains in the skin and continues to emit anti-coagulant secretions. They'll be on your legs, too.'

Reluctantly, Tiller undid his belt and dropped his trousers.

'Christ,' he said, looking down at the revolting, swollen objects clinging to his thighs and calves. 'I knew Burma was bad, but I didn't know it was this bad.'

'You'll get used to it,' said Sandy, handing him his cigarette. 'It's the flies I can't stand. I tell you in this fucking country the real enemy is disease, the monsoon and dear old mother nature – not the fucking Japs.'

5

They found the cache of rice soon after the sun had risen above the Arakan Yomas mountains, which stretched across the horizon in front of them, dividing the Arakan from the rest of Burma. A thin trickle of the greyish-white grains from a torn bag led them off the main trail into some undergrowth and after a few hundred yards they came upon a disused bamboo hut – a *basha* in the local army parlance – that stood on stilts in the middle of a small clearing. Sandy wanted to enter the hut but Taffy stopped him.

'It could be booby-trapped,' he said. 'Take Dopey, circle round the clearing and check that there aren't any other *bashas* nearby.'

As the other two men moved off, Tiller and Taffy walked cautiously towards the hut, their carbines at the ready. It was unlikely that the Japanese would booby-trap the path because any animal could set it off – but, as Taffy said, you never knew with the Japs.

They walked carefully round the hut, keeping their distance, before approaching and peering up through gaps in its floor.

'There must be a couple of hundred bags of the stuff,' Taffy said. 'Enough to feed a regiment for a week. I can't see if there's anything else in there, though.'

'Do we look?' Tiller asked. He noticed that the

ramshackle door, approached by a short flight of rickety bamboo steps, was tightly closed.

'If there's a booby-trap it will be on the door,' Taffy reminded him. 'Standard Jap procedure to put one there. The natives know it and keep clear.'

'Let's see,' said Tiller. He climbed the steps and walked right up to the closed door. He had cleared dozens of booby-traps in his time. The Italians were especially ingenious in planting them, and one of their favourite devices was made of wood and contained just enough explosive to blow a man's foot off. It was both cheap and effective – a rare combination, for it cost next to nothing to make and left the opposing side with a lot of wounded men who were a drain on resources. Such ingenuity had appealed to Tiller. After all, why kill a man when it is so much more effective to maim him?

He ran his hand carefully and lightly round the bamboo frame of the door. At the top right-hand corner his fingers came in contact with a thin, taut wire.

'There's one here all right,' he called down to Taffy, who was watching him intently. 'It's probably a pull switch which operates when the door is opened.'

He cut the wire with a small pair of pliers, one of the implements on a versatile knife he always carried, and then began feeling round the door again.

'If the Japs are like everyone else, there will be a second one,' he said.

'They're not,' said Taffy with feeling. 'They're not like anyone else, Tiger, I can tell you that. But you're right. They always use two triggering devices.'

As Taffy was speaking, Tiller's probing fingers found a second wire. Once he had severed this he pulled on the bamboo door, which squeaked on its leather hinges as it swung open. He found both pull switches, which had been jammed into either side of the door, then traced the severed wires from them up to a book-sized package lashed to the bamboo wall above the door. Tiller ran his fingertips around it to make sure that the device was not attached to another booby-trap. Satisfied, he carefully untied it and carried it into the daylight.

'That would blow a man's head off very neatly,' he said, laying it on the ground. 'What explosives do the Japs use?'

'*Shimose*, mostly,' Taffy replied, squatting on his heels to look at the device more closely. 'A form of lyddite.'

'Christ, don't they have anything more modern than that?' Tiller said, surprised. 'These pull switches are as good as any I've seen.'

He threw the two small metal objects on the ground next to the packet of explosive.

'OSS stores, I expect,' Taffy said. 'The Japs have captured a lot of stuff from the Chinese, apparently.'

He picked up one of the switches and turned it over. 'Yes, here you are.' He showed Tiller a tiny hallmark on the metal. 'That's an OSS device, all right.'

'OSS?' Tiller queried. He had never heard of any outfit with these initials.

'Office of Strategic Services,' Taffy replied. 'A Yank organization. They're everywhere in South-East Asia now, trying to raise guerrilla bands and so on. They're meant to be hush-hush but everyone knows about them.'

Sandy and Dopey broke through the undergrowth and came towards them.

'No other *bashas*,' said Sandy, 'and no sign of any other caches. But we've found a couple of good spots to site the Bren if we're going to set up an ambush here.'

Taffy entered the *basha* cautiously and shone his torch into every corner, but was soon back with the others.

'There's only the rice in there,' he said. 'I reckon they'll come for it as quickly as possible. It already smells a bit.'

'What will they do?' Tiller asked.

'Hijack some local labour and bring them in a couple of lorries to the nearest road after dark,' Taffy said promptly. 'The locals will load the rice and the Japs will then drive off. The labourers will have to walk home. It's unlikely there will be more than half a dozen Japs. They can't spare the men.'

'If you're right, Taffy, we can't set up an orthodox ambush,' said Tiller. 'We won't know who we're shooting at – Japs or Burmese.'

'Well, the Burmese are collaborating, aren't they?' said Dopey harshly. 'They'll only be getting what they deserve.'

Taffy gave him a long, hard look and Dopey shrugged and turned away.

'What we must do,' said Tiller as he carefully replaced the booby-trap and rewired it, 'is ambush the lorries once they're loaded with the rice. We won't set it up here at all.'

'Makes sense,' Taffy said, 'provided we can find the road.'

They found it eventually, though it took them most of the afternoon. It proved to be no more than a track for bullock carts that threaded its way down through the Arakan plain from the Yomas. It looked infrequently used and was much overgrown, but faint tyre marks among the wheel ruts of the local carts showed that the Japanese had recently been there.

The track was, Taffy said, too close to Japanese positions to start a fire-fight. They would just have to find a way of mounting a silent ambush and destroying the rice. Nevertheless, they sited the Bren gun so that the lorries would have no chance of escaping from its field of fire if the silent ambush went wrong. They made their plans and then sat and waited.

As the day progressed, the towering masses of monsoon clouds built over them. At one time thunder rolled around the peaks of the Yomas in the distance, and a torrent of rain swept over them which then cleared. The sun, hanging low in the sky now, looked bleary at the edges, and the air was steamy and dank.

Tiller took a swig from his water bottle and wondered how long the Japs would be in coming. He didn't fancy sitting in this sauna-like atmosphere for any longer than he needed to, for soon, as night fell, the mosquitoes would find them.

But just as the sun dipped below the horizon they heard the sound of engines. They were a long way off but quite distinct. By the time the lorries arrived it was quite dark. There were two of them, with their lights off, and open at the back. Just as Taffy had said, they were crowded with chattering Burmese – at least twenty of them, of all sizes and ages, all men or boys.

The SBS patrol watched them clamber down and crowd together while the Japanese shouted at them and at each other. No one seemed in much of a hurry. A Japanese officer wearing a cloth peaked cap and a long, curved sword at his side paced up and down while his subordinates organized the Burmese. Tiller drew a bead on him with his M2 and felt the restraining hand of Taffy on his arm.

Tiller turned his head and grinned reassuringly at his fellow sergeant, then lowered the carbine. Taffy must think him a fucking beginner if he thought he was going to ruin the whole operation by killing the officer.

Still, on reflection, Tiller understood Taffy being cautious. Better safe than sorry. It took time to get to know a new man in such a tight-knit team. Even a highly trained, élite outfit like the SBS was not exempt from finding itself harbouring a man who, for whatever reason, panicked or made an elementary mistake, or failed to pull his weight at a critical moment during an action. In an ordinary unit these men were tolerated, even protected from authority, but no one trusted them under fire, and they knew they were not trusted.

In the SBS, where everyone was a volunteer, such men were given a second chance, but never a third. After a second error they were returned to their units, discreetly, without comment. The work was too dangerous to carry passengers.

At long last the Burmese were marshalled into some sort of order and, led by one of the Japanese, set off down the path towards the *basha*. The officer went last, after ordering the two drivers to remain in their vehicles.

Somehow – and Tiller realized how fucking stupid they'd been – he and Taffy had thought the drivers would go with the rest, assuming that the Japanese would want as many hands as possible to shift the rice quickly.

Tiller could begin to see what Taffy meant when he said the Japanese always did the unexpected. They had different thought processes, was how Taffy put it. But there was probably some standing order in the Japanese army that drivers had to remain with their vehicles at all times. Whatever the reason, it meant the SBS patrol couldn't remove the distributor heads from the lorries' engines as they had planned to do. Which in turn meant that it was going to be difficult in the dark, and with the Burmese still milling about, to stop them from being driven off without opening fire on them.

Tiller felt Taffy tap him on the leg and he began to wriggle back slowly from his ambush position. Taffy put his mouth to Tiller's ear and whispered: 'What shall we do? Hope for the best?'

Tiller shook his head. He never hoped for the best. A man had to create his own luck.

'We'll take out the drivers now. Remove the distributor heads, and then wait for the remaining Japs to come back. There will be four of us and four of them. Much better that way.'

'I'll come with you.'

Again Tiller shook his head. 'One of us has to tell the others.'

Tiller, feeling Taffy hesitate in the dark, gripped his shoulder. 'I've done quite a bit of silent killing, Taffy. Better let me do it.'

Taffy grunted his reluctant agreement. 'Good luck,'

he whispered and moved off into the dark to where the Bren gun had been set up.

Tiller propped his carbine against a tree, loosened his commando knife in its sheath, and took from his pocket the length of cheesewire with its wooden handles at either end. He didn't want to use his knife if he could help it. Using the garrotte was just as quick and efficient – a man was unconscious in seven seconds, dead in fifteen – and a lot less messy than using his knife, expertly though he had been taught to handle it.

He slid silently down the bank towards the two lorries. They were parked about twenty feet apart, pointing back the way they had come. The driver of the rear one was leaning against its tailgate, smoking. Tiller could see the glow of his cigarette. He should be no problem, Tiller decided. But where was the other driver?

Tiller moved cautiously towards the first lorry. When he came level with its cab he could see that the driver was asleep, his head leaning on the driving wheel. Momentarily, Tiller considered dealing with him first, because it seemed the easier of the two options. But his training had been thorough and he remembered the advice of his instructor in such a situation. Always take the one who is awake first. If anything goes wrong it will take the sleeping one longer to react. Any noise created by dispatching the first might rouse the sleeper but he wouldn't know what was happening. He might even come and investigate, presenting an easy target.

Tiller moved back to a position where he was opposite the second Japanese. He could see that the man was getting impatient, for he kept looking at his watch. Tiller knew that the SBS patrol, by circling in search of the road, had taken very much longer to find it. It now occurred to him that the distance between the lorries and the *basha* was probably not all that far. He would have to hurry.

He moved from the undergrowth and crouched by the side of the lorry's cab, took a deep breath, and then eased himself gradually towards the end of the vehicle. He could now see that the driver was still leaning against the open tailgate. If he remained in that position it would be impossible for Tiller to use the garrotte. He wished now he had someone working with him who could distract the driver so that he could approach him from behind. Perhaps he was going to have to use his knife, after all.

He bent down and found a small stone, and as he reached the rear of the lorry he flicked it over the driver's head. He didn't hear it drop but the driver must have, for he stood upright and turned towards the sound. That was all Tiller needed. In one quick movement he threw the wire over the man's head and drew it tight around his neck while at the same time pushing his knee hard into his lower back.

The driver scrabbled desperately, Tiller overbalanced and the man landed on top of him, gurgling and wriggling. Desperation lent Tiller a strength he didn't know he had and he exerted every ounce of his muscle power on the handles of the cheesewire.

For a second or so it was touch and go whether the Japanese would be able to lessen the pressure of the wire on his windpipe by squirming around. But Tiller hung on and the man's strength quickly waned. The heels of his boots drummed on the ground and then quite suddenly, like a balloon with the air released from it, he went limp.

Tiller held tight as he counted, then rolled the Japanese off him and stood up. He bent down and felt the man's carotid artery on the right side of his neck. He was dead.

Tiller grabbed him by the collar and pulled him into the ditch. He had always thought the Japanese were a small people, but this fellow was large and powerfully built. He had, he realized, a lot to learn about his new enemy.

As he stood and listened he could feel the sweat trickling down his sides and legs, and could still smell the dead driver in his nostrils. He could not hear anything, but he knew he had to act quickly, for the rice-bearers would be back at any moment.

Throwing caution aside, he moved up to the cab of the first lorry and tapped on the window. The driver's head jerked up and he tumbled out of the cab, stuttering something in Japanese. Tiller chopped him under his ear with the side of his open hand, turned the stunned man round, and broke his neck.

As Tiller dragged the body into the ditch the others scrambled down from their positions.

'Good work, Tiger,' Taffy said softly.

'What now?' Sandy asked.

'We'll take the others as quietly as we can without alarming the Burmese too much,' said Tiller. 'Use your pistols if you want to. If you press the muzzle right into the Japs' uniforms it's as good as using a silencer. I'm going to position myself over there and will take out the Japanese bringing up the rear. It'll be the officer probably. Once I've done that I'll signal you and you can finish off the other three.'

'How will you signal us?' Taffy asked. Tiller produced a curved silver whistle-like object that the SBS teams were issued with in the Mediterranean theatre to signal to each other during an operation.

'Ever used one of these?' he asked Taffy.

The sergeant nodded. 'But they don't have that species of waterfowl over here,' he objected.

'Who's to know?' Tiller retorted. 'The Japs aren't going to have time to ask the Burmese about it, are they?'

He left the others to sort out where they wanted to position themselves and walked off down the trail. He calculated roughly the distance the returning party would be strung out along the path and added fifty yards, then found a place to hide and settled down to wait. He did not have to wait long, for within five minutes he heard the chatter of the Burmese as they approached. They appeared out of the night in single file, all of them carrying two sacks, the younger ones three stacked on top of their heads.

One of the Japanese – he seemed to be some sort of junior NCO – was leading the party and he kept turning round and urging the Burmese on. Tiller counted them as they passed, and for a nasty moment thought the other Japanese must all be bringing up the rear together. But then, about two-thirds of the way along the column, there was a short gap before two more Japanese appeared.

As they passed, Tiller noted with satisfaction that neither was the officer. The officer had looked an arrogant bastard strutting around.

The party straggling along the path seemed end-less. There must have been more Burmese than they thought. But then there was another gap and the officer came along. He was smoking a cigarette and seemed in no hurry at all. Tiller waited until he had exhaled the smoke – he didn't want him spluttering and coughing – and then clamped his hand over his mouth and drove his knife deeply into his right kidney.

The Japanese sagged and expired without any pro-test or struggle, and the Burmese porter ahead of him never faltered in his stride. Tiller waited until the porter had disappeared into the night before moving the body to the side of the trail. He wiped his knife on the dead man's tunic, returned it to its sheath, and produced the duck call. It certainly made a curious sound.

Tiller searched the officer, tucked his papers into his pocket, then hurried back along the trail. He was confident he wouldn't be needed, but he wanted to be there all the same. He rounded a corner and saw the white lungi of the last Burmese in the party well ahead of him. Then he heard three shots – two stifled, one louder – and as if by magic the Burmese were gone. They had simply evaporated into the night without a word.

Tiller broke into a run and arrived at the lorries as the other three SBS men were searching the bodies of the three dead Japanese. Two bags of rice lay in the back of the second lorry and others were scattered around the opening. Of the Burmese there was no sign.

'How many bags do you reckon they were carrying?' Taffy asked Tiller.

'Less than half of the total, no more.'

Taffy grunted. 'Yeah, I reckon that's right. I suppose we should destroy what's here.'

'Take too much time,' said Tiller. 'Anyway, the locals will take it before the Japs do. They could do with it. But we'll have to destroy what's still in the *basha*.'

They siphoned the petrol out of the lorries' tanks into cans they found in the back of one of them. They scattered the contents of one can over both vehicles while Taffy took two incendiary devices out of his knapsack.

'More OSS stores,' he said to Tiller, showing him the small, flat, black celluloid cases, no larger than a small pocket notebook. Tiller took one and weighed it in his hand. It weighed, he guessed, not much more than half a pound and was less than six inches long and half that in width. He noticed the time pencils positioned on either side of the device.

'What delay are these?' he asked.

Taffy peered at them in the dark. 'One's red. That's only twenty minutes. The other's yellow. That's roughly six and a half hours, so I'll use that one. If the Burmese return for the rice they will have come and gone by then.'

'Very neat,' said Tiller admiringly. 'What are they called?'

Taffy shrugged. 'Just pocket incendiaries, I think. They've got what the Yanks call napalm in them.'

'Napalm?' Tiller had never heard of the word.

'Naphthalic and palmitic,' Taffy explained. 'They're acids which turn petrol into a kind of jelly.'

He removed the yellow-tagged time pencil, squeezed the tube to break the glass ampoule inside it, and carefully

74

replaced it in its groove alongside the incendiary device's black case. He primed the second device in the same way and then placed one under the driver's seat in each lorry.

The first hint of dawn was in the sky above the mountains when they reached the *basha*. They doused it with petrol and set it alight. As they watched the building go up in flames, a series of violent explosions rocked the air, making Tiller jump sideways towards the nearest cover.

Sandy laughed. 'Pockets of air in the bamboo, Sarge. They expand and explode. Sounds just like small-arms fire. I tell you, Sarge, Burma's full of oddities. You'll get used to it.'

6

'Good. In fact, excellent.' Major Jim Danforth leant forward in his chair and dropped the report on to his desk.

Outside in the compound that housed the local military establishments at Cox's Bazar the singsong chatter of Indian soldiers mixed with the chirrup of the local frog population. Together they made a soothing, almost somnolent sound that drifted through the open windows of the SBS officer's tiny office. A hoopoe flew in its undulating way into a nearby tree, disturbing a family of monkeys, which screeched angrily at the salmon-pink bird.

Tiller wiped the sweat from his forehead and, out of the corner of his eye, watched a gecko traverse the wall behind his commanding officer. It moved in jerks. For minutes at a time it stayed motionless, as if it had been hung there, then would suddenly dart forward a few inches at incredible speed before halting again. Once or twice its tongue flicked in and out, though whether it was testing the space in front of it, or was catching something invisible to the human eye, Tiller couldn't tell. That's right, carefully does it, he said to it approvingly: the well-known adage 'time spent in reconnaissance is never wasted' applied as much to a gecko as it did to an SBS man.

'Thank you, sir.'

'About half a ton, you reckon?'

'That's what Sergeant Welsh calculated. Didn't the Burmese crew know?'

'They're still being interrogated,' said Danforth. 'The trouble is, you have to use two interpreters: one to translate from Arakanese into Burmese, the other from Burmese into English. It takes an hour to ask a question and another hour to get an answer. Bloody typical.'

Typical of what exactly, Danforth didn't say.

'There was an interpreter with us who seemed to speak English and the lingo,' Tiller said.

'Tantok, you mean? He speaks a little English, but he won't interrogate anyone. His sympathies lie with the locals, really.'

Tiller remembered the tall, grave, dignified figure of the captain of the *sandoway* as he had peered down at him over the side of his ship.

'What will happen to them, sir?'

'The crew? The captain will be fined and the ship will probably be impounded.'

'I suppose they were only trying to earn their living,' Tiller muttered. 'And I don't suppose the Japs gave them much choice.'

'True. But if the Japs caught any Burmese working for us,' Danforth reminded him, 'they'd shoot them out of hand. We don't want to antagonize the locals – the British colonial government sitting on its collective arse in Simla keeps reminding us not to – but equally we can't allow them to aid and abet the Japs to supply their front-line troops. We try and steer a middle path. We end up satisfying no one. Bloody typical.'

The gecko jerked across the wall. The fan whirring

noisily and laboriously in the middle of the ceiling stirred the humid air without noticeably cooling it.

'I wanted to have a word with you, Tiger. I know you're only attached to us pro tem, but Taffy has spoken highly of you. Frankly, I want to hang on to you for as long as possible. There's something quite big in the air and I could use you for it. In the meantime I'd give you your own ML and your own patrol. How about it?'

Tiller hesitated. Hasler wouldn't be arriving in Ceylon for some weeks. He now had the dreaded word 'instructor' on his records, which meant, in theory, any senior officer in the Far East theatre could make a request for him on a temporary basis. Once that occurred he might be lost in a jungle of red tape from which even Blondie might not be able to extricate him. Much better to remain here, where there was at least some action, until Blondie called for him.

'Fine, sir. Thank you.'

'Good. There's someone I want you to meet.'

Danforth pressed a button on his intercom. 'Ask Mr Coates to come in, will you.'

As he leant back in his chair a satisfied smile played on Danforth's face. Though HO – hostilities only – he had taken to soldiering as the proverbial duck to water, and had taken to the SBS in particular. Trained by Roger Pountney, he had survived some of the early raids in the Mediterranean, and had done his stint as an instructor at Ardrossan–Saltcoats in Ayrshire before joining Z SBS – one of Pountney's offshoots – in Algiers. Z SBS specialized in clandestine warfare, ferrying agents into France and Italy from

Allied submarines, and sometimes – if the agents were lucky – in picking them up again.

Danforth's time in Z SBS had highlighted for him the essential difference between the SBS and the SAS, whom many in the military hierarchy thought of as the land equivalent of the SBS. The SBS worked discreetly, in pairs, essentially alone, while the SAS's job was to work and fight together to create mayhem behind enemy lines. This basic difference in approach necessitated different types of men, something the high-ups did not always appreciate. So it sometimes occurred that the wrong sort of men appeared in the ranks of the SBS. It could have been that Tiller was one of them. Danforth now knew he was not.

'You wanted to see me, Major?'

The crisp, authoritative voice made Tiller turn in his chair. The man standing by the door was in civilian clothes – khaki shirt and shorts, knee-length khaki socks – but he wore a revolver at his hip and carried a thick, black walking stick with an unusually shaped crook.

Danforth leapt to his feet, crossed the room, and pumped the civilian's hand warmly. 'Good to see you, Dick. Come in, come in.' The man accepted a chair on the other side to Danforth's desk from where Tiller was sitting. He had a deeply creased, leathery face, a close-clipped moustache, vigorous black hair slightly tinged with grey, and eyes like gimlets. They bored into Tiller as Danforth made the introductions, taking in Tiller's parachute wings and DCM ribbon without visible change of expression.

Tiller nodded awkwardly. He knew without thinking how to react in front of men dressed in uniform,

whether they were generals or corporals. But civilians
– especially one in a combat zone – always made him
uneasy. War at the sharp end was the business of
soldiers, that's how he saw it.

'Mr Coates is – was – a forestry officer in Burma,'
Danforth explained. 'Part of the colonial government.'

'Game warden too,' Coates added, 'until the buggers
sacked me.' He cleared his throat harshly as if he was
about to spit out the memory of it.'

'Quite,' said Danforth easily. Tiller got the immediate impression that the SBS major knew and liked
Coates, and understood his testiness. 'Except your
file, Dick,' he said gently, 'has it worded "voluntary
retirement after a distinguished career which earned
him a well-earned OBE", or something similar. I much
prefer that version.'

'You may. I don't,' Coates said curtly. 'Mealy-
mouthed buggers. Never ever said what they meant.
I was sacked. Given the boot. It's as simple as that.'

The gecko, perhaps not accustomed to all the movement in the room, had decided to beat a retreat. It had
turned round but must have then forgotten where it
had come from, for it stayed frozen at the same height
as the slowly circulating fan. Tiller tried to suppress
a smile.

'And what are you grinning at, young man?' Coates
said, glaring across the room.

'I always like to hear someone speaking the truth,
sir,' said Tiller. He called this prickly old sod 'sir'
because he had been brought up by his grandfather to
respect his elders, and Coates must be, Tiller reckoned,
all of forty-five. He glanced at Danforth. 'Sorry, sir, am
I speaking out of turn?'

'Not at all. Tiger. I think you two will get along famously.'

Tiller stiffened inwardly. He opened his mouth and then shut it again. He felt like the gecko, not entirely sure which way to move.

Coates, however, pounced. 'You mean, I'll be working with Sergeant Tiller?'

Danforth nodded. 'Any objections?'

Coates cleared his throat and briefly smoothed his moustache. 'Looks a bit young, that's all. How long have you been in Burma, Sergeant?'

Tiller told him.

'Two weeks. Two *weeks*?' Coates seemed amazed that anyone could be anywhere only two weeks. 'You know how long I've been in Burma? Twenty-five years.'

'That's why we've taken up your kind offer to help,' Danforth said tactfully. 'We need your experience.'

Danforth turned to Tiller. 'Mr Coates is fluent in Arakanese. He knows the Arakan and its people intimately. He also knows just about everything there is to know about the Japanese because he helped fight them in 1942. He'll be working alongside you on the kind of operations you'll be doing. But you're in charge, Tiger. Dick understands that, don't you, Dick?'

'What are these operations exactly?' Tiller asked.

'As you know, we're primarily here to harass the Japs' coastal supply lines. Fifteenth Corps is planning to make a big push in the area now to try and capture Akyab before the monsoon proper begins. So we've had orders not to scale down our activities because of the monsoon but to increase them to obtain as much information about Japanese dispositions as possible.

That might mean occasionally going inland – not just keeping to the rivers – both to capture Japanese personnel for interrogation and to send in jitter parties.'

'Jitter parties?' Tiller asked.

'Small groups of men who'll attack Jap rear positions. Make them edgy, uncertain. The Japs used them a lot in Burma in 1942 and we've taken a leaf from their book. It means working with the local people more than the kind of patrol you've been on so far. But we've also got to try and stop the locals warning the Japanese of our presence.'

'How do they do that?'

'They see an ML approaching at dusk and when it gets dark they simply light a bonfire. The Japs then know there's an ML in the area and they lie low in one of the *chaungs* until the ML's passed. It's very crude but very effective and we've got to stop it. Too many supplies are still getting through to the Japs.'

'And who's going to make up the rest of the team, sir?'

'You happy to have Sandy and Dopey? Taffy doesn't mind.'

In their different ways both SBS men had proved themselves during that last patrol. Tiller nodded his agreement. 'That's fine with me.'

'Good. We'll go down to the ML now so that I can brief you and the skipper on the patrol tonight.'

Outside, the towering clouds loomed above the harbour, threatening yet another downpour.

'When do you reckon the monsoon proper will arrive, Dick?' Danforth asked Coates.

The civilian studied the clouds. 'Not long. Another week or so. It's going to be early this year.'

'After this morning's downpour, I thought it had already arrived,' Tiller commented.

'You ain't seen nothing yet, Tiger,' Danforth said. 'I was here at the tail end of last year's monsoon and what came down this morning was just a light shower. Up to two hundred inches can fall in the Arakan in a year. That's a hell of a lot of water.'

Their ML had recently arrived from Simonstown via Chittagong. You could tell which of its crew hadn't been in Burma long, Tiller thought. In the Western Desert white knees indicated a new arrival. Here, the skins of some of the crew had not yet acquired the yellowish tinge that appeared after a few months on Mepacrine.

The ML's skipper greeted them with a casual salute and a warm smile. A small monkey, perched on his shoulder, chattered noisily at them. Its bright, button eyes watched them warily as they shook hands with its owner, who introduced himself as Lieutenant David Locker. 'Inevitably known as Davy Jones after the locker, I'm afraid,' he said with a friendly grin, his South African accent very distinct.

Under his beard Locker's skin was quite yellow and it transpired that he was an old hand on the Arakan coast.

The monkey bounced and chattered as Coates peered at it. 'A rhesus – am I right?' he said, but it wasn't really a question.

'If you say so,' said the South African with his strange nasal twang. 'We all call him Nabob. We traded him for a hundred cigarettes when we stopped at Calcutta. I'll show you round.'

One ML was very much like another in layout,

but there was an atmosphere unique to each. Tiller felt it at once in the way the crew reacted. Most of them were new to Burma, but they'd already been long enough with their captain to catch his obvious enthusiasm for his job. They were alert, smartly turned out, and the ML was spotless – quite unusual in a new vessel which must have been sailed straight from the builder's yard.

At one point Locker drew Tiller to one side. 'We'll be working together a lot. In harbour it's best to keep to the formalities, but at sea and on patrol I'm Davy to you and your patrol.'

'And I'm Tiger.'

Who's this civvy character, Tiger?' Jones nodded behind him at Coates, who was examining the three-pounder on the foredeck.

'Someone the major foisted on me. He's a sort of guide.'

Tiller expected the lieutenant to object, perhaps almost hoped he would. He assumed naval officers didn't like civilians aboard their ships any more than he liked having one as part of his patrol. Instead, the South African said: 'Good idea. I know the coastline from here right down to Sandoway, and most of the rivers, but you'll need someone who knows the area if you go inland.'

In the tiny wardroom Danforth spread out a large-scale map of the area to the south of Cox's Bazar. 'This is the River Mayu, which you patrolled the other night, Tiger. But I want you to move further south and go up the Kaladan. As you can see, like the Mayu it runs from north to south, so it's a convenient artery into Japanese-held territory. Akyab, at its entrance, is still in Japanese hands, but we're not sure how strong they are inland. The Kaladan's navigable right up to Paletwa, but that's already fallen to Fifteenth Corps. You know the Kaladan, Davy?'

The South African shook his head. 'Never been up it. We don't usually operate so far from base.'

'Familiar to you, Dick?'

Coates nodded. 'It's a maze of islands and *chaungs*,' he replied.

'It's also a main artery for Jap supplies,' said Danforth, 'but that's not why we're sending you up here. We need to know how strongly the Japs are holding the area inland. Latest intelligence suggests they still hold Apaukwa. The best way of doing that is to take a Jap prisoner.'

'I thought that was almost impossible,' said Tiller.

'It's easier than it was,' said Danforth. 'Jap morale is pretty low now that they are on the run. So the ordinary soldier is tending to surrender, not commit *hara-kiri*.'

Tiller wondered what sort of army they were up against if suicide was a sign of high morale.

'*Seppaku* is the correct term,' Coates interjected without taking his eyes off the map.

'Whatever it's called, it's messy,' said Danforth. 'So don't go for an officer or a senior NCO even though they're likely to know more. Take a junior NCO or an ordinary soldier. Because being made a prisoner of war is such a disgrace the ordinary soldier has had no training in how to counter interrogation. So it's easy enough to get out of them what they do know.'

Davy was busy measuring the distance from the sea to Apaukwa. 'That's a good sixty miles,' he said. 'It's going to be a long patrol.'

'We'll expect you to be away a week, perhaps more,' Danforth confirmed. He turned to his SBS men. 'Take three Mk II canoes but no heavy automatic weapons. You're not going there to cause mayhem. It'll be a typical SBS operation. And don't forget your Mepacrine and condoms.'

'Condoms?' Tiller queried. 'What . . . ?'

'They are the only way to keep your watch, compass and matches dry on patrol,' Danforth explained, and then grinned at Tiller and said: 'What else were you thinking you might need them for, Tiger?'

They sailed from Cox's Bazar the following evening and an alert lookout on the ML saw the first flare of the bonfire just as the bottom rim of the sun touched the horizon to starboard. The fire was almost abeam of the ML and it flickered momentarily, hardly visible to the naked eye, before it disappeared.

Davy trained his binoculars on the hillside from where the lick of flame had appeared, and mouthed an expletive which made Nabob hop and chitter on his shoulder.

'Fuck it,' he said loudly.

They were well south of the River Naaf, off a part of the Arakan that could be held by either Fifteenth Corps or the Japanese. Either way, the last thing Davy wanted was for the chain of bonfires to precede his arrival off Akyab. Especially as they were going to have to lie up for the day under camouflage netting before preceding at dusk up the river. The Japs didn't have much offensive sea power in the area, but they still had some bombers. If they knew where the ML was lying it was possible they might try to attack it from the air.

'Are you sure it's a signal fire?' Tiller asked. He was standing next to Davy on the ML's open bridge.

'Well, there's only one way to find out,' Davy answered. 'Port thirty. Increase speed to fifteen knots,' he said into the voice pipe. 'We're going in and I'll put you ashore in the rubber dinghy to deal with it, Tiger. It'll take you and two others. Is that enough?'

Tiller nodded, though he had no idea if it would be or not.

'They won't be Japs,' said Davy reassuringly, 'and probably not ordinary natives either. Often they're members of the Burma National Army who do this sort of thing – a collaborationist outfit.'

The coastline loomed up in the gathering dark and the ML slowed to a stop. The rubber dinghy was launched over the side and the crewman scrambled down into it. Coates appeared on deck, buckling on his revolver.

'I assume you'll be wanting me,' he said.

'Not this time, Dick,' Tiller answered. It had never occurred to him that Coates would even think he might be needed. 'No room in the dinghy, I'm afraid.'

Coates grunted something and turned away.

Tiller, Sandy and Dopey lowered themselves cautiously into the rubber dinghy, which bounced alarmingly on the water. Each was armed with an M2 carbine and hand-grenades. The crewman rowed them silently to the beach, some fifty yards away, and said he would return for them when they signalled to the ML from the beach.

The beach was quite firm but immediately to their right they could see the beginnings of a mangrove swamp which probably hid the muddy estuary of a small *chaung*. They moved inland on a compass course, their automatic carbines at the ready, and were soon making their way through sparse, chest-high elephant grass interspersed with denser clumps of bamboo. In the darkness ahead an owl hooted twice.

As the ground began to rise the elephant grass grew thicker and higher, and here and there palm trees rose up tall into the night sky. The elephant grass made it difficult to see any distance ahead and Tiller, who was holding the pocket compass in front of him, was careful to ensure they kept their bearings.

After a while the elephant grass became shorter and more sparse and Tiller could see that the ground now started to rise sharply up to the hilltop where the fire had been lit. There was no sign of it now.

Tiller turned and said in a low voice: 'We won't go straight up. Too obvious. We'll skirt round and approach from inland.'

Sandy and Dopey nodded.

'Don't fire unless you're fired upon,' Tiller added.

They followed the contour of the hill inland, but a swampy area soon forced them to take a higher route. The ground squelched under their feet and mangrove roots snared their boots. Behind him Tiller heard Sandy stumble and swear under his breath, and he could feel the sweat cascading down his face. He wiped his forehead with his sleeve and felt the sweat sting his eyes. Again, somewhere ahead of them, an owl hooted twice.

The nature of the ground gradually forced the three men higher and higher until they came to a flattened area, some sort of vegetable garden, long abandoned. They skirted it and then turned directly uphill.

As they approached the summit the hillside became bare of vegetation. At one point Tiller dropped on to his haunches and waved the other two down. He studied the shape of the hilltop against the night sky but could see nothing moving. He got up and moved slowly forward, his ears straining for any unfamiliar sound. About twenty feet from the top he waved the other two down and moved forward by himself in a crouching position before crawling the last few yards to the top.

Beyond the ridge there was a large dip in the ground before it rose again. Beyond, Tiller could see the waters of the Bay of Bengal. Now he understood why they had only seen a momentary flicker of the flame: the signallers had built the fire well below the second ridge in the middle of the horseshoe-shaped hollow. Provided the flames were kept to a reasonable height, the only direction it could be seen from was the south. He probed the darkness around the glowing fire but could see no movement.

Tiller turned and beckoned to the other two.

'What do you reckon?' he whispered when they joined him. 'Looks deserted to me.'

'Perhaps they've got a nice little ambush laid on for us,' Sandy whispered.

'You mean from that ridge? That's the only possible place.'

'I'll take a look-see,' Dopey suggested and Tiller nodded.

Dopey slid away into the dark.

The other two waited, half expecting the rattle of automatic fire. But nothing happened and a few minutes later Dopey was back shaking his head.

'Not a dicky-bird,' he murmured.

'Strange,' said Tiller. 'Perhaps they heard us coming and just made a bunk for it.'

'Sounds reasonable,' said Sandy. 'Let's put that fire out and get the hell out of here.'

While the other two covered him Tiller moved forward and inspected the fire. It had been well laid and a pile of branches was stacked beside it. Tiller seized one and began scattering the burning logs. Then he scooped up loose sand and earth and quickly managed to douse the fire completely. He gathered up the spare branches, lugged them up to the far ridge and threw them over the edge into the mangrove swamp below. It seemed a rather pointless exercise, but it was, he supposed, better than nothing.

They could not wait for the signallers to return, but by way of a deterrent Tiller quickly laid an elementary booby-trap with a trip-wire and two of his grenades. It was an old trick which he had been taught at the start of the war. He tied the trip-wire to two rocks so that it stretched at ankle height across the path to where the fire had been laid. Then he took out the safety-pin of one of the hand-grenades, pressed its handle into the ground and weighed it with one of the stones. He then repeated the process with the other grenade. Anyone hitting the trip-wire would dislodge the stones, allowing the handles to fly off and activate the grenades' fuses. It was a crude and not very effective booby-trap, as the grenades would expend most of their fragmentation power on the ground, but it was better than nothing.

The SBS patrol retraced their steps as quickly as possible and were wading through the elephant grass near the beach when they heard the owl hoot for the third time. Tiller paused.

'What is it, Sarge?' Sandy breathed in his ear.

What was it?

Tiller's sixth sense told him something was not right, but the alien environment made him doubt his own intuition. The air was leaden with heat and in the distance thunder rumbled. He realized then that they were retracing their footsteps exactly – always a basic error.

He indicated for the other two to follow him and moved off to the left. If it meant wading through the edge of the mangrove swamp, so be it.

They emerged from the chest-high elephant grass right where the mud and the mangrove began and as they did so light automatic fire opened up on them from their right.

Phut, phut, phut. The bullets struck the elephant grass behind them as they dived for cover into the mud and mangrove.

To Tiller's surprise he heard the fire being returned from the mangroves in front of them. Then the twin Oerlikons on the ML opened up with a stream of 20mm tracer shells that seared through the elephant grass. There were two piercing screams, followed by silence.

Tiller waited and then levered himself up cautiously. There was a movement ahead of him and he found himself facing Coates and the fourth member of the SBS team.

Coates was resting his carbine on his right shoulder, his forefinger resting on the trigger guard. Tiller had often seen photographs of big-game hunters carrying their weapons in a similar fashion.

'What the fuck . . . ?' he began.

'I'm glad you at least had the sense to come back a different way,' Coates said brusquely. 'Let's see what damage we've done.'

He strode off through the elephant grass, followed by the others.

A hundred yards along the beach they came across a carefully prepared ambush position. Two men in a uniform Tiller had never seen before lay dead in front of it and a third lay on his back some yards away. He was still alive but he died in one final spasm as they came up to him. By his side was a Japanese light machine-gun with a haversack full of spare magazines. There was a smell of burnt grass where the Oerlikon tracer shells had singed the undergrowth.

'Burma National Army,' said Coates turning over one of the bodies with his boot. 'You were lucky to get away with that, Sergeant.'

'How did you get ashore?' said Tiller. He thought he'd made it plain to Coates that he had had no need of him.

'In the rubber dinghy, of course. Danforth told me to stick to you like glue. Immediately I got ashore and heard that owl call I knew you were in trouble.'

Coates spread out the rain capes belonging to two of the dead Burmese and began methodically searching the bodies, throwing any documents he found on one of the capes and any weapons he found on the other. Tiller noticed that he went about his task with practised ease.

'But why?' he asked. 'It was just an ordinary owl.'

Coates glanced up and gave Tiller what even in the dark Tiller could see was a withering look. 'You don't get screech owls on the coast. Only inland. Don't you know that? No, there's no reason why you should. Anyway, once we knew what was happening they never stood a chance. But then neither would you have if you'd come back the same way.'

'Glad I did something right,' Tiller retorted. He felt rather like a schoolboy being reproved by his form master.

Coates shrugged, wrapped up the two heaps in the two capes and tied a knot in them. He handed the one containing weapons to Sandy.

'Dump those on the way back,' he said. 'I'll take the documents and look through them later.'

He pointed to the light machine-gun and haversack, and said to Dopey: 'You take those. They might come in useful.'

Dopey glanced at Tiller, who nodded.

'Right,' said Coates, 'let's signal for the dinghy.'

Back on the ML Coates disappeared below with the documents and Tiller joined Davy on the bridge as the ML surged slowly ahead.

'Quite a character, that bloke,' Davy said cheerfully. 'He was clucking around after you like an old hen. He didn't think you were safe ashore on your own. It seems he was right, too.'

The ML skipper glanced mischievously at Tiller, who just said: 'We'll have to step on it if we're going to get to that island by dawn.'

When they reached the northern end of Akyab island it took them some time to find a convenient *chaung* to lie up in. As they drew the camouflage netting over the ML the first glimmer of light was already showing above the Yomas. It was a black morning with towering cumulus clouds and no sooner had the crew finished putting the netting in place than the heavens opened and Tiller, lying in a bunk immediately under the deck, fell asleep to the rhythm of the rain pounding above him.

7

Tiller was awake and half sitting up immediately the crewman's hand touched his shoulder. He could still hear the drumming of heavy rain on the deck above him.

'The skipper said you'd probably want to know that we're underway, Sarge.'

'I thought we weren't going to move until after dusk,' said Tiller, swinging his legs off the bunk. He could feel the movement of the ML as it sliced through the waves.

'It is after dusk,' said the crewman with a grin. 'You've been out for twelve hours. Mr Coates said to leave you.'

What the fuck was it to do with Coates? Tiller wondered irritably as he pulled on his boots.

'There's some hot soup in the wardroom,' said the crewman.

Tiller thanked him and buckled on his belt with its commando knife and .45 pistol attached to it. The wardroom was only for officers but Davy ran his ship his way and the entire SBS patrol, including Coates, had been given automatic entry into it. They were all there now, eating tinned soup and bread.

Coates glanced up and said: 'You had a good sleep,'

in his matter-of-fact way. He looked as fresh as he had the previous evening.

'I hope we all did,' Tiller replied. 'We won't be getting much from now on.'

'Never sleep much anyway,' Coates said offhandedly. 'Spent most of the day going through the documents from those Burmese.'

'Anything of interest?'

'It's obvious the Japs are in the process of moving a BNA regiment into the area to try and counter our activities.'

'What is this Burma National Army exactly?' Sandy asked him. 'We know they're collaborators, but where did they spring from?'

Coates was in his element explaining the pre-war Burmese independent movement, the 'Thirty Comrades' who had formed the Burma Independence Army to fight for freedom from British rule, and how the Japanese had used this small force for internal security after they had invaded the country. Once Burma had been conquered, he explained, the Japanese turned the Army into the Burma Defence Army, which became the Burma National Army when Burma was granted independence by the Japanese the previous year.

'Is that right?' Tiller queried. 'I thought the Japs ruled the country as the occupying power.'

'So they do in reality,' said Coates. 'But the Burmese are only just beginning to realize that. Incidentally, it's only the ethnic Burmese who collaborate. Most of the hill tribes like the Karens and Kachins loathe the Japs.'

'Complicated business,' said Tiller, but in his mind anyone in uniform firing a weapon at him was fair game.

'War always is,' Coates grunted.

By the time they'd finished their meal the rain had stopped and Tiller went on to the bridge to join Davy. Akyab island was now just a thin line on the horizon to port; ahead lay the six-mile-wide estuary of the Kaladan. The South African took Tiller below and spread out a chart of the river.

'Plenty of depth under our keel for at least thirty miles,' he said. 'We should easily cover that distance in the dark, provided we don't encounter any Jap river traffic. If we do, then we'll just have to lie low up one of these *chaungs* for another day.'

'And after thirty miles?'

'It begins to get shallow and, as you can see, it also starts to narrow quite a bit. I wouldn't like to take you much further than, say, here.'

He pointed to a bend in the river near the outflow of a small *chaung*. 'You could either cut across land to Apaukwa or go by canoe.'

Tiller studied the chart. Thirty miles by ML was more than three hours at normal cruising speed. By canoe it was nine hours, perhaps more, depending on the current. If the ground was flat it would be quicker to walk, but only Coates would know that.

But when they asked his opinion, having called him into the chart room, the forester immediately shook his head. 'It's flat all right, but it's all paddy-fields, ankle deep in water, perhaps deeper. Quicker to go on the river. It's always quicker by river in Burma.'

It seemed sound advice and Tiller thanked him.

'I assume this time I'm going with you.' Coates made it a statement of fact.

Tiller grinned. 'Glad to have you along, sir.'

'Don't call me sir,' said Coates. 'It makes me sound old. Dick's my name.'

Tiller asked him if he had ever been in a canoe. 'Once spent three weeks going down the Irrawaddy in one,' was the gruff reply. 'Can handle a paddle as well as the next man.' And with that Coates stumped out of the chart room.

Davy and Tiller exchanged amused glances. 'Cantankerous old sod,' said Davy, but there was a note of admiration in his voice.

By midnight the ML was past Akyab town, an area heavily patrolled by Japanese patrol boats, and had entered the river, though it was too wide to see both banks. Davy kept to the middle of the stream. The water was calm but the tide was ebbing strongly and this held the ML back at first. However, in the early morning the tide began to flood and the ML soon ate up the miles and although it was still pitch-dark it became possible to see the outline of both banks of the river clearly. All night, the gun crews stayed closed up on the three-pounder forward and the twin Oerlikons, which were positioned aft of the funnel, but there had been no sign of any river traffic.

Before dawn broke, Davy took the ML into a small *chaung*, anchored her clear of an outcrop of mangrove and threw the camouflage netting over her. Sheets of rain blown by the prevailing south-westerly monsoon wind whipped across the *chaung* and hammered at the ML's deck but brought no relief from the humid heat that hung over the ship.

By dusk the rain had cleared and the sun went down, a lurid orange orb, its colour reflected on the massive clouds that dominated the western horizon.

In the chart room Davy pointed out to Tiller the *chaung* in which they were sheltering and then, with his dividers, measured how much further upstream the ML could safely go.

'Just a couple of hours' steaming,' he said. 'We'll go into this *chaung* here to wait for you. It winds fairly close to Apaukwa and it's certainly big enough for the cockles. I'll take you up it as far as I can. How long do you think you're going to be?'

'We'll have to lie up tomorrow,' Tiller replied. 'You'd better give us seventy-two hours.'

Davy nodded. 'We can hang on that long provided we're not spotted.'

'Do the Japs have many air patrols?' Tiller asked.

'The sky's ours, more or less,' Davy replied cheerfully. 'Don't worry. We'll be waiting for you.'

Before the last glimmer of light had left the sky the ML edged its way back into the main stream and headed up river. The guns' crews were all closed up to their weapons and on the bridge lookouts scanned both banks with night binoculars. The ML's speed was cut right down and its engines just gave a low burble. One hour went by, then two. Davy cut the vessel's speed until it was only just moving against the sluggish current.

'There,' said one of the crew in an undertone, pointing across the river. Davy nodded and gave orders for the ML to change course.

The *chaung* did not seem much narrower than the main river but it soon became shallower and at one point the ML ran gently on to a sandbank. It came off easily enough when its engines were reversed but Davy said to Tiller: 'I can't risk going any further up. Sorry.'

He turned the ML round, its propellers churning up the muddy waters and eased it expertly across the *chaung* before giving the order to put the engines in neutral. The freed clutch set up its usual unsettling whine.

'Slow astern,' Davy said into the voice pipe and the ML came to a halt close to the eastern bank where it had been built up to channel the monsoon waters into the main river.

Tall palms – called *danis*, Coates said – and much shorter mango trees studded the bank. One palm, nearly uprooted by the cyclones that sometimes raged across the area, had been blown at a precarious angle over the *chaung*. Its large leaves, used by the natives to roof their *bashas*, would help hide the ML from the air.

Davy ordered the clutch to be briefly engaged and the ML slid towards the tree.

'Slow astern.'

When the ship had lost all way but before it could start drifting, its anchor was let go and the chain rattled noisily in the hawse-pipe. The anchor dropped into the murky water with a loud splash.

'I want two warps ashore as well.'

The rubber dinghy was launched and the warps secured to the nearest trees. A silence settled on the *chaung*.

'Let's get those cockles in the water,' said Tiller quietly to his men, and the three Mk II canoes were slipped over the side.

Tiller had taken a trace of the *chaung* and the surrounding area from Davy's chart, and he now showed this to Sandy and Dopey before they started off.

'I reckon it's not more than about four hours' paddling,' he said, indicating the way up the *chaung* with a pencil. 'We'll lie up at dawn around here. I'll lead and take Mr Coates with me. Sandy, you have Tiny, as you're number two and take up the rear.'

Tiny Joad, the fourth member of the SBS patrol, was a tough, six-foot-two guardsman with a liking for unarmed combat.

'Dopey, you follow me in the spare cockle with the stores.'

In turn, they descended the rope ladder and dropped expertly into the cockles' circular cockpits and then, with brisk strokes of the double paddles, made for the middle of the *chaung*. When all three were assembled there they formed line astern and began the long trek up the waterway.

The darkness was intense and the black tangle of the mangrove swamps which lined both sides of the murky water seemed to close in on them the further upstream they went.

'Watch out for crocodiles,' said Coates in Tiller's ear. 'They're shy creatures, but it's best to avoid hitting any if you can.'

From the way Coates spoke Tiller felt that he was enjoying himself hugely. The older man certainly had no trouble keeping up with Tiller's rate of paddling.

'Are any of them man-eaters?' Tiller asked over his shoulder, half in jest.

'Certainly,' came the terse reply. 'And the biggest ones around here can grow up to thirty feet long.'

It struck Tiller then that Sandy was right: disease, the monsoon and mother nature, as he so quaintly called it, were far bigger hazards than the Japanese. At Cox's

Bazar all new arrivals were lectured by the chief medical officer. Besides warning of the dire consequences of malaria if Mepacrine was not taken daily, he had listed some of the more common medical problems, explaining their symptoms and their effects. Tiller could only remember some of them, but dengue fever and the ulcers that developed from any sort of open wound stuck in his memory as having particularly unpleasant consequences. And there was also something called the mango fly, the medical officer had added, which liked to lay its eggs under your eyelids.

'Our main problem won't be the crocs,' said Coates, cutting across Tiller's thoughts. 'It'll be getting over that jungle-covered ridge that divides this *chaung* from Apaukwa.'

They paddled until dawn and then rafted up under a large arch of undergrowth which hung over the syrupy black water. At daylight Tiller and Coates splashed through the mud of the mangrove swamp and on to firmer ground.

'We can either cut across to the ridge from here,' said Coates, 'or go further up the *chaung* in the cockles.'

They studied the tracing from the chart and calculated the quickest way was overland, as the *chaung* swung away from the ridge before returning and running alongside it.

'The first bit will be the easiest,' said Coates, surveying the land in front of them. 'It's drier than I thought it would be.'

They decided to start immediately, and to take Sandy with them. The other two would wait with the cockles. If the trio did not return within twenty-four hours then the other two would make the reconnaissance before returning to the ML.

They skirted some paddy-fields, wet underfoot, and then gained higher ground, where the sun slanted through a mixture of teak and cedar trees. Then the going became more difficult, for the undergrowth was a mass of knotted bamboo canes and elephant grass, and they took it in turns to lead the way.

The heat and humidity, and the exertion of cutting their way through the undergrowth with their kukris – the traditional curved knives carried by the Gurkhas – left the two SBS men drenched in sweat and gasping for breath. The forester, quite unperturbed, moved forward at a steady pace, chopping rhythmically at the undergrowth. Once a wild pig almost ran through Tiller's legs in fright, but otherwise they saw and heard only the occasional bird and the incessant chattering of monkeys swinging in the trees above. In the jungle, Coates told them, you had to stay dead still to see what was there around you.

Soon the scattering of trees quickly gave way to more open country and they could see the ridge above them. They rested for an hour and brewed some tea on the small Primus Tiller carried.

When Tiller had difficulty in lighting a match Sandy said: 'With Indian matches eight things can happen. They light: highly unusual. The head breaks off. There is no head. The stick breaks in half. The head ignites and the flame runs straight up the stick and burns your fingers. The head ignites but the flame goes out at once. The head splutters and is consumed without there being any flame. The head flies off, alight, and burns either you or your clothes.'

After all these things had happened, some more than once, Tiller managed to get a match to light properly and they had their tea. But as they started towards the ridge the rain swept down on them, drenching them to the skin, and the jungle closed in on them once more. When the rain stopped the ground steamed like a cauldron.

It was late afternoon by the time they reached the top of the ridge and were able to look down on the *bashas* of the township that were dotted across the open plain below them. Most of them were huddled near a bamboo bridge which spanned a *chaung*. In the *chaung* were a number of sampans tied up alongside a jetty. One was being unloaded with rice by a group of natives watched by several Japanese soldiers. There was also a group of *bashas* around the sole stone building, which was directly below them.

'A school?' Tiller asked.

'Missionary church, more likely,' Coates replied. 'The Japs will have taken it over.'

They counted the military traffic that crossed the bridge and noted the different types of vehicles. The track leading to and from it seemed to have been heavily used. It ran, a winding red scar, towards the Yomas. The church seemed to be a headquarters of some kind, for the drivers of both convoys and individual vehicles always stopped and entered it before proceeding.

'Looks a worthwhile target,' said Coates, scribbling in his notebook. 'The RAF will want to know about it.'

Towards dusk natives began to return from the fields. Several hung on to the back of a full-grown elephant while others were crowded into a bullock cart.

They streamed across the bridge and disappeared into the *bashas*. By now the sampan had been unloaded and replaced by another. The labourers were still at work removing the bags of rice from it when the darkness swallowed them up.

'Where do we think is the best place to pick up a prisoner?' Tiller asked the others. They were back behind the highest part of the ridge and were brewing water for their K-rations.

'What about the Japs watching the rice being unloaded?' Sandy suggested. 'It wouldn't be too much of a problem to snaffle one of them.'

'Or snatch someone who comes out of that head-quarters,' Tiller said. 'You might get someone useful.'

'There's a storm drain which runs right by it,' added Coates. 'It would not be difficult to approach.'

'You want to come, Dick?' Tiller asked Coates, using the forester's Christian name for the first time. Coates allowed the question to hang in the air for a moment, and then shrugged. 'You're the boss, Sergeant, but I could be useful.'

They ate their K-rations in silence. Sandy, in an attempt to break the monotony of their taste, heated all his together: coffee, powdered milk, fruit bar, compressed dried ham and egg.

'What's it taste like?' Tiller asked.

'Same as usual,' Sandy answered gloomily.

They decided that the time to strike would be soon after midnight. This would give them plenty of time to regain the ridge in the darkness while giving them daylight to find their way back to the canoes. They found a comparatively dry spot in which to shelter, but when they could not sleep Coates explained to them how elephants were captured and tamed.

'It's done by experts who are licensed by the government to capture elephants within a given area of, say, a thousand square miles,' he said. 'An area that size is worked over for about three years and then is left alone for another six. When a wild herd is found a stockade is built and the licensees' workers – usually Karens, who are the most skilled – drive the herd towards it. It's done at night, as the elephants are less likely to stampede then. Also, they can't see the stockade until it is too late. Even so, quite a proportion of a herd usually escapes being trapped. Those that are trapped are removed into training cages as quickly as possible.'

'How the hell is that done?' Tiller asked. He couldn't see how you could move an elephant anywhere it did not want to go.

'They move them with ropes which they put around their legs and heads,' Coates replied. 'It's quite marvellous to watch and requires tremendous skill and courage. Once the elephant's in the cage it's allotted two keepers, who feed it by hand, tend to its wounds and sleep by it. Within days, if the keepers are any good, they are on friendly terms with the animal and it is then allowed out of the cage and tethered to a tree. As it grows tamer so it is allowed more freedom. They're basically very docile, affectionate creatures. But the licensees only take young elephants, those under seven feet in height. The older ones, say over eight feet, can't take the shock of capture and often die.'

'Is it true an elephant never forgets?' Sandy asked.

'It's true,' said Coates.

* * *

At midnight they slipped down the ridge, along the storm drain, and into the township. The *bashas* were all in darkness but a light burnt in the stone building. Outside it two Japanese soldiers stood by the door. Their bayonets – extraordinarily long and clumsy by British standards – were fixed to their rifles, which were slung over their shoulders. They acted as if they were a long way behind the front line and did not seem particularly alert.

'What do you think?' Tiller whispered to Coates. He had become accustomed to consulting the older man.

Coates shook his head. 'We'd have to take both and they'd soon be missed.'

Tiller nodded his agreement. They waited for someone to come out of the building but no one did. After half an hour they gave up.

'There must be garrison troops,' Tiller said. 'Let's scout around.'

They skirted the stone building and soon came upon a small encampment of Japanese army tents which they would not have been able to see from the ridge. They were considering what to do next when the problem was solved for them. A Japanese, dressed only in his underpants, staggered out of the nearest tent and made for the bushes where they were crouching. He had obviously had too much sake, for he was unsteady on his feet. A stream of urine splashed noisily on to the ground and the man grunted with relief. As he turned, hitching up his pants, Sandy's cosh felled him. He pitched forward without a sound and they dragged him into the bushes and then tied his hands and legs and gagged him. He was a small man, light-boned.

Tiller and Sandy took it in turns to carry him to the

bottom of the ridge, where they constructed a crude litter to carry him up to the top. Once they were beyond its crest they put their prisoner on the ground. He had already shown signs of coming round and after a couple of minutes he opened his eyes. At first he started up uncomprehendingly, then terror flooded into his face and he struggled violently to free himself. Coates put a restraining boot on his shoulder and then bent down and spoke to him haltingly in Japanese. Gradually, the man's terror turned to bewilderment and he stopped struggling. Coates took out a knife and cut the rope binding the man's legs, allowing him to stagger to his feet.

'He won't cause any problem,' Coates said, snapping the blade of his knife closed. 'I've told him if he does, I'll put this knife between his ribs.'

As daylight broke behind them they began making their way back to the waiting canoes. It took much of the day, for the Japanese, though he was wearing sandals, found it hard to keep up. At midday they rested for an hour, ate cold rice they had brought with them, and brewed tea. They loosened the prisoner's gag and gave him a couple of handfuls of rice and half a mug of tea. If he was grateful, he didn't show it and Tiller had no compunction in putting the gag back in position as soon as he had finished.

'Do we know who or what he is?' he asked Coates.

'A lance-corporal in their Signals Corps,' the forester replied. 'Could be very useful to us, but my Japanese isn't good enough to interrogate him properly.'

They were sitting under a palm tree in a small clearing. Tiller loosened his boots and leant back on his elbows. 'Five minutes, you two. Then we must get going.'

The heat and the tension of the patrol made his body heavy with exhaustion. His eyelids flickered and closed, and he felt the back of his head rest on the earth. The world seemed suspended in sleep when from a distance he heard Coates say very decisively: 'Don't move, Sergeant. Stay quite still,' and the swish of the forester's kukri as it passed by his head.

Tiller rolled and was on his feet in an instant, his hands grappling for his carbine. Coates sheathed his kukri calmly and stepped behind him. Something was writhing in the long grass, but Tiller couldn't see what exactly until the forester picked it up and dangled it in front of him. It was the headless remains of a snake about four feet long.

'A Russell's viper,' Coates informed him. 'I don't suppose it was doing anything other than going about its business. But if you'd moved you could have frightened it and it might have struck.'

Tiller stared in fascination at the still-writhing body. 'Poisonous?'

'Very,' said Coates calmly. 'If it bit you on an outer extremity I dare say I could have saved you. You'd have had no chance, though, if it had struck your head.'

'Well, thanks,' Tiller muttered.

Coates found the severed head with its distinctive 'V' and picked it up. He carefully inserted the blade of his pocket knife into the snake's mouth and pressed on the sac of poison, which dribbled from the creature's forked tongue.

'Fascinating to think that such a small amount of liquid can kill a healthy man in half a minute,' he said.

He threw the head into the undergrowth. 'We should really keep the body. Cooked in herbs, it makes a very tasty dish.'

'Don't let's bother,' said Tiller.

They reached the canoes in the late afternoon and at dusk they began the return journey to the ML with their prisoner jammed into the front cockpit of the spare cockle.

The ML merged so well with its surroundings in the dark that they were almost past it before they saw it. Willing hands helped them aboard and the Japanese was hustled below. The canoes were then hauled on to the deck and stowed, the mooring warps were released and hauled in, the anchor was weighed, and Davy edged the ML carefully into the middle of the *chaung*.

'We're going to have to keep going when it gets light,' he said to Tiller. 'I'd prefer to do that than risk passing through the estuary in daylight, as the Jap sea patrols are bound to spot us and they might be able to call on some Bettys to help them.'

'Bettys?' Tiller queried.

'The Japanese Navy's Mitsubishi light bomber. No one could pronounce the names of some of these Jap machines, so they've all been given code-names. Anyway, let's just hope it's raining by daylight so there's low visibility over the river.'

But dawn broke fine and clear – one of those sparkling days that occasionally occurred, so Coates said, before the monsoon set in properly – and around mid-morning, with the ML moving at near maximum speed, the stern lookout shouted: 'Aircraft approaching, sir.'

Davy swung round, focused his binoculars on the two fast-approaching dots, and pressed the knob which sounded the klaxon for action stations. The aircraft were still too far away to be identified but they were flying wing-tip straight down the river towards the ML.

'They must be Japs,' Davy said to Tiller, who had scrambled on to the bridge with his carbine when the klaxon had sounded. 'No Allied aircraft would fly that low over Jap-held territory.'

The pilots had seen the ML, for they banked in opposite directions. Their outlines now made them easy to identify and the red Japanese roundels on the underside of their wings could be plainly seen.

'Zeros, sir,' the lookout in the stern yelled excitedly.

'Shit,' said Davy. He had hoped they would come straight at the ML together. By approaching from separate directions they would split his fire-power. Nearly all the Japanese Navy's experienced pilots had long since been lost in the great Pacific naval battles but their tactics showed that the two now manoeuvring to attack him were not novices.

'Hoist the battle ensign,' he shouted, and the white ensign of the Royal Navy was quickly raised on the short mast abaft the bridge. Davy then allotted his armament their targets and said to Tiller: 'You're better off below. An M2 isn't much use against a Zero flying at 400mph.'

'You're going to need every bullet in the air that you can manage,' Tiller retorted.

Davy shrugged. 'Please yourself. Here's a spare tin helmet. Not that it'll do you much good.'

By now the two fighters were about a mile off on

either quarter and once abreast of the ML they changed course for it. The whine of their engines filled the air as they dipped their noses towards their target. Davy waited and then shouted into the voice pipe: 'Full ahead, give her everything she's got.'

For several seconds nothing happened and then the ML began to surge ahead. As she did so the first fighter opened fire, but the ML's change of pace had confused the pilot and the bullets hammered harmlessly into the ML's broadening wake. As it fired, the Oerlikons opened up on it, the twin barrels spitting out 20mm shells.

The second Zero waited longer and was therefore more accurate. Its bullets ripped into the funnel and spattered the bridge, and one of the crewman manning the port-side twin Lewis gun toppled and fell. But the pilot held his course just a fraction of a second too long and the heavy machine-gun in the stern of the ML raked its fuselage efficiently.

The Zero's pilot must have been hit, or perhaps he just panicked, for he made the fatal mistake of turning right across the ML instead of left. It was just what the three-pounder crew in the bows had been hoping and waiting for, as they could not bring their weapon to bear on any target which attacked from astern or either quarter. But now the second Zero was exposed to their fire and before it could sheer off they pumped two shells into it. The aircraft bucked and slewed and then swerved away, trailing smoke. Tiller, kneeling as he worked on the hit Lewis gunner, heard the ML's crew cheering wildly. The gunner was dead, Tiller discovered, and dragged his body away from the gun.

'Watch for that other bugger,' Davy yelled at the top

of his voice. The first Zero was long gone, but now they could see it a mile away, barrelling skyward to gain height. The sun glinted on its wings and its engine revved into a high-pitched scream. It looked, Tiller had to admit to himself as he wedged himself into position behind the port-side twin Lewis gun, a very beautiful piece of equipment.

Tiller gripped the gun, made sure the ninety-seven-round pan magazine was properly attached, and aligned the Zero in the large circular central sights positioned between the distinctive air-cooling jackets which covered each of its barrels. He had never used a Lewis before and he just hoped it was as accurate as the praise he had heard heaped on it.

The Zero reached the height the pilot wanted and then carved through the sky until it was on a straight run towards the ML. With the second Zero limping into the distance, all the ML's armament was able to concentrate on the first one. Even the three-pounder was able to train on it, but the pilot pressed home his attack. Tiller smelt the acrid tang of cordite as he fired the twin Lewis and was dimly aware that splinters from the bridge were flying past him in the air; someone cried out; spent cartridges cascaded on to the deck beside him and the quick-firing weapon bucked under his grip.

The Zero's engine rose to a climax and for a fraction of a second, as it passed overhead, its shadow fell across the ML. Then its sound quickly faded into the distance and the fighter was lost in the heat haze that shimmered on the horizon.

'He's had enough,' Davy yelled. 'The bugger's had enough.'

The crew cheered and then the lookout shouted: 'The other one hasn't though, sir. Here he comes.'

The second Zero had swung round and was coming back. It was definitely wobbly in the air and smoke was belching from its engine. It bucked and shuddered but somehow the pilot kept it on its course. Davy watched it, shading his eyes from the sun. The aircraft dipped towards the ML, coming at such an angle that its intentions were obvious.

'Jesus,' Davy shouted, 'it's a kamikaze.'

The Zero was belching smoke but still it came on, despite the fusillade being fired at it.

'Hard a starboard,' Davy shouted into the voice pipe. 'Give her every bloody rev you can.'

The ML headed for the bank furthest from the approaching aircraft. Tiller watched in amazement. Davy appeared to be driving the ML aground. The Zero swung crazily in the sky as the pilot tried to aim it like a missile at the vessel.

'Hard a port,' Davy yelled into the voice pipe, and the ML slewed round. Now the Zero and the ML were on a collision course.

But the Japanese pilot had either not calculated what the ML would do, or could not get the controls of his doomed aircraft to react quickly enough. The Zero screeched towards them and everyone except Davy threw themselves on to the deck. It missed the ML by twenty feet or so and hit the far bank with a blinding explosion.

'One down and one to go,' Davy yelled.

But the other Zero did not return.

8

As Coates had predicted, the monsoon proper arrived early. A week after the ML returned from its mission a huge turmoil of cumulonimbus clouds boiled over the whole sky and the rain tumbled down in a seemingly unending torrent that turned the ground at Cox's Bazar into a muddy morass. On most days it stopped occasionally and the sun shone briefly, a watery yellow ball that made the ground steam and the air damp and clinging. But within hours the black clouds, with their flat bases and monumental peaks, would gather again.

Every so often a cyclone swept through the area, accompanied by rumbling thunder and flashes of lightning that lit up the whole sky. Then the south-westerly monsoon winds blew fiercely off the Bay of Bengal, driving the rain almost horizontally and bending and contorting the palm trees and scattering their leaves.

On these occasions the sea became as tumultuous as the sky: white-flecked, boiling, black. It seemed impossible that any ship could stay afloat in such conditions. But the cyclone always blew itself out as quickly as it had come, leaving a lurching swell, unpleasant but manageable.

'No army could fight in this, surely,' said Davy to Danforth, watching the rain tipping down outside

Danforth's office. The other ML skippers and the SBS patrol leaders murmured their agreement. War had become completely mechanized and it was difficult to see how any vehicle could move in such conditions.

'Don't you believe it,' Danforth replied. 'Since Supremo's taken over he's given orders that fighting is to continue throughout the monsoon period. There's to be no let-up at all. Which is why we're all gathered here this morning. We've got the Japs on the run and we've got to keep them running. We mustn't give them any time to recover. Fifteenth Corps is planning something big. I don't know the details, of course, but my guess is that it's going to make an all-out drive down the Arakan shortly. Our task will be to continue to harass the Japanese supply lines and their lines of communication.'

'Easier said than done in this weather,' grumbled one of the ML skippers.

'We're not doing too badly,' said Danforth easily. 'We've already forced the Japanese to detach a regiment of the Burma National Army to counter our activities. However, Fifteenth Corps is keen that we draw off as many Japanese troops as possible. So they have asked us to mount what is primarily a deception operation. We are to capture and hold an island off the coastline to make it look as if we are going to use it as a base for raiding the mainland. It would be a move which the Japanese, hopefully, could not afford to ignore.'

'Which island is it?' the same ML skipper asked, and Danforth picked up a wooden pointer from his desk and indicated the island on a map hanging on the wall. 'Ramree. Here.'

There was a moment's stunned silence. Then Taffy said: 'But, sir, that's almost down to Sandoway. Must be a good fifty miles behind Jap lines.'

'Exactly,' said Danforth cheerfully. 'If you want to hit them below the belt it's no use giving them a jab on the nose. This will be a jitter party they won't forget.'

'If we capture it, sir, how do we manage to hang on to it?' Tiller asked. Presumably, Fifteenth Corps did not expect the SBS Group to defend an island some forty-five miles long by fifteen wide which was within spitting distance of the Japanese-held mainland. It numbered only sixteen men in total.

'From that Jap who was captured last week, we're fairly sure it's only lightly held at the moment,' said Danforth reassuringly. 'But we're going to have to put in a recce patrol first, to make sure. If we're right we start the deception operation to make the Japs think we have landed in force. If they look like making a full-scale assault from the mainland to take it back, we won't attempt to hold it. But we will have succeeded in our objective of drawing off troops from their front line.'

'You mean we're the cheese in the mousetrap?' Tiller said.

'Exactly, Tiger. Any light Japanese reinforcements from the mainland will be dealt with by the RAF and by our ML patrols.'

'Will *we* get any reinforcements, sir, once we're on the island?'

Danforth rubbed his cheek. 'If necessary. The Eastern Fleet is now back at Ceylon from Mombasa. God knows why. Perhaps the powers that be think the

117

Japs might raid Ceylon again, as they did a couple of years back. But the fleet does have the capability of lifting a Marine Commando that's available in Ceylon. Certainly the deception plan is to make the Japs think the Commando is going to be used for a landing. We'll see.'

'The Japs aren't crazy enough to mount another raid, are they?' one of the ML skippers said. 'Without air supremacy, that's kamikaze tactics.'

Danforth shrugged. 'Perhaps. But remember, they still have the most powerful battleships in the world at their disposal.'

'What's this word "kamikaze" mean?' Tiller asked Davy when the briefing broke up. 'You used it to describe that Zero pilot.'

'Kamikaze? It's a suicide tactic the Jap air force has begun using. They crash their aircraft on to our ships. It's very effective.'

'So kamikaze is Japanese for topping yourself?'

Davy shook his head. 'Means divine wind. It's what they called the typhoon which prevented Genghis Khan from invading Japan in the thirteenth century.'

'Very poetic,' said Tiller. 'They've got some imagination, those Japs.'

To get the better of your opponents you had to understand them, anticipate how they thought and how they would react, he reflected. This was especially true of small-scale operations that the SBS specialized in. The Japs were different from the Germans or the Italians and Tiller was only too well aware that he still hadn't adjusted his fighting habits to take account of this difference. That was dangerous and he knew it. Both the Americans and the British had vastly

118

underestimated the military skill of the Japanese at the beginning of the war. It was not a mistake that any Allied serviceman made in 1944. Or if he did, he most likely did not live to make it again. But it was one thing to realize the Japanese were good and to respect their skill and bravery; it was quite another to understand what made them tick. Tiller wondered if he ever would.

'Got a moment, you two,' Danforth called over to them as the others filed out of his office and into a downpour. It was raining so hard that the noise of the water drumming on the corrugated-iron roof filled the room. The gutters could not cope and were spilling the water everywhere.

Davy and Tiller turned and Danforth said: 'I know you've only just got back, but this is the op I wanted you for, Tiger. I want you to recce Ramree and clear it of Japs if there are only a handful there. I'm going to give you extra men. If the Japs hold the island in force I shall need some estimate of how many there are there, what state of readiness they're in and where, if necessary, we could land the back-up force.'

'What would a back-up force be landing in, sir?' Tiller asked.

'LCAs or LCPs. Two LSTs plus an escort force is available at Trincomalee to bring the Marines to Ramree. You've just got to find the right place for them to land.'

Tiller looked doubtful. He knew both the LCA – Landing Craft Assault – and its American equivalent, the LCP – Landing Craft Personnel – had very shallow draughts. Provided he could find a suitable beach on Ramree, with firm terrain, the right gradient and no sandbanks, the back-up force could be landed in these craft easily enough. But their mother ships, the LST – Landing Ship Tank – were two hundred feet long. If there weren't any suitable landing beaches facing the Bay of Bengal, it could be tricky finding enough open water for them to operate from, for on its landward side Ramree was a mass of tiny islands and solid mangrove swamp.

'That's a job for a COPP team,' said Tiller doubtfully.

'I know,' agreed Danforth, 'but the nearest COPP team is at Algiers, I believe. Supremo says we can't wait for them. If he says we can't wait for them we can't. Anyway, you know enough about COPP work, Tiger, to make a fist of it. It's the best we can do in the time available. I've got some photo recce shots for you to look at.'

He led them to a table and extracted a number of vertical aerial reconnaissance photographs from a large brown envelope. They were taken quite low – the pilot obviously was not worried about Japanese anti-aircraft fire – and were remarkably clear, given the monsoon conditions.

'Taken last week during a break in the weather. They're of the island's only harbour and the main town, Kyaukpyu,' – Danforth pronounced it 'Chalkpu' – 'which surrounds it. There are also some likely landing beaches for your recce team, Tiger, and for the back-up force.'

They took turns in looking at the photographs through stereoscopic lenses. Viewing the overlaps of succeeding photographs with the lenses gave a three-dimensional effect. A trained photographic interpreter could extract astonishingly detailed information from them.

'The interpreters have measured the depth of water over these beaches,' said Danforth, 'but their gradients and firmness will have to be checked if we're going to use them.'

'How the hell can they know the depth of a beach from an aerial photograph?' Davy asked.

'It's called the direct wave velocity method,' Danforth explained. 'In shallow water the velocity of a wave is a function of the water depth. The slower it is the shallower the beach. If the interval between successive photographs is known, and if individual crests can be identified in successive ones, their velocities can be measured and so can the depths over which they are passing.'

'I shouldn't have asked,' said Davy.

Tiller was more interested in the aerials of the town as that was where the Japanese on the island would have their main defences. He knew he had the expertise to land safely on the beaches, even if it meant going through quite high surf, and that was all that mattered to him for the moment. If the back-up force had to be landed at a later date, that was something that could be planned after he had had time to reconnoitre the best beaches. In the meantime the town was where the Japanese would be. He pulled the photographs towards him and reached for the stereoscopic lenses. Davy peered over his shoulder.

'Looks in ruins,' said Davy.

Danforth nodded. 'It is. But have you looked carefully at the harbour?'

Davy bent over them again.

'Did you see anything, Tiger?'

Tiller shook his head. 'It looks empty to me.'

'And to me,' Davy added, straightening up.

'You're right. Now look at these.'

Danforth extracted more photographs from another envelope. 'Taken forty-eight hours ago. Arrived this morning. See any difference?'

Davy and Tiller bent over the new photographs in turn, and both shook their heads.

'Look. See this shadow? And this one here? And another here?'

'Just shadows, surely?'

'Not so, so the boffins tell us. They're native boats. *Mergui*, probably, for local coastal trade. But that one there might be something bigger, a *tavoy* schooner perhaps.'

'What does that indicate? There are Jap reinforcements there?' Davy asked.

Danforth shook his head. 'RAF Intelligence think not. They're much more likely to be country boats the Japs have commandeered to take food from Ramree to the mainland. Whatever they are they need to be destroyed. If it wasn't for the monsoon the RAF might find the aircraft to do it, but it's a hundred to one against them having clear enough weather for long enough to do it. Anyway, if there was they would be too busy supporting Fifteenth Corps. No, it's a job for us. Right up your street, Tiger.'

'I'd say,' agreed Tiller. A pulse of excitement went through him at the prospect.

'It'll be a good opportunity to use those new collapsible canoes, Tiger. But I'm not going to risk you using those in the surf, so Davy will put you ashore in the motor surf boats.'

Tiller nodded his agreement. The previous week four large bergen rucksacks had arrived at Danforth's office. Each contained a sixteen-foot collapsible canoe which weighed only 104lb. Ingeniously constructed from shaped plywood frames which were fitted together by lengths of metal pipe, a canoe could be put together in less than five minutes by its two-man crew.

'Take plenty of toys with you,' said Davy, referring to the limpet mines the SBS employed to destroy shipping.

Tiller shook his head. 'A limpet's no use against a *mergui* – or any local boat for that matter.'

Davy looked surprised. 'Why's that?'

'They've all got wooden hulls,' Danforth said. 'A limpet will only fix itself to a steel hull.'

Davy laughed. 'Of course. I should have thought of that. Even I know magnets won't hold to wood. So what will you do? Or do you want me to come into the harbour and do the job?'

'Certainly not,' said Danforth sharply. 'We're not going to risk an ML.'

Tiller shrugged his indifference at Davy's question. 'The easiest thing is probably to capture them and sink them with a PE charge. I don't see any problem.'

'Well, there is a problem actually, Tiger,' Danforth said. 'Destroying native craft being used by the Japanese is one thing. Sinking them in a Burmese harbour is quite another. The government has issued an edict on it, as a matter of fact.'

'Government?' Tiller queried in bewilderment. 'What government?'

'The Burmese government-in-exile.'

'You mean the lot that sacked Dick?' Davy said.
'Well, stuff them.'

Tiller nodded his agreement. He'd never heard of
a civilian colonial government interfering in military
operations.

'Sorry, boys,' Danforth said firmly. 'Now that we're
in the process of retaking Burma, the colonial government is having more and more say in what we can and
can't do. And we can't sink native shipping without
good reason.'

'So we have to allow them to sail and then try and
intercept them?'

Danforth smiled. 'That's the theory. But we've come
up with a better idea. Stick the equivalent of a limpet
mine on the hull with a long enough time delay and the
ships will sink at sea. No one will be any the wiser.'

'Trouble is, sir, as you well know, we don't have
the equivalent of a limpet mine that works on wooden
hulls,' said Tiller in exasperation.

'You're right again, Tiger. *We* don't have such a
device, but the Yanks have it.'

Tiller stared at him, amazed. 'They do?'

Danforth pressed his intercom. 'Is Master-Sergeant
Lee White out there? He is? Send him in, please.'

Almost instantly, there was a knock on the door
and before Danforth could respond a tall, lean man
in his late twenties, dressed in bush shirt and trousers,
entered. He saluted Danforth with an abrupt, exagger-
ated salute. It looked odd to Tiller because he wasn't
wearing a cap.

'Major?'

The drawl was Texan, straight from some B movie;
the man's jaws chomped on chewing gum. He looked

124

both at ease and totally alert, light on his feet. With a quick motion he unslung a rucksack from his shoulder and put it on the table.

'Thanks for waiting, Sergeant. We need your advice.'

'Sure. How can I help?'

'Master-Sergeant White is a member of the Office of Strategic Services,' Danforth told Davy and Tiller.

Tiller remembered Taffy's remark about the OSS when they had found the booby-trap. A hush-hush Yank outfit, he'd said.

'It was the OSS who kindly supplied us with the collapsible canoes,' Danforth added. He turned to White. 'We're going to be testing them out soon. We'll give you a full report on them.'

Tiller stretched out his hand to the Texan and introduced himself, then Davy did likewise. Like Tiller, the sergeant wore a pistol and a fighting knife on his belt. The pistol was a regulation Colt .45 automatic, but the knife was longer and narrower than Tiller's and was contained in a 'pancake flapper' sheath.

'We are going to dispose of some native craft,' Danforth said. 'We need an explosive device with a time delay that can be fixed to a wooden hull. You boys have such a store, am I right?'

'Sure have,' said White. He sat down and opened the rucksack. 'We call it a Pin-Up Girl.'

He slid the device out on to the table. To Tiller it looked like an ordinary limpet, but without the usual six magnets.

'It's slightly lighter than our standard limpet,' the OSS man said. 'And of course our limpet is an almost exact copy of yours. Except, unlike the Brits, we use a celluloid case. And we use Torpex explosive because PE reacts with celluloid.'

'But how do you attach it to a wooden hull?' Tiller asked.

The American turned the device over and pointed to a socket fastened along one side of it in which lay a thick, five-inch-long iron bolt. 'This is all you do,' he said, then deftly swivelled the socket until it was at right angles to the case. The socket locked itself into place with a click.

'See that trigger under the slot where you attach the placing rod?'

Tiller nodded. The American pointed to the ring of the safety-pin which retained the spring-loaded bolt in its place in the socket.

'You just slide the ring over it. Unhooking the placing rod automatically pulls up the trigger, which pulls out the safety-pin holding back a spring. When the spring is released it drives the bolt into the hull and the Pin-Up Girl is ready for action.'

Tiller turned the device over. He hoped it was as simple as the Texan made it out to be.

'Very ingenious,' he said, trying not to sound grudging. He wondered why the boys at Welwyn Garden City, who had managed to come up with something as crackpot as the Welman, had not thought of such a useful device. At least they might not have given it such a daft name.

The Texan rummaged around in his rucksack and placed on the table half-a-dozen tall, oval tins, very like those used for cigars. He slid the top off one of them. 'And these are the time pencils.'

'Are yours the same as ours?' Tiller asked, drawing one out from the tin.

The Texan grinned. 'Guess we like to think they're better. We've used a different corrosive and slightly thicker wire to try and make them less vulnerable to changes in temperature.'

'And the colour codes. Are they different?'

The Texan shook his head. 'The same as yours. Red for half an hour, then white, green, yellow and blue for two, six, twelve and twenty-four hours.'

'What else have you got, Sergeant?' asked Danforth.

The American grinned. 'What would you like, Major? Some footshooters . . . a box of caccolubes, perhaps?'

'Caccolubes? What on earth are they?'

The American dug into his rucksack again and produced a small tin box. He opened it to reveal five egg-shaped rubber sacs, each of which was about two and a half inches long. 'Means bad lubricant. We also call them turtles' eggs. Drop them in a gas tank, the rubber disintegrates and the contents are mixed with the fuel. After fifty miles or so the truck comes to a grinding halt. By which time the engine is ruined. Can be used against any sort of engine.'

Tiller poked at one with his finger. 'So what's in them?'

'Thirty grams of a mixture of finely ground aluminum-magnesium alloy and ground cork. We've also been working on a new type of incendiary device.'

He placed a six-inch rectangular greased waterproof cardboard carton on the table. Tiller picked it up gingerly and weighed it in his hand.

'Only weighs $1.1/4$lb,' the Texan informed him. 'We call it the City Slicker.'

'What does it do?'

'It's used to ignite fuel oil slicks on the water. It's perfectly safe until water-fused.'

'Water-fused?'

'That's what activates it: water,' the American explained patiently. 'See this flap? You just lift it before you chuck it in the slick. After one minute the water activates the chemicals inside, which, in turn, ignites the oil. Very effective against a damaged enemy vessel or aircraft. Useful, too, to cause a diversion.'

'Can you let us have some Pin-Up Girls?' Danforth asked eagerly.

'Sure. As many as you want,' the Texan said cheerfully. 'I guess the caccolubes don't fit with your type of operations but the City Slicker could be useful to you. This one is a prototype and we're looking for someone to test it under operational conditions. The colonel thought you guys might be able to find a suitable target to try it out on.'

Danforth and Tiller exchanged glances. Tiller nodded. Danforth said: 'I'm sure we could.'

The American slid the box across the table to Tiller. 'There you are, buddy. All yours. How many Pin-Up Girls will you need?'

'A dozen,' said Tiller. 'That should see us through this op.'

'I'll see that they're here by noon tomorrow.'

'Tell us what else you people have developed that may be of use to the SBS,' Danforth requested. 'Tiger, take some notes, will you?'

The OSS, it seemed, had been working on a number

128

of ingenious devices, including a rubber inflatable powered by a new silent outboard engine, and was eager to have them tested in the field. When he had finished describing them and answered the inevitable questions, the Texan picked up his rucksack, saluted Danforth and said: 'Pleasure doing business with you, gentlemen. Any time.'

Two days later, as dawn broke, two MLs, in line astern, nosed cautiously out of the crowded anchorage of Cox's Bazar. The rain had temporarily relented and Tiller stood by Davy on the bridge watching Nabob, perched on his master's shoulder, eating the remains of a piece of fruit. The monkey watched him with knowing button eyes.

On the deck amidships two SBS Mk II canoes, covered in tarpaulins, were lashed to the stanchions just in case they were needed.

'You're a belt and braces man, aren't you, Tiger,' Davy had remarked to Tiller when he had said he wanted to take them along.

And Tiller had shrugged and replied: 'You bet I am. Those Yank canoes have never been used operationally.'

A number of Burmese rowing a large, crudely made boat stopped to wave. Tiller waved back. Nabob chittered angrily.

'Like the bloody rush hour in Cape Town, this place,' Davy muttered. 'Have you ever seen so many boats? The whole bloody population of the Arakan seems to live afloat. And some of the crates they go to sea in look as if they've been tied together with bits of string.'

'That's almost exactly how they do make them,'

said Coates, sucking noisily on the stem of his old briar pipe. 'Haven't you ever looked closely at one of their country boats? Fascinating. They stitch the planks together with cane.'

'Christ,' muttered Tiller. 'Remind me not to get a lift in any of them.'

'They're as seaworthy as this tub,' snapped Coates.

'That's not saying much,' Davy grumbled. 'Anything above a force six and I run for shelter.'

'Who turns out all these boats?' Tiller asked Coates, peering down at a mass of working craft huddled together by a quay. 'And what do they call them?'

'Generically, they're called *chok-hle*,' said Coates. 'Which literally means "stitched boat". The type we've just passed is called a *kistie*. The hull is hollowed out from the trunk of a tree. Then the owner floats the *hle-don*, or rough hull, down stream to the *chok-thama*, or boat stitcher. He bores a line of holes along the edge of each plank and builds up the hull by lacing the planks together with bamboo cane. Any gaps between the planks or the holes are caulked with bamboo bark.'

'Are you seriously saying they go to sea in them?' Tiller queried.

Coates smiled and shook his head. 'No, they're used in the *chaungs* mostly. It's the *tavoy* and other schooners like the *sandoway* and the *mergui* that are used for coastal trading.'

An ominous swell lifted and rolled the MLs as they left the shelter of the harbour, and the horizon was black with monsoon clouds. They headed south instead of following the south-east line of the coast, so that they were soon out of sight of land.

All day they rolled through the monsoon swell,

watching the heavy veils of rain, driven by a stiff south-westerly, sweeping across the sullen waters of the Bay of Bengal. Occasionally there was a glimmer of sun before the clouds closed in again, but at least at sea the air was fresher, less damp and cloying.

Tiller went below to get something to eat and found that the wardroom had been converted into a small operating theatre. Everything was covered in white sheets and a surgeon-lieutenant – instantly recognizable by the thin red stripe between the two gold stripes on his sleeves – was checking his surgical instruments with an Indian sick-berth attendant. The surgeon glanced up and grinned when he saw Tiller's look of surprise: 'Standard procedure on an op of any size. Didn't you know?'

Tiller shook his head. He thought of the Lewis gun operator whose place he had taken on the River Kaladan and wondered if an operating theatre could have saved him. But he knew it could not have. They had buried him at sea in a brief but dignified ceremony, the weighted, canvas-wrapped body being slid into the waves from a plank. The burial had been watched in silence with bared heads by the few members of the crew not at their action stations.

'If you're looking for some nosh it's being handed out from the galley,' said the surgeon.

Tiller thanked him and retreated hurriedly from the humidity of the wardroom, its lingering smell of antiseptic and its gleaming instruments a grim reminder of the dangers ahead. He went to the galley and was given a doorstep of a sandwich and a mug of tea, which he took on deck. He made his way aft. The Oerlikon crew were stood down but preferred, despite the rain, to sit around their gun eating their sandwiches to going below. They nodded to him in a friendly way. His skill with the Lewis gun had not gone unnoticed and his efforts to save the life of the gunner had been appreciated.

Further aft one of the wireless operators attached to the SBS for the operation hung over the side looking pale. To distract him from the ML's lurching motion Tiller asked him what deception methods he proposed to use.

'Usual stunt,' the signals corporal said. 'I'll just exchange messages with my oppo and sent out ones to a fake subordinate HQ. The Japs are quite capable of decrypting several of our low-grade ciphers, so we'll use one we know they've cracked. They're shit hot on traffic analysis and it's the volume of signals that attracts their attention, not so much the contents. I shall only be acting as a brigade HQ, so the volume won't be that great. Bloody hard work while it lasts, though.'

Tiller asked what traffic analysis was; he hadn't heard the term before.

'Monitoring the level of signals and their networks,' the signaller explained. 'The Japs might not be able to decipher all the signals immediately, but from the quantity and type they'll be deceived into thinking that a Commando Brigade HQ is controlling a landing of some size on Ramree.'

'But they must know we might try and pull a stunt like that,' Tiller protested. He didn't much like the thought of what might happen if the Japs double-guessed them.

The signaller was reassuring. 'They couldn't know

for certain, any more than we could be certain of them pulling the same trick. But the signals deception would be only a small part of a much larger deception scheme, and the other factors have to be right. For instance, we will have made sure the Japs know we have a Commando Brigade in Ceylon with a lifting capability to Ramree. What's more, we will have made sure they will have been able to monitor that lifting capability in Ceylon. Who knows, Naval HQ at Trincomalee may have broken wireless silence by signalling the LSTs and their escort force after they supposedly had left harbour. We give the Japs all the pieces of the jigsaw puzzle and leave it to them to fit it together.'

'I had no idea,' said Tiller. 'Who thinks up these cunning schemes?'

'A naval commander called Fleming,' said the signaller promptly. 'I know him because I've worked with him. Runs an outfit called D Division in Ceylon. D for deception. He thinks up all sorts of deception radio tricks.'

As they talked the dull greyness of the day faded suddenly into night. Of the sunset there had been no sign. Tiller went below, reassured that he and his tiny force were being well looked after by the powers that be. The SBS might be the cheese in the mousetrap but the trap seemed a powerfully made and well-designed one.

He slept soundly for four hours and then dressed in the two-piece swimming suit which the SBS used in tropical climates. It was made of a light, waterproof material which gave some protection to the body from sharp rocks and, more importantly, from the several species of fish which could administer particularly vicious stings. The jacket was fitted with an inflatable rubber lifebelt. On his feet he wore light rope-soled canvas shoes. These were so much better, he had found, than the rubber commando boots he had worn in the Mediterranean. Rubber was slippery and leather quickly rotted in the jungle heat. But, with rope soles, the wetter they got the harder they became. Even Coates had grudgingly admitted that they were better than the calf-length canvas jungle boots he wore, though he refused to use them.

Tiller then filled the many pockets of the suit. Pencils, plastic board which served as waterproof writing paper, COPP measuring reel, compass, emergency rations, torch, spare pistol magazines, citronella oil to ward off the mosquitoes and sandflies, standard dressing for bullet wounds, the City Slicker, and a small plastic container which diffused shark repellent in the water, were all fitted in somehow. Then he buckled on his belt with his .45 pistol on one side and his commando knife on the other, and finally donned a kapok lifebelt which protected the rubber one that was part of his jacket, and which gave additional, unpuncturable buoyancy should he need it. He packed his rucksack with a cheese-cloth mosquito net, a change of clothes, a towel, a blanket and a medical kit. He also stuffed in the rudimentary two pieces of escape and evasion equipment carried by all personnel on operations, though he had doubts about their practicality. These were a silk British flag known as a 'blood chit' because any Burmese safely delivering back its owner would be financially rewarded, and what was known as a 'pointee-talkee' phrase book.

Tiller returned to the bridge to find that Coates was

still jammed into one corner, sucking his empty pipe, a seemingly indefatigable watcher of events. At the other end of the bridge Davy was drinking a mug of tea and feeding Nabob bits of biscuit. Rain hung in the air. The wind had dropped and with it the swell.

'How much longer?' Tiller asked Davy. Davy glanced at his watch and then across to his navigator, a fresh-faced RNVR sub-lieutenant, who said immediately: 'We reach the DR position in fifty minutes, skipper.'

'I'll make a final check on all the equipment,' said Tiller. He went aft and ticked off on his list the two collapsible canoes in their rucksacks, the crate of Pin-Up Girls which the OSS had delivered so promptly, the wireless with which he would communicate with the ML, and the boxes of extra rations and ammunition.

The wireless operators would stay aboard the ML until the SBS team had reconnoitred the island. If given the all-clear for the deception operation to proceed, one of the operators would be landed with his wireless equipment while the other stayed on the ML. The one afloat would begin broadcasting as if the Brigade HQ was directing a landing.

While Tiller was checking his equipment two of the ML's crew began to prepare to lower the motor surf boat from the davits in the ML's stern. It was twenty feet long, and was equipped with a five-horsepower Stewart and Turner petrol engine which ran silently because the exhaust outlet, on the starboard side, was below water level. Constructed of wood, the boat had a flat bottom and high bows, and was designed, as its name implied, to land troops and equipment through surf.

Exactly fifty minutes later the ML slowed to a halt. The other ML drew alongside it and both lowered their motor surf boats into the dark, oily water. Up ahead Tiller could just make out the shadowy coastline of Ramree.

9

In the half light of a murky dawn the two motor surf boats dipped and careered in the swell as they neared the shore. Occasionally their rolling motion lifted their exhaust pipes out of the water, which made them emit a curious, animal-like coughing sound. To those aboard the craft it sounded horrendously loud. But Tiller knew that even if there was anyone ashore the sound would be completely drowned by the breaking surf which now thundered directly ahead of them.

The roar of the surf steadily increased. Then the waves around the boats began to break and they were suddenly pitched into a lather of foam. It was like being flung on to one of those funfair rides which tossed you in all directions. The curled tops hung threateningly over the gyrating, bouncing craft and the hiss as they broke all but drowned out the warning shouts of the crewmen to their passengers to hold tight. But the boats rode the turmoil well and though plenty of spray swept over them no solid water came aboard.

The interpreters of the reconnaissance photographs had earmarked the beach as one suitable for landing, but they had not been able to calculate the expected height of the surf. However, their prediction that the beach shelved gradually and that there would be no excessive undertow or lateral current proved correct, for the crews were able to guide their boats right into the beach without having to worry about veering and presenting a side to the wind and waves.

The crews jumped into the shallow water and held the boats bow-on to the beach while the SBS patrol leapt ashore and made a dash for the sparse under-growth that lined the beach, their weapons at the ready. Coates, carrying his black walking stick, his carbine slung over his shoulder and his empty pipe stuck upside down in his mouth, was the last to jump ashore.

The men spread out quickly to search the area. Fifty yards inland they found two *bashas* on stilts – fishermen's huts, judging by the odour that lingered in them – but no sign of their occupants. By now the dawn had given way to a grey, humid, wet morning. In its murky light they carefully extended their search inland but found nothing but a series of partially completed defences behind which lay large, uncultivated paddy-fields.

By the time the patrol had returned to the beach the crewmen had unloaded the collapsible canoes, the wireless and other equipment from the surf boats, and had returned to the MLs, which had now retreated beyond the horizon to await the outcome of the operation.

The patrol set off in single file along the fringes of the beach towards Kyaukpyu. They stumbled through the thick, muddy mangrove, cursing the tangled stumps that snared their feet. The smell of rotting vegetation and dankness hung in the air.

They made several deviations to reconnoitre areas which might have been occupied by the Japanese. Even for Coates it was unknown territory, though the terrain was similar to more open parts of the Arakan coastal mainland. They trudged on for hours, soaked by the rain and their own sweat. Once they came upon a favourite form of Japanese defence: a deep ditch and row upon row of *panjis*, bamboo stakes, sharpened and hardened by fire. But there was no sign of any Japanese.

At one point they saw several vultures circling to gain height in a thermal above some open paddy-fields and on investigation found the skeletal remains of what Coates said was probably a water buffalo lying in an irrigation ditch. It had been picked clean and the bones were as white as if they had been scrubbed. Its eyeless sockets were still swarming with ants, intent on finding the last vestige of edible tissue. Nearby the party found the remains of a fire and an empty Japanese cigarette packet.

'So they are here,' said Tiller. 'Somewhere.'

He looked up at the vultures which circled over their heads and felt an urge to empty his carbine at them.

Coates, as if guessing what he was thinking, looked up too and said: 'Cunning bastards, they always hang around just out of range.'

They picked over the fire and concluded that the Japanese had indeed been there. The remnants of a few bones showed that it was probably they who had killed the water buffalo, though it could have been a leopard or tiger, Coates said, as they sometimes preyed on native cattle.

In the early afternoon, still some distance from the town, they came upon the first signs they had seen that the island was still inhabited: a small group of *bashas* set on the usual stilts among neglected vegetable gardens. A large, dark-brown pig rooting in the mud and debris under one of the *bashas* showed that someone must be living there, but at first the SBS team could find no sign of life. However, in the last *basha*, the smallest and most decrepit, they found an old couple squatting on the floor who hardly bothered to look up until Coates addressed them in Arakanese. Then they became quite animated, gesticulating in one direction and then another, their weathered faces creased in smiles of welcome that revealed almost toothless gums.

'They say Kyaukpyu is deserted and has been ever since the Japanese arrived,' said Coates. 'Most of its inhabitants fled to the mainland.'

'No Japs?' Tiller asked. He could hear the disappointment in his voice. So did Coates, who smiled briefly and said: 'Not quite, Tiger. It sounds as if you'll get a crack at our Nippon friends. They say a Jap patrol passed through here a week or so back. Around nine of them, from what I can gather.'

'But they're not here in strength?'

Coates shrugged. 'Difficult to say. They are very simple people. They would not know what was going on outside their own community. They also say that about two cooking pots of rice from here there is another group of *bashas* where a few of the inhabitants have decided to stay. Probably because they are too old to move, like this couple. They might know something.'

'Two cooking pots of rice?' Tiller queried.

'They don't have clocks around here,' Coates explained. 'Instead they measure walking distances by how long it takes to boil a pot of rice. One pot takes about twenty minutes.'

'Which direction?'

Coates turned to the old couple, who gestured vaguely inland. He thanked them gravely and they bowed and smiled. Then they argued with Coates, but he firmly shook his head and eventually they wandered off.

'They wanted to give us food,' the forester told Tiller. 'It's the custom in these parts. I told them our religion didn't allow us to eat before sundown. I don't think they believed me, but were mightily relieved as they obviously have hardly got enough food to feed themselves.'

'We'll have a look at this other place,' said Tiller, 'but it will mean bivouacking somewhere for the night.'

'What about here?' Sandy suggested.

'Not in these *bashas*,' Coates said firmly. 'Too easy to pick up a skin disease or dysentery. The edge of the beach is best.'

Other members of the patrol, who had been scouring the immediate area for any sign of the Japanese, returned without finding anything. Two SBS men were left behind with the collapsible canoes to prepare a bivouac near the beach for the others and then Tiller found the path that led inland, and struck out along it.

At first the jungle was dark and gloomy but then suddenly the monsoon clouds parted and the sun, already past its apex, shone with a piercing heat through the jungle canopy. Steam rose from the vegetation as if it was being cooked and insects hummed and buzzed around them, and high up in the trees a band of monkeys gibbered loudly and bounced from one branch to another. The ground was slippery with mud but the undergrowth remained relatively sparse and the path was clearly marked.

They walked, keeping a distance of some yards between them and taking it in turns to lead. At one point, when Coates was in front, he stopped, squatted and warned the others to drop down, then pointed with his stick.

'I just saw a namesake of yours,' he said quietly to Tiller when he came up cautiously to join him. 'It came from the left.'

The two men moved forward cautiously until they came to the animal's spoor. Coates bent down and looked at the outsized cats' paws that could be plainly seen in the mud. 'Full grown, I'd say. Curious.'

'Why?' Tiller felt uneasy and vulnerable, and gestured to the rest of the team to spread out from the path.

Coates straightened. 'If we'd disturbed it, it would hardly have come in our direction, would it?'

'You mean someone else did.'

'Perhaps.' Coates was not a man to commit himself. Tiller wondered what would have happened if the tiger had come right up on one of the team.

Anticipating Tiller's question, Coates said: 'They do sometimes attack. It happens. There are three types of tiger: those which feed on cattle, those which feed on game, and the man-eaters. The last are rare and only attack humans if they have bad teeth or if they're too old, or too infirm or injured to catch their natural prey. Rogue tigers are rarer than rogue elephants, though.

142

And rogue elephants aren't common. I've known three in twenty-five years.'

Half an hour later, just as the sun had begun to slip behind the tops of the trees to their right, the path led into a clearing which had a number of small *bashas* built under the larger trees. Scraggy chickens skittered in fright from the centre of the clearing, where they had been feeding, and the long shadows swallowed them up.

Coates called out something. His voice echoed among the trees without at first bringing any response. Then he shouted something more harshly and an old man appeared from one of the *bashas* and climbed slowly down the bamboo steps to the ground. He bowed to Coates, who shook him by the hand.

The villager was as old as the earlier couple. He had a sparse, straggling goatee which he kept combing through nervously with his fingers and his lungi hung awkwardly about his thin body like a curtain.

'He's the headman,' Coates explained. 'But there's no one here except him and his wife. He says the Japanese have not visited the place but the local policeman came once. He's sure there are no Japanese in Kyaukpyu, which he confirms has been deserted by the population.'

'I don't trust him,' Tiller said. There was something about the man that made him wary of him.

Coates looked at Tiller sharply. 'You've got a good sixth sense, haven't you, Tiger?'

Tiller grinned. 'It's kept me alive so far.'

'I might make an adequate hunter out of you in peacetime,' said Coates grudgingly.

He spoke rapidly to the man, who began to point

towards the town. Coates thanked him elaborately and the man returned to his *basha*. 'He says to take that path there. It's the quickest and easiest to the town.'

'What do you think?' It was the first time Tiller had asked the older man's advice automatically.

Coates shrugged. 'Many headmen are in the pay of the Japanese. It's better to approach the town from the beach.'

'I agree,' said Tiller. 'We'll take the path until we're out of sight. Then we'll cut back to the coast.'

It was almost dark by the time they found their way back to their rendezvous. The two SBS men who had remained had prepared simple bivouacs by using branches cut from nearby trees to make simple lean-to huts which they had roofed with plantain leaves. Inside each hut a groundsheet had been suspended on short poles to make a bed and above these were hung the mosquito nets.

The patrol took care to change into dry clothes and to examine their feet before covering themselves in citronella oil as an extra precaution against the biting insects. They took it in turns to stand guard, but nothing disturbed them except the subdued roar of the rollers breaking on the beach and clamour of the frogs in the undergrowth.

At the first glimmer of dawn the patrol started out again. The monsoon rain was falling heavily and cast a grey pall over the landscape. After an hour they came across a wide *chaung* which still had only a trickle of water in it. Instead of crossing it Coates recommended following it inland, as this would bring them behind whatever had driven the tiger towards them the day before.

They walked steadily for another hour before Tiller stopped them to survey the opposite side of the *chaung*. It seemed a good place to cross but as they began to move towards the bank a burst of machine-gun fire sent them diving for cover.

'Where is it?' Tiller shouted to Dopey, who was acting as point man. Dopey, crouching behind a tree, indicated a small hill on the far side of the *chaung* with the barrel of his carbine. Tiller cautiously scanned the hillside but it was quite some distance from them and had plenty of cover for a machine-gun. He couldn't see anything moving. He wondered why the gunner had opened fire at such extreme range when he had little or no chance of hitting any of the patrol.

Coates, who had crawled up beside him, said: 'It's a Type 92, what the Yanks call a "woodpecker".'

'Trust the Yanks to come up with some fancy name for it. How can you tell?'

'Low rate of fire,' said Coates briefly, his eyes continuing to scan the hilltop. 'Makes it sound like a woodpecker pecking away.'

'It was fast enough for me,' said Tiller, only too aware of the weapon's distinctive knock, knock, knock, which made it quite different from any other machine-gun he had heard before. 'Why the fuck fire at us at that range?'

'It's a favourite trick of the Japs. Open fire from a feature they know you will try and outflank and where there is an obvious and easy method of doing it. That's where the real ambush will be.'

'You mean they expect us to take shelter in the *chaung* and outflank them by going up it?'

'You've got it in one, Tiger.'

'And the ambush will be overlooking the *chaung*.'

'Bull's-eye again.'

'So let's find where the bastards have laid it,' said Tiller and indicated that the patrol should follow him away from the *chaung* and into the mangrove on the right of the path.

It was hard going, and slow too, but within half an hour they had moved in a wide semicircle and managed to manoeuvre themselves behind the area where the Japanese, in all probability, lay in wait for them beside the *chaung*.

Sandy was sent ahead to scout while the patrol rested. He returned, after what seemed an interminable time, with a grin on his face. He held up the fingers and thumb of one hand and the four fingers of the other. Tiller nodded and waved him forward, and then beckoned for the others to follow. He had no doubt that his men, though outnumbered, could deal with nine Japanese, especially if the patrol was able to surprise them.

'Drop back, Dick,' he whispered to Coates. He didn't want the old boy to take deliberate risks and get himself killed; for one thing, he was too useful to the team now. For a moment Coates hesitated, but then shrugged and hung back to allow the others to pass him.

Sandy led the patrol through dense undergrowth and then up a slight incline. Near the top of it he threw himself down and crawled towards the skyline. The others followed suit, spreading out laterally as they did so. Tiller stayed with Sandy and eased himself alongside the Australian, whose head was flattened against the coarse grass of the incline.

Sandy nodded upwards and Tiller slowly, with infinite care, moved himself into a position from where he could look over the incline and down into a hollow which overlooked the *chaung*.

The Japanese were a lot closer than Tiller had imagined. Worse, they had with them what he recognized as a Taisho medium machine-gun mounted on a tripod. It was sited to fire down the *chaung* but could, he knew, be quickly swivelled in any direction.

Doubtless the Japanese officer in charge thought he would do all the damage with the Taisho, but supporting the machine-gun team were half a dozen infantrymen. These were armed with the standard 6.5mm Arisaka rifle, but instead of lying in the normal prone position, they were, Tiller was surprised to see, all squatting on the ground among the elephant grass, their rifles raised to their shoulders, their elbows resting on their knees. One of them also had what looked like a small mortar. Their attention was entirely focused on the *chaung*.

Carefully, Tiller glanced around the hollow, which was fringed with what Coates called paddy-field teak trees – those of no value for Burma's timber industry. The spread of their branches had kept the vegetation from growing under them. The ground there, Tiller saw immediately, was much too bare to hide any additional troops and there were certainly none hiding behind the solid bright brown trunks.

For a moment he savoured the situation and then slid back. He put his mouth to Sandy's ear: 'We'll go in behind our grenades.'

147

'Do we want a prisoner?' Sandy whispered back.

Tiller shook his head. 'Only if they surrender.'

The others were looking at Tiller. Tiller couldn't see Coates, but assumed he had got the message and was keeping out of the way. He detached his two 36 grenades from his belt and showed them to the others to make sure they knew what he was doing. Then he took out the pins and held them in either hand and rose slowly to his feet. Sandy did the same. Tiller lobbed both grenades at the Japanese below him, and Sandy followed suit.

As the four grenades were still curving through the air a shot rang out and then a second. Simultaneously, Tiller heard the crack of a bullet and something plucked at his shoulder, and out of the corner of his eye, as he brought his carbine to bear on the Japanese below him, he saw something fall from one of the teak trees.

Then the grenades exploded and all hell broke loose.

Two of the Japanese who had been hit by the flying shrapnel from the grenades began screaming – a high-pitched, animal sound the like of which Tiller had never heard before – and then he and the other members of the team were charging down the incline, emptying their magazines into the waiting ambushers.

One of the team of two machine-gunners was uninjured and he frantically spun his heavy weapon round on its tripod to meet the oncoming charge. He got off a short burst but then the twisted ammunition belt jammed the firing mechanism.

Tiller could see the terror in the machine-gunner's face as he lifted his carbine. He felt it jolt in his shoulder

148

and the man pitched forward over the breech of his gun. Tiller swung the M2 away but could see no other obvious targets.

Then, immediately in front of Tiller, the Japanese officer in charge rose from the undergrowth. He must have been wounded by one of the grenades, for his jacket was ripped and one side of his face was covered in blood. In one hand he held his long, slightly curved sword. He ran straight at Tiller, screaming at the top of his voice.

'*Banzai! Banzai!*'

To Tiller's astonishment the two remaining Japanese who had not been killed or wounded, instead of running away or surrendering, took up the cry and also began charging up the slope towards the SBS men now stationary above them. They screamed as they ran, the sun glinting on the grotesquely long bayonets fixed to their rifles. But first one fell and then the other, so that only the officer, intent on reaching Tiller, remained.

For a split second fear surged through Tiller like an electric shock. He sighted his carbine and pressed the trigger. But the weapon either jammed or the magazine was empty. The Japanese was nearly on him now and Tiller's position screened the man from Sandy's weapon. Tiller fancied he could see the look of triumph on the officer's face and smell the foulness of his breath. Slowly, deliberately, the man paused, raised his sword with both his hands and swung it. Instinctively Tiller ducked and heard the swish of the blade as it passed above him.

The Japanese was tall and powerfully built but the heavy sword and his wound made him stagger out of control for just long enough for Tiller to ram the muzzle of his carbine into his face with all his force. Crying out pitifully, the man raised his hands instinctively and dropped his sword.

Tiller reversed his carbine and smashed the stock against the man's head, knocking his khaki forage cap off his shaven skull. The man staggered and as Tiller stepped backwards to draw his pistol, Sandy was able to get a clear enough view to shoot him with a burst from his carbine. The man sagged to the ground, grappled blindly for his sword, tried to regain his feet, rolled over once, and lay still.

The shooting stopped as suddenly as it had begun and a silence settled on the hollow which was broken only by the sobbing of the one surviving Japanese, who lay in the undergrowth.

The SBS patrol deployed instantly to search the area for any other survivors. But the machine-gun crew on the hilltop had decamped and there was no trace of any other Japanese. Tiller, driven to distraction by the dying sobs of the wounded Japanese, started to walk over to where he lay to see what he could do to help the man, but was stopped by a warning shout from Sandy.

'Keep back, Tiger, for Christ's sake. Keep away from him.'

Tiller stopped and turned and saw Dopey moving round until he had a clear view of the dying Japanese. Dopey raised his rifle.

'Jesus, don't do that,' Tiller heard himself shout indignantly. He felt fury flood through him that a trained SBS man like Dopey would shoot a wounded man. He'd fucking crucify him when they got back.

Dopey ignored him. He squeezed the trigger of the

150

carbine once. The shot rang loud in the stillness of the clearing and the sobbing stopped. For a moment the silence returned and then there was a shattering explosion as the grenade rolled out of the dead man's hand. Its acrid smoke drifted up towards the watching SBS patrol.

'Christ almighty,' Tiller exclaimed quietly.

Dopey came back, refilling the magazine of his carbine as he walked.

'One of their little tricks,' he said nonchalantly. 'If they're wounded they hope you're going to be compassionate enough to try and help them. So they hold a primed hand-grenade until you're close enough to receive it in the face. Then they blow themselves up and take you with them. They won't be taken prisoner.'

'Christ almighty,' Tiller said again. He went over to Sandy, who was searching the dead officer. 'Thanks, Sandy.'

'Stubborn bastards, aren't they,' said the Australian casually, throwing the officer's documents up to Tiller. 'Don't know when to give up.'

As he caught the documents Tiller felt a sharp pain in his shoulder. He glanced down, and saw that his shirt was soaked in blood.

'That sniper nicked you,' said Sandy. 'You'd better watch out.'

Aware that in that climate even the smallest cut could become infected, Tiller took out the bulky first-aid dressing from his pocket and handed it to Sandy. Sandy placed the pad over the graze and bound it tight with the bandage attached to it.

'What sniper?'

'You all right?' Coates asked as he approached. He carried his rifle, as he always seemed to, tucked under his arm like a shotgun. His empty pipe, bowl downwards, was hanging from one corner of his mouth.

'Sure. What sniper?' Tiller felt irrationally angry that something had happened which he knew nothing about.

'Sniper in one of those paddy-field teak trees,' Coates said, removing the pipe and pointing the stem at one of them. 'I thought I'd better watch out for them. It's another of the little tricks of the trade the Japs get up to. Surprisingly, that one hadn't tied himself to the tree as they usually do. They like doing the unexpected when they're not being thoroughly predictable.'

'It was certainly that. You got him?'

'Well, no one else was going to,' Coates said sharply. 'And as you seemed intent on keeping me out of harm's way I thought I'd better make myself useful somehow.'

'You sure as hell did that,' said Tiller. 'You must have picked him off immediately he'd fired.'

'Young man, I've picked off – as you call it – a charging tiger inside four seconds. That's all the time it gave me. That Jap sniper wouldn't have given you much longer. They know always to shoot first whoever is in charge.'

Tiller accepted the rebuke without comment. He flicked through the officer's documents quickly. Sandy had found a diary on the dead body in which some of the leaves were marked with pressed flowers. On the pages were short poems in Japanese characters.

Tiller passed it over to Coates, who said: 'This is the form of poem they call haiku. See, each poem is divided into three parts.'

'Code of some sort?' Tiller asked.

Coates shook his head. 'I doubt it. Probably genuine ones he wrote himself.' He paused and read one of them.

Tiller peered over Coates's shoulder and looked at the delicate pressed flowers and the precise, neat strokes of the Japanese characters on the rice-paper of the diary.

'Love poems,' said Coates. 'Want a translation?'

In his mind's eye Tiller saw again the officer's face contorted in hatred as he ran at him screaming and waving his sword. He shook his head. He wondered if he would ever understand his new enemy.

The SBS began searching all the bodies, taking great care to make sure that none was booby-trapped. Tiller had never seen a fully clothed Japanese soldier at close quarters before. He noted the drabness of their uniforms, the curious canvas shoes with heavy rubber soles in which the big toe was separated from the rest of the foot – Sandy said they were called *tobi* – and the long khaki woollen puttees that they all wore from the top of their *tobi* to just below the knee.

As Tiller watched, two of the SBS unwound body belts from under the jackets of the dead men. They threw one of them to him to examine. It was made of silk and was finely stitched with Japanese characters. Tiller showed it to Coates.

'It's called a *senninbari*,' Coates said. 'Which means a thousand stitches. Their wives and sweethearts make them. The inscriptions they sew on them are supposed to bring luck.'

Tiller shook his head in silent astonishment.

After they had searched all the bodies they buried

them quickly in a communal grave. Tiller decided the Taisho machine-gun might come in handy, so this was dismantled. But Coates insisted that the other Japanese weapons should not be left lying around for the locals to gather. So they took out any moving parts and threw them into the jungle, and then dug a pit and threw the weapons in it, and covered them up.

'What's this then?' Tiller held up the small mortar – it was no more than two feet in length – by its curved base plate before he threw it into the pit.

'Fifty-mill grenade launcher,' said Sandy. 'We call it a knee mortar.'

'The Japs are lousy shots,' said Coates, 'which is why they like squatting and not lying prone as we do. Gives them a more stable base. But what they lack in accuracy with their rifles they make up for with the use of that nifty little weapon.'

'Is it fired from the knee, then?' Tiller asked. He noticed that the base plate seemed conveniently shaped to place on a man's thigh when he was kneeling.

Coates laughed. 'Christ, no! I've seen others make that mistake. They ended up in hospital. Some twit in Intelligence translated "leg" as "knee". The Japs call it a "leg mortar" because they carry it strapped to one leg in a canvas container.'

Tiller threw the mortar into the pit and filled it in. Then he beckoned for the others to follow him. The machine-gun team that had escaped from the hillock would alert any Japanese in Kyaukpyu and he wanted to press on across the *chaung* as quickly as possible in order to locate Kyaukpyu harbour and launch the operation. They could expect further opposition and he wanted to press home his advantage before the Japanese could organize another reception for them. Also, his shoulder was getting stiff and he was worried that it might become infected. Sandy had scattered sulphonamide powder on the wound before he had bound it up but there was no guarantee it would work.

They skirted a whole succession of empty paddy-fields before coming to the first *bashas* of the deserted town and moved round these until they reached the coast on the far side. By now the remains of the day were fading from the sky. As it darkened, the clear patches filled with a sprinkling of stars and sporadically the full moon came from behind a cloud and, to Tiller's consternation, flooded the ground with a pale light. The last thing he wanted, or expected, was to have to attack the boats in moonlight.

They inched their way cautiously into the town, wary of where they stepped, alert for any signs of booby-traps. The walls of some of the *bashas* had fallen down; others were roofless or covered in weeds, and the unpaved road between them was a tangle of grass and roots. A rat skittered across in front of them but otherwise there was no sign of life.

After a few hundred yards the road widened, the *bashas* gave way to several stone buildings, nearly all without their roofs, and soon it was apparent that the SBS patrol was approaching the centre of the deserted town. This was next to the harbour, which looked like a large lagoon.

The moonlight shimmered on the waters of the harbour and they could see several wavering lights glinting from the boats anchored there. Tiller, who was acting as point man, counted eight of them. Some were quite big and would need two Pin-Up Girls to sink them, which meant he barely had enough devices.

He halted the patrol and went ahead by himself to reconnoitre, but apart from some empty oil drums which lay piled in a pool of stinking oil and water, there was little to see. He decided it was best to withdraw a little way down the street they had walked along and to occupy one of the stone buildings that had retained its roof. The patrol searched all the nearby buildings and eventually returned with a young, cowering native, who was closely questioned by Coates.

'He says the Japanese are all aboard the boats preparing to sail,' Coates told Tiller, who was helping Sandy and Dopey assemble the collapsible canoes. 'There are none ashore.'

'What are the cargoes on the boats?'

'Rice mainly, which they must have known was in the town's storehouse. But also anything they could find that is edible. They've been here about a week.'

'How many of them, does he know? How did they get here?'

Coates shot the questions at the native.

'He says most of them came in the boats. There are no natives aboard any of them. But some arrived in a landing-craft which then left. Those are probably our friends we met by the *chaung*.'

'Do we believe him?'

Coates shrugged. 'They roped him in and the few others still living here to help them load the boats. I suppose he's got a fair picture of what's going on. He's hopping mad that the Japs have pinched all their food. So he's not a collaborator. Not unless he's a bloody good actor.'

Tiller thought of the time pencils he had with him. 'And he says they're preparing to set sail tonight?'

'Yes. The boats are fully loaded, so my guess is they'll wait for the moon to set and then push off. It's only a couple of hours to the mainland but they wouldn't want to risk being caught by any of our sea patrols in moonlight in open water.'

Tiller's shoulder was beginning to ache intolerably. 'That means we've got to paddle out to them, lay the Pin-Ups, and then escape, all in what amounts to broad daylight,' he said.

'We'll set up the Taisho so we can give you covering fire if necessary. Are you using both canoes?'

Tiller nodded.

'That'll leave three of us ashore. That should be enough. There can't be many Japs aboard those boats.'

'But they'll be expecting an attack,' Tiller reminded him.

'They might have been expecting one while they were ashore,' said Coates. 'They won't be expecting the kind you're planning on. They probably think they're as safe as houses out on the water.'

Tiller remained doubtful. 'No sailor's so fucking stupid as to think that.'

'They won't be sailors,' Coates predicted confidently. 'The Japanese Navy doesn't concern itself with helping to feed the Japanese Army. The two services loathe each other even more than they loathe us. They'll be army personnel.'

Sandy came up to them. 'The canoes are ready,

Sarge,' he said. 'Six Pin-Ups in each. Shall we take them down to the harbour?'

Tiller nodded. He turned to Coates. 'How long before the moon sets, Dick?'

'Three hours,' Coates said immediately.

'I want six-hour time pencils for the Pin-Ups,' Tiller said to Sandy. 'If they aren't well out to sea at that time, then the Burmese government will have to go stuff itself. I'll follow you down. Let's find a good place to set up the machine-gun, Dick.'

They found a roofless stone building next to the harbour which from its first floor gave a clear all-round view of it and called two of the SBS patrol up with the Taisho.

'On no account fire until I send up a red Very light,' Tiller told them. 'Then engage first the boat that's showing the most fight. But be bloody careful. I don't want to be shot up by you two bastards.'

The men grinned and secured the machine-gun's tripod firmly by piling rubble around its feet. They had identified it as an even older model than the 'woodpecker'. Tiller had been told at the firearms school in Chittagong that they had been phased out of the Japanese Army some years before. Obviously the Japanese in the Arakan were mostly equipped with obsolete weapons.

All SBS men in the Far East theatre had been trained to handle Japanese weapons and now, in readiness for the action they hoped would come, they stripped down the mechanism expertly, oiled it and reassembled it.

'Where will you be?' Tiller asked Coates after they returned to their temporary headquarters.

'I'll go to the other end of the harbour,' Coates

replied. 'Then I can cover you if you decide to land there after laying the Pin-Ups.'

Tiller hesitated and then asked: 'What were those Japs shouting when they charged us? A war cry of some sort, was it?'

'*Banzai*,' said Coates. 'A *Banzai* charge is the last act of a defeated force. They just charge the opposition regardless. It's a death cry more than a war cry. Comes from the Japanese "*Tenno heika banzai*", which means "long live the Emperor". The Japs consider their emperor a deity, as you know.'

'Jesus,' said Tiller quietly. He could not get the contorted face of the Japanese officer as he ran towards him out of his mind.

The SBS men had launched the two collapsible canoes in deep shadow on the edge of the harbour, sheltered by a cluster of tall reeds. Dopey and his crewman were already in their canoe, their paddles resting across it. Sandy crouched by the other one and, after Tiller had climbed into the rear cockpit, slid quickly into the front one. Then, with a few swift strokes, they left the reeds and rafted up while they considered the best line of attack.

They were now so low in the water it was difficult to see their targets and they decided it was safer for both canoes to keep together until they were near enough to see where exactly the craft were anchored.

Tiller led the way. He moved around the edge of the harbour so that the silhouettes of the canoes merged with the low land that rimmed it. As they paddled, the monsoon cloud covered the moon and before long it began to rain.

10

'*Dareka Okiteru?*'

The shout rang out across the dark water like a challenge. Tiller and Sandy froze in mid-stroke and slumped forward to minimize their profile.

'*Dareka Okiteru?*'

The beam from a powerful torch stabbed the darkness from one of the boats which was anchored to the left of the canoes. It seemed to waver uncertainly before being directed on to the deck of another boat anchored on the extreme left of the group. Tiller raised his head with infinite care and could just see the dark shadow of the Japanese holding the torch.

'*Dareka Okiteru?*'

The torch sliced away to another boat and caught in its beam a soldier sitting on the deck with his rifle across his knees. He protected his eyes from the shaft of light and shouted back: '*Damare. Nenasai.*'

The words were harsh and urgent but the figures showed no urgent action. Were they words of warning? Tiller felt the adrenalin begin to pump through him. The Japanese might have seen them, or heard something. He couldn't tell. As a precaution he began undoing the toggles that secured his carbine to the inside of the canoe.

Using single paddles, the two teams had cautiously

circled the edge of the harbour in the pouring rain until they had come to the narrow entrance with its rough-built stone piers on either side. There had been no sign of any guards on land or of any harbour patrol. All the canoeists' targets were anchored in the middle of the harbour, huddled together as if for protection. Only one light now showed, from a boat in the middle.

Their targets had seemed a long way away, hopelessly out of reach, and Tiller had thought then, with a flash of insight, that it was not only the Japanese who committed suicide: they just made a ritual out of it. And why not?

Then, as they had crossed the harbour mouth, he had seen an indistinct blur to their left, a small island perhaps, between themselves and the Japanese. As they had approached it the rain had ceased as quickly as it had come and he could see it was a bombed-out hull of a small merchant ship. Under his breath he had thanked the RAF with all his heart, for the wreck had meant the canoeists had at least an outside chance of reaching their targets.

They had sheltered behind the half-sunk ship as long as they dared, hoping against hope that another veil of rain would sweep across the harbour to protect them. But the sky, although partially covered, so that the moonlight was intermittent, remained obstinately clear of rain clouds, and eventually Tiller had indicated it was time to start. He had decided to attack the three boats huddled together to their left, plus a smaller one anchored apart which he suspected was the headquarters ship, and Dopey should attack the other four. Each canoe would act independently. There was no question of one helping the other in an emergency if it meant abandoning the operation. That was how they had been trained. They all knew the rules and must now follow them without question.

Just as they had left the security of the wreck the moon had gone behind a bank of cloud and Tiller had thought that perhaps after all they stood a chance. But then the Japanese officer, or whoever he was, had started shouting . . .

Now the torch switched to another ship, sweeping along its decks in search of a sentry.

'*Dareka Okiteru?*' the Japanese repeated. He sounded almost plaintive.

There was no answer. He called out again. This time a long stream of what could only have been abuse echoed across the water in reply. The torch wavered uncertainly before it was snapped off, and Tiller could just make out its holder going below.

Tiller waited a moment before straightening up. He listened intently but he heard only the gentle slap of the water on the edge of the cockle and Sandy breathing heavily behind him. Ahead he could see the tops of the masts of the Japanese ships moving in gentle arcs across a clear patch of night sky. Satisfied, he took a deep gulp of humid monsoon air and dug his paddle carefully into the water.

Suddenly the moon, which was now beginning to wane, bathed the harbour with the brightness of a searchlight. Tiller hesitated in mid-stroke and Sandy urged in his ear: 'Keep going. Head for the *mergui* on the extreme left. We know there's no sentry on deck.'

Banzai, Tiller shouted to himself. *Banzai*, Tiger.

He dug in quickly now, and felt the pain of his

shoulder jar through his arm. The phosphorescence on the water danced and glittered, but he calculated that the quicker they got there the better – and by moving fast they had less chance of being hit if they were seen.

It was further than he had thought, but then they were suddenly in the shadow of the eighty-foot native schooner thrown by the moon on the water, and Tiller had to slow the canoe down with his blade. Gently, slowly, they drifted alongside, and then rested.

The tide was beginning to ebb so that it thrust the canoe against the side of the *mergui*, making it easy for Sandy to steady the canoe while Tiller prepared one of the Pin-Up Girls.

Tiller squeezed the soft copper tubing of the time pencils to crush their inner capsules. He then replaced them in their slots, silently approving the American precaution of using two delay mechanisms. Too often in the past he had laid explosives which had failed to explode because the temperamental time pencils had not functioned.

He wondered if he had allowed the correct amount of time – the warm water would speed up the ammonium chloride eating through the fine wire that retained the spring-loaded firing pin – and decided that he had. At the best of times pencil fuses were rather hit-or-miss devices, but on this occasion timing was not crucial.

The next part of the operation was crucial. He did not know if all the crew were asleep in the *mergui's* crude deck house, situated near the stern, but it seemed logical that they would all be there to keep out of the worst of the monsoon weather. It therefore made sense, to avoid alerting the crew, to fix the Pin-Up as far from them as possible, and he indicated to Sandy that he wanted to move the canoe up to the bows. Sandy nodded his agreement and moved the canoe slowly down the length of the vessel.

Silently, Tiller withdrew the pieces of the placing rod from their position in the bows of the canoe and connected them together. He attached the Pin-Up to the end of the rod and waited for the canoe to drift to a halt near the bows. He remembered the Texan telling him it was exactly the same principle as placing a limpet and he slowly lowered the Pin-Up on the end of the placing rod into the water.

The canoe tipped alarmingly, but Sandy managed to shift his weight sufficiently to compensate without losing his fingertip grip on the roughly hewn edges of the *mergui's* planking. If it had been a steel hull, Tiller thought, Sandy would have had a magnetic holdfast to keep a grip on the ship's side. The Yanks might be clever, but they had failed to think of that, and he wondered, as he made his first attempt to disconnect the placing rod, if they had ever used their clever device operationally.

At first the placing rod refused to disconnect itself and he had to lever it upwards again with more force. This time it came away from the Pin-Up and simultaneously there was a distinct vibration as the bolt was driven into the wooden hull. Tiller heard Sandy's sharp involuntary intake of breath as the boat trembled momentarily under his hand.

Tiller tensed, waiting for the inevitable shout of alarm from the deck of the *mergui*, for he was sure that the thud of the bolt into the planks must have been heard or felt by at least one of its crew. If they were discovered it would be no use trying to fight. The only chance then would be to dive under the vessel and try to get to the shore unseen.

The seconds ticked by. Tiller glanced back at Sandy, who shrugged and grimaced. It looked as if they had got away with it.

Tiller withdrew the placing rod from the water and slid it along the canoe's deck. One down, Tiller thought – just three to go.

The two boats next to the *mergui* were much bigger and would need two Pin-Up Girls to be sure of sinking them.

'*Tavoys*,' Sandy whispered in Tiller's ear as they moved cautiously towards the schooners.

The moon, low in the sky, was behind another bank of cloud now and Tiller, elated by their success so far, felt further encouraged by the darkness that now engulfed them. He knew that on a dark night SBS canoes, when their crew took the prone position, were indistinguishable from floating logs.

The thickness of the planking of the first schooner – which, Tiller judged, was well over a hundred feet long – muffled the sound and dampened the vibration of the first Pin-Up's bolt as it was driven home just near where they judged the engine was positioned, and then they placed another near the rudder.

The second schooner lay near the first one. It was slightly longer than the first, and although a tough ocean-going vessel it looked in poor condition. From a gash in its side Tiller deduced it must have recently been in a collision.

This time they placed the first charge near the bows. Then they moved aft, looking for the exhaust pipe, which would indicate the position of the engine. When they found the pipe Sandy steadied the canoe while Tiller prepared the placing rod and attached a Pin-Up Girl to it. Then, just as he was leaning over to lower the device into the water, Sandy's grasp slipped.

Instinctively, Sandy grabbed at the *tavoy's* side but in the split second it took for him to restore the canoe's stability the canoe tipped. It caught Tiller off balance and he felt the Pin-Up Girl slide off the placing rod, and into the water.

Tiller cursed silently. He had one device remaining and he had to use that on the final target, as it was almost certainly the headquarters ship. One Pin-Up Girl wouldn't sink the *tavoy* and he wished now he'd placed the first one by the engine, where it would have done the maximum damage. Too late now.

He looked down into the water as if half hoping the device would be floating on the surface, and saw something he had not noticed before. He tapped Sandy on the shoulder. Sandy leant back and Tiller whispered: 'Oil.'

Now that he had spotted it, the large, black, greasy puddle, stretching out beyond the schooner's stern, was easy to discern. The collision must have ruptured its fuel tank. Tiller thought of using the City Slicker but then dismissed the idea. It would have prevented them sinking the headquarters ship and would probably have scuppered any chance of Dopey finishing his tasks and escaping. They turned the canoe round and sheltered under the *tavoy's* raked bows while they studied their final target.

They could see now that it was another *mergui*, smaller than the first, easily identifiable by its high

166

poop and not unlike an Elizabethan man-of-war. A light glowed from its cabin and there was movement on its deck. Tiller looked across the stretch of open water and considered their options while Sandy held the canoe steady under the schooner's bow.

The tide was flowing out of the harbour more swiftly now, but to allow the canoe to drift with it towards the *mergui* was too risky and too slow. But it was a help that at least they had the tide with them and would not have to paddle against it.

Looking across at the *mergui*, which was anchored by the stern as well as the bow, it seemed highly unlikely to Tiller that the hammer blow of the bolt being driven into the planking would go unnoticed on such a small craft, especially as some of its occupants were still awake. So they would have to work on the assumption they might be discovered. He indicated that Sandy should bend forward and he then whispered his plan in his ear.

Sandy knew the odds but nodded his agreement. He let go the schooner's bobstay, and they began to paddle across the open water towards the *mergui*.

At that point, as Tiller said afterwards, God intervened in such a decisive way that he felt there was, after all, a kindly man in heaven with a long, white beard. For the monsoon rains returned with a vengeance. They came abruptly, out of nowhere it seemed, a rushing, roaring downpour that churned up the water around them and cut visibility to a few yards. Thunder rumbled overhead. Tiller hastily extracted his pocket compass and during a vivid flicker of lightning managed to take a bearing of the *mergui* before it vanished behind a veil of torrential tropical rain.

Looking at it from the *tavoy*, the *mergui* had seemed almost on the horizon, but as the rain continued to hammer down, its outline suddenly appeared ahead of them. Now Tiller had to practically shout to be heard above the roar of the rain and the claps of thunder.

'Forget the plan,' he said to Sandy. 'We'll make it.'

'Thank Christ for that,' Sandy replied. 'I didn't fancy our chances of swimming ashore.'

The storm had driven below whoever had been on the *mergui's* deck but the light in the cabin continued to flicker and blink intermittently as the rain lightened and then came down with renewed ferocity.

They came alongside right under the high stern that made a *mergui* so easily distinguishable from the other types of native craft, and let the canoe drift with the tide towards the bow.

Unlike the fore-and-aft-rigged *tavoy*, the *mergui* was rigged with Chinese lugsails, so it did not have a bowsprit. But its bows were raked to such an extreme that Sandy had no difficulty in keeping a firm grip on them while Tiller planted the last Pin-Up Girl. He lowered the device on the placing rod and then waited until another gust of wind and rain swept across the vessel before lifting the placing rod to disengage it. But however hard he tried he could not get it to disconnect and trigger the bolt.

Quite suddenly the rain stopped, the wind dropped to a stiff breeze, and the sky cleared around the last remnants of the moon.

Then behind them, from one of Dopey's targets, Tiller heard a Japanese shout a challenge. There was a single shot, then a burst from what he knew was a

M2 carbine, and a longer burst from a Japanese Type 100 sub-machine-gun.

Above them the crew of the *mergui* erupted on deck, shouting instructions at one another.

Sandy said urgently in his ear: 'Do we swim for it?'

'No point now,' whispered Tiller, consigning the placing rod and the Pin-Up Girl to the bottom of the harbour. 'Let's take this fucking junk instead.'

He pulled his carbine from its place and then tossed a 36 grenade on to the deck of the *mergui*. Stealth and evasion was the hallmark of the SBS but on occasion direct action was necessary. Now was such a time.

Sandy whooped his delight and threw two more grenades in quick succession. They went off with a thump that shook the *mergui* from stem to stern.

While debris was still clattering on to the deck and into the water the two SBS men swung themselves on board, deliberately tipping over the canoe as they did so. It sank instantly.

When the SBS men appeared over the bows the two Japanese who had survived the grenades panicked and jumped or fell into the water. Tiller shot one with his carbine; the other went under and did not come up again. With his carbine Sandy covered the three Japanese lying on the deck, but as he edged closer to them he could see that they were dead.

The firing and shouting behind the two SBS men continued sporadically but the moon was now too low in the night sky to shed any proper light on what was happening. Lights and shouts of command or alarm seemed to be coming from all corners of the harbour. A machine-gun from one of the ships opened fire on the shore, its tracer bullets arcing prettily over the water.

Another began firing into the sky as if the gunner thought the attack had come from that direction.

'Search the deck house,' Tiller ordered. Sandy lifted his hand and moved aft while Tiller searched the dead Japanese before rolling them into the water.

Sandy came out of the cabin.

'That's the lot,' he said. 'It must have been the HQ ship. There are charts all over the place and a wireless set.'

'Has it got an engine?'

'You must be joking.'

'Then we'll sail it ashore. I don't fancy swimming.'

'Too right,' said Sandy. 'You'll fancy it even less if you look over the stern.'

Tiller went aft and saw, directly under the counter, the dismembered remains of what had once been a human body being tossed about amid a churning, frothing mass of water.

'What the fuck . . . ?'

'Hammerheads,' said Sandy. 'Not a pretty sight, is it? I didn't like to tell you they'd be around when you were planning to swim for it.'

Tiller turned away in disgust. 'Get ready to sever the bow-anchor warp while I hoist one of the lugsails. When it starts filling, cut the stern one. There's quite a wind blowing, so you're going to have to be quick or we might tear the stern out of her.'

'I'll be quick all right, Sarge,' Sandy replied laconically. 'We're about to have visitors.'

He pointed to an open boat which had emerged from the shadows of the first *tavoy*. It was still too far away from them to make out any details except that it was being rowed.

'What armament has this floating sieve got, I wonder?' Tiller asked, glancing round him.

'Fuck all that I can see,' Sandy replied.

'Well, we'll just run the buggers down.'

'What about Dopey?'

'What about him?' Tiller snarled. 'You know the rules. Anyway, he's upwind of us, and without an engine there's nothing we can do.'

Sandy saw the sense in that. He unsheathed his *parang* knife and moved forward. Tiller tugged on the rope halyard of the mainmast and found that the square sail, crudely made of bamboo matting strengthened by battens, could be easily hoisted on its yard. He pulled it up quickly, made the halyard fast, and ran aft to find the rope that controlled the sail. When he found it he held it with one hand and the tiller with the other. He felt the strain on the rope as the sail filled and shouted for Sandy to cut the warp that held the bow anchor.

'All gone for'ard, Tiger!' Sandy shouted, and Tiller smiled at his delight at being in such a scrap. Good for Sandy – the Aussie was all right.

For a moment the *mergui* hovered as the tide kept it head to wind, but then it bore away quickly and the single sail, filled with wind, made the mast creak and groan under the stress.

Sandy scrambled aft as the *mergui* swung round and, as Tiller struggled to control the vessel, sliced through the aft anchor warp with one powerful stroke of his *parang*.

'All gone aft!'

Now that the *mergui* was free it gathered speed quickly and Tiller sailed it straight at the oncoming boat. He could see now that it was being rowed by six men and that there was a Japanese crouched in the bows with some type of light machine-gun. In the stern stood another wearing a forage cap and a long sword.

The two craft converged quickly. The Japanese in the stern shouted something and the boat altered course in an effort to avoid a collision. The soldier in the bows opened up with his machine-gun. Chips of wood flew off the *mergui* but the angle was not right for the machine-gunner to be able to fire at the two SBS men crouched by its helm.

Tiller pushed the helm towards him and followed the boat, pointing the bows of the *mergui* straight at its middle. Even in the darkness he fancied he saw the mouth of the officer open in astonishment just before the *mergui* hit.

There was a crunch and a jolt, shouting, then silence as the *mergui* careered on into the darkness.

'More fucking shark fodder,' Sandy said with satisfaction.

'The trouble with you Aussies,' said Tiller, who was beginning to enjoy himself, 'is that you're crude and foul-mouthed, and without any sympathy for those less fortunate than yourselves.'

'Know where you'll find sympathy, Tiger?' Sandy chuckled. 'I'll tell you, mate. It's in the dictionary between "shit" and "syphilis". Where are we heading?'

'Back to where we came from,' said Tiller. 'I hope.'

The second *tavoy* was looming up ahead of them when a stream of tracer erupted from it. It was something heavy – a 20mm cannon of some sort. Even the Japanese couldn't miss at that range.

'Shit,' said Tiller, instinctively ducking.

'Someone's on the ball,' Sandy said calmly. 'Not before time, I'd say.'

A second burst went through the *mergui's* sail, but Tiller, instead of altering course away from the *tavoy*, put the *mergui's* helm down and sailed straight for it.

'Christ!' Sandy yelled out. 'What are you doing, Tiger?'

Tiller pulled out the City Slicker. 'Shut up, and chuck this in the oil slick as we pass. Make sure you open the flap first.'

As one Pin-Up Girl wasn't going to sink the *tavoy*, he'd bloody well burn it instead. In for a penny, in for a pound. The government in exile would have to take a running jump at its collective self.

The *mergui's* change of course surprised the Japanese aboard the schooner as much as it had Sandy, and it took the gunner time to adjust his aim. A third burst flew over the *mergui* but then the gunner got the range and the *mergui* shook as the shells began thumping into its hull. Then they were too near for the gunner to depress his gun. The schooner loomed up and then disappeared behind them.

'Bombs away!' Sandy yelled.

Tiller heard the crack of rifle bullets over him and he ducked into the cockpit. Then the whole sky seemed to light up and the firing stopped. Tiller looked round and saw the water around the *tavoy* was one large sheet of flame.

'That was less than a minute,' Tiller said. 'I'll tell that bloody Texan what I think of him and his fancy devices.'

As he spoke, he saw the shore looming up ahead.

The *mergui*, filling rapidly with water, was hard to control. Tiller wrestled with the helm.

'Hold on!'

Its torn sail flapping noisily, the *mergui* surged through the water. Then it grounded, staggered free and drove on before hitting some underwater obstruction which jarred it from bow to stern. The mast snapped and the sail fell with a splintering crash on to the deck, so that pieces of bamboo matting flew into the air and were blown away into the night. It sent both SBS men sprawling and Tiller's carbine flew across the cockpit and into the deck house.

But still the *mergui* kept going until at last it was driven by the wind right through the rushes and on to the beach almost exactly at the place they had left in the canoe three hours before.

As they jumped on to the beach and ran up to the building where the others were waiting for them, the moon dipped below the horizon and the flickering flames of the burning schooner shot into the night sky.

Half an hour later the remaining native boats weighed anchor one by one and began slowly threading their way out of the harbour.

11

'Hello, American boys. How are you enjoying yourselves today? Aren't you missing your home comforts?
And what about your girls? Who do you think is taking
them out while you're away?'

The female voice was smooth, seductive and strongly
tinged with an American accent. It was not hard to
imagine what she looked like at the microphone: smiling
and friendly, everyone's buddy. But sexy too, very sexy.

'Do you know you're dying in your thousands so
that your British ally can regain her empire in Asia?
Of course you do. Because we know you American
boys have a good joke about it. You say that SEAC
really stands for Save England's Asiatic Colonies.'

The announcer paused.

Then she went on in a more serious tone: 'That's
not much of a joke when you're dying in the mud, as
so many of you are. Yet even as you listen the British
are back in Burma, a country which we the Japanese
made free and independent last year. They are back
practising their old colonial ways, making the local
people slaves again. They have found a new way to
do this in the Arakan, boys. They burn and wreck the
fishermen's boats to deprive them of a living. Not very
nice, is it? Is that sort of behaviour worth dying for?'

The man in the white linen suit bent forward and

snapped off the wireless. Danforth had introduced him to Tiller as Mr Hollis, a Colonial Office Civil Affairs Officer from the government in exile. But to Tiller he looked like someone who had stepped straight out of a Hollywood movie – Cary Grant, perhaps, or some other dapper film star. His suit was uncreased, the triangle of silk handkerchief which poked neatly out of his breast pocket matched the tie that was loosely knotted around the collar of his crisp white shirt.

'Not good, gentlemen,' he said now, settling back in his seat. 'Not good at all.'

Danforth, whose wireless it was, raised his eyebrows. 'Who was that cute little number?'

'She's just one of several females who broadcast propaganda from Japan. Tokyo Rose, our American friends call her. Different versions of that particular piece have been broadcast over the air for the last week. They must think it worth repeating.'

The atmosphere in Danforth's office was unusually formal. Tiller had been introduced to the visitor, but had not been waved to a chair as he usually was. Standing at ease, he watched the rain falling out of the sky outside the office, its drumming on the tin roof making it necessary to speak loudly.

Danforth got up from behind his desk and paced back and forth. 'You say Corporal Douglas laid all his charges but was then seen by a sentry aboard one of his targets?'

Tiller nodded. 'Yes, sir,' he replied in his most formal manner.

'Who raised the alarm?'

'Well, he shot at him, sir, but missed.'

'In the meantime you were about to lay the last charge on your last target?'

'That's correct, sir.'

'But immediately surprise was lost you decided instead to overwhelm the Japanese aboard the boat?'

'Yes, sir.'

'Which led to the boat being driven ashore?'

'Yes, sir.'

'What made you decide not to lay the charge?' Hollis asked.

Tiller considered whether to answer this. He accepted that the inquiry had to be carried out, that Danforth had no alternative but to have this officious little creep in his office, and that he, Tiller, had to be questioned by him. But Tiller had already put everything in his report. It seemed a waste of time to repeat it all again.

There was a long silence. Danforth, still striding up and down, looked at Tiller and nodded his encouragement.

'It's all in my report,' said Tiller reluctantly.

'I would like to hear it myself,' said Hollis.

'I couldn't get the charge to fix itself to the hull,' said Tiller.

Hollis looked at Danforth sharply. 'I take it that all your men are fully trained, Major?'

The implication was not lost on Danforth or Tiller. Tiller bristled and Danforth said quickly: 'It is a new device that the Americans have made. We agreed to test it out for them. It is still in the development stage.'

Hollis's foxy expression could not disguise his disappointment at this news. He couldn't blame Tiller

177

for its failure then and he couldn't blame the Americans because – well, because he couldn't. He tried another tack.

'You could have abandoned the operation at that point, could you not?'

Tiller stiffened. 'My orders were to plant delay devices on all Japanese shipping in the harbour. This I did.'

Hollis tapped his fingernails on the table. Even he was beginning to find it hot, for he took out his silk handkerchief and dabbed it delicately on his forehead. 'But your orders were also to ensure that there should be no evidence that local shipping was being destroyed by British forces. Is that correct?'

'But . . .' Tiller began.

'Is that correct, Sergeant?'

The drill sergeant's voice from all those years ago resonated in the recesses of Tiller's mind: 'You 'orrible little man, you. What are you? 'Orrible, that's what you are.'

With a great effort he said, very quietly: 'That's correct.'

He was very glad for Hollis's sake that Dopey and his partner had got back safely without a scratch on them, otherwise he would have been inclined to break the man's neck then and there. He decided to add bureaucracy to Sandy's list of disease, the monsoon and mother nature that the SBS were fighting. It was surprising the Japs got a look in at all.

Hollis now swung round to Danforth, who paused in his pacing. 'I'm sure you'll appreciate, Major, that the Burmese government takes this matter very seriously. Very seriously indeed. It could have grave implications for its long-term postwar policies in this area. I'm sure you'll be carrying out your own disciplinary procedures but . . .'

Hollis had overstepped the mark and Danforth interrupted him with the sharpness of a razor. 'I won't be.'

Hollis looked surprised, not so much by what Danforth had said but by the undisguised hostility with which he said it. 'I must say,' he began, but was interrupted by a knock on the door.

'Come,' said Danforth.

Coates put his head round the door. 'I just . . .' he said, but stopped when he saw Hollis in his crisp white suit. 'Well, well, well. Look who we have here.'

'Ah, yes,' said Danforth. 'Thanks for coming, Dick. Come in and shut the door.'

But Coates had already done so. To Tiller it looked as if he had closed it as he would a trap in which he had caught a particularly prized wild animal.

'This is Richard Coates, our district adviser.'

'Oh, we know each other,' Coates said softly. 'Don't we, Hollis?'

Hollis shifted uneasily from one foot to the other, and nodded.

'Long time no see, Hollis. How's Simla?'

'Cooler than here,' said Hollis.

'I bet it is,' said Coates. 'Cooler and a lot more comfortable. Safer, too. Where are you billeted? At the Grand or at the Simla Palace?'

Hollis ran a forefinger round the inside of his collar. 'The Palace, actually.'

'Very nice,' said Coates softly. He took his pipe out of his pocket and tried to light it. Two matches broke and one fizzed on to the floor before he succeeded. But not for a moment did Coates take his eyes from the civil servant's face.

'Mr Hollis is here on behalf of the Burmese government,' Danforth explained. He was either not aware of the tension between the two civilians or was pretending to ignore it.

'You mean the *British* Burmese government,' Coates interrupted him. 'There is a difference now, you know, Jim – whether we like it or not.'

'The Burmese government in exile is the only one recognized by the Allies,' Hollis said stiffly. 'Only the Axis powers have recognized the Burmese collaborationist government.'

Coates waved this airly aside with the stem of his pipe. 'Of course, of course. Just my little joke.'

Tiller watched with amusement as the two men squared up to one another like fighting cocks.

'He's investigating the wrecking of that *mergui* in Kyaukpyu harbour last month,' Danforth intervened quickly. 'You were on that op, weren't you?'

'Indeed,' said Coates. 'Brilliantly conceived and carried out, if you want my humble opinion, even though we did not manage to draw off Japanese troops from the mainland as we had hoped. Do we know whether any of those boats got to the mainland?'

'It looks unlikely,' said Danforth. 'Our sea patrols have seen plenty of wreckage in the area. But the collaborationist government cannot prove that we disposed of them.'

'But I am sure they will be telling the natives who owned them that it was the British who did it,' Hollis said sharply. 'However, that is neither here nor there.

I am investigating the wrecked *mergui*. As a carbine and grenade fragments were found on this vessel that is sufficient proof that it was British personnel who were responsible for its loss. The British Burmese government is being accused of deliberately inciting the British forces to adopt a policy which deprives native fishermen of their living.'

'Nothing unusual in that, surely?' said Coates, fiddling with his pipe, his eyes still on Hollis.

Hollis was caught off guard. 'I don't understand?'

'The government. Depriving people of their living. You are quite adept at it yourself, aren't you?'

Hollis flushed. 'Now look here, Coates,' he blustered. 'I can't see what . . .'

'Shall we just settle the matter in hand,' Danforth interrupted soothingly. 'I asked Mr Coates here as he was an eyewitness,' he said to Hollis. 'He will be able to give you as independent an opinion as it is possible to have.'

He turned to Coates. 'Would you say that the wreck of the *mergui* was unavoidable, Dick?'

'Yes,' said Coates without hesitation. 'Once the Japanese were aware they were being attacked there was, in my opinion, no chance of Sergeant Tiller escaping unnoticed. He took, under the circumstances, the only possible action which was not positively suicidal.'

'Suicidal?' Hollis picked up the word immediately. 'Surely, that's quite irrelevant. What matters is to carry out orders. It seems to me that if Sergeant Tiller was unable to carry out his, then he should have abandoned the attack on the vessel and tried to withdraw from the scene. If necessary, he could have swum ashore. All your men are expert swimmers, are they not, Major?'

Danforth did not trust himself to say anything. He just nodded.

Coates was not so restrained. 'Sergeant Tiller was wounded in the shoulder. Even you must know, Hollis, that blood and movement in the water attracts sharks. I would not have laid my odds on Sergeant Tiller and his partner reaching the shore. For them to have tried would have been suicidal. There is no other word for it.'

Danforth glanced across at Hollis, who was writing in a notebook. 'Mr Hollis, are there any further questions you would like to ask?'

The Civil Affairs Officer hesitated. 'I suppose none of you know why that schooner went up in flames? Nothing to do with you, I suppose?'

Tiller opened his mouth and shut it again. Coates tamped down the tobacco in his pipe and said scornfully: 'How do you suppose a canoe could set alight a hundred-and-twenty-foot schooner, Hollis? You know how unreliable Indian matches are.'

As if to prove his point, Coates picked up the broken matches with which he had failed to light his pipe and placed them delicately on the table in front of Hollis with a smile. Hollis snapped his notebook shut angrily, and stood up.

'Is there anything else we can do for you?' Danforth asked with exquisite courtesy.

'Thank you, no. I have no doubt, Major Danforth, that you will be hearing further about this matter.'

'Silly little prick,' Coates said when the door had shut behind the civil servant.

'You two were obviously already acquainted,' Danforth said with a grin as he sat down behind his desk with a sigh of relief. He waved Coates and Tiller into chairs. 'How's your shoulder, Tiger?'

Tiller had spent six weeks in the local hospital after his wound had become infected. 'Fine now, sir, thank you.'

'Good, because I think it's best if we move you on. Our Mr Hollis is a persistent individual. He seems to forget there is a war to be fought and it's people like you and me who have to fight it. If he insists on an official inquiry, I have no doubt as to what the outcome will be, but it will mean withdrawing you from operations while it's held and lots of bumf flying around.'

Danforth stood up and went over to the window.

'By coincidence I heard from an old friend of yours and mine yesterday, Major Hasler.'

Tiller had forgotten about Blondie and his plans for a Special Operations Group. The interview at Combined Operations seemed a long time ago now.

'He wants you to join him in Ceylon as soon as possible.'

'But, sir . . .'

Danforth turned and spread his hands. 'It might be better if you're out of the way until all this has blown over, Tiger.'

Tiller nodded reluctantly, not disguising the twinge of disappointment he felt. He had just begun to enjoy himself in the Arakan. The work of A Group SBS rather suited his abilities and he was, he thought, just beginning to get the hang of things.

Danforth watched Tiller's reaction and tapped a

pencil on his teeth. 'I must confess I did everything I could to keep you here. But now that Hollis is intent on stirring things up I think it's best for you to go. There's a lorry going to Chittagong this afternoon. The RAF will fly you to Kandy from there. Think you can be ready?'

Tiller reluctantly agreed that he could be. 'Did Major Hasler say what he wanted me for?' he asked. The thought that after all he was destined to become a Welman instructor filled him with dread.

Danforth shook his head: 'I have no idea. I assumed you would know.'

'I think it's for me to become a Welman instructor with this new Special Operations Group.'

Danforth raised his eyebrows. 'They've got Welmans in Ceylon, have they? I wonder why.'

12

The Liberator bomber lurched clumsily into the air from the muddy airstrip, the noise of its four engines filling the fuselage with a barrage of sound as it climbed steadily towards the great bank of monsoon cloud that lay directly in its path.

Tiller breathed a sigh of relief. It had taken nearly two days before a sufficient break in the rain allowed the aircraft to take off. He had spent them in the tin-roofed hut which served as the sergeants' mess, watching the rain beat down outside; or playing gin rummy for too much money with the flying crews of the Special Duties squadron based on the strip.

The crews of the SD squadron – American, Australian Canadian, and New Zealanders as well as British – had been quite open about their work, discussing in front of him both its hazards and its technical difficulties. They answered without hesitation his questions about their operations, for as soon as they had seen his parachute wings he had been immediately accepted by them. It was then that Tiller heard of Force 136 for the first time and the guerrilla war against the Japanese that, with the Force's help, was being waged in the Burmese hills.

The crews had also talked of 'drop zones' and 'updraughts', of 'joes' and 'nickels', of 'The Hump' and 'undershoot', of operations with codenames like

'Badger' and 'Character', and of the 'Moonlight War' which the Dakota and Liberator crews were continually waging – not against the Japanese but against the Burmese monsoon. They called it the 'Moonlight War' because they needed the light of the moon to see their drop zones, and could not operate without it.

It had not taken long for Tiller to learn that 'joes' were Force 136 agents, 'nickels' were propaganda leaflets, and that 'The Hump' was the nickname for the air supply route between northern India and China. This meant flying across the Himalayas in all weathers; accidents were common.

Someone tapped him on the shoulder. It was the dispatcher, who had an easy ride today as the aircraft was empty of both cargo and joes.

'The skipper says do you want to go into the cockpit?' he shouted above the roar of the engines.

Tiller nodded and followed the dispatcher forward. The dispatcher opened the padded cockpit door to let Tiller in and then closed it behind him. On Tiller's immediate right was the navigator, who looked up from the radar screen with its slowly sweeping trace and nodded to him. Ahead, with their backs to him, were the pilot and co-pilot, their instruments reflecting a pale green on the windows of the cockpit.

The pilot, a young American US Army Air Force lieutenant, had already turned over the controls to his co-pilot and, with a cigar in one hand, was leaning back in his seat contemplating a huge colour photograph of a nubile, and almost totally naked, woman, which was stuck to the roof of the cockpit above his head.

When Tiller appeared he stood up, and pointed to his seat. 'Take it easy, Sergeant,' he shouted. 'I'm going to get my head down. Too much beer last night.'

Tiller knew the co-pilot, a flight sergeant, from the sessions of gin rummy. The pilot grinned and stuck up his thumb and then bent and twiddled the knob of a trim tab. The Liberator neared the great bank of clouds and Tiller, wanting to have a last look at the ground, peered out of the cockpit window and watched the Burmese coast running jaggedly below him. Then the plane banked and they were heading into the Bay of Bengal, and moments later the cloud closed in. It whipped, vapour-like, by the windows of the cockpit and the Liberator bucked like a bronco. Tiller could see the whiteness of the second pilot's knuckles as he gripped the rudder and remembered the ML crewman's casual comment about how easily the wings of an aircraft could be torn from their roots in a monsoon storm.

For three hours they jolted and bumped through the vapour, an occasional flicker of lightning the only relief in the near blackness. Then, quite suddenly, the clouds parted and below them the Bay of Bengal was spread out like a great plate of shimmering steel. To their right, beyond the horizon, was the Indian coastline. Heading northwards towards it were three lines of dots in arrowhead formation.

The co-pilot pointed them out to Tiller and shouted: 'Convoy.'

'Where would it be from?'

'Melbourne, probably. They offload at Calcutta, then the cargo's taken by rail to Dimapur and Chittagong for distribution to the Fourteenth Army. That convoy route is the lifeline for the Burma offensive and for the Nationalist Chinese. Cut that and it's the equivalent of cutting our jugular.'

Intrigued, Tiller peered down at the tiny dots. The ships were isolated specks amid the vast expanse of water. 'It looks a vulnerable jugular,' he said. 'How do we protect them?'

'Air patrols mostly. Liberators flying out of Colombo and Calcutta. But of course they have a pretty strong anti-submarine escort with them. Not that the Japs often use their subs to attack anything as ordinary as a merchant ship. Not in the true tradition of the Samurai spirit.'

Tiller looked puzzled.

'Never heard of the Samurai?' said the co-pilot. 'Old Japanese warrior caste. All the Japs have been conditioned to follow the Samurai tradition of fearlessness and self-sacrifice. The *Banzai* charge and all that.'

Tiller remembered the *Banzai* charge and the look on the Japanese officer's face. 'And suicide,' he added.

The co-pilot laughed. 'It seems to us to amount to that sometimes. To them it's a form of personal courage. It leads them to despise any form of defensive warfare. Silly bastards have lost all their best pilots. Know why?'

Tiller shook his head.

'Because they refused to have armoured cockpits as the armour slowed their aircraft down. What kind of logic is that?'

Tiller shook his head in wonderment. 'It's hard to get inside their heads,' he said.

The co-pilot told him to look out of the other side of the cockpit. Tiller peered through the haze and could dimly see on the horizon a long string of islands.

'The Andamans,' the co-pilot shouted.

'Long way from anywhere,' Tiller shouted back. 'Do we even bother to garrison them?'

The co-pilot glanced up at him with an amused smile. 'Didn't you know, the Japs hold the Andamans. That's the tip of the knife at our jugular, Sergeant. There are always plans afoot to recapture them but somehow it never happens.'

Then, as abruptly as they had parted, the clouds closed in once more and the rest of the flight to Kandy took place in the gloom of monsoon rain. It was still lashing down when the Liberator descended through the cloud. Even so, from the air, Ceylon looked green and inviting.

'The altitude of Kandy is 2000 feet,' said the co-pilot, 'so it won't be too hot.'

Immediately the Liberator had landed there was a hum of activity about the airstrip that Tiller had never come across anywhere else. The long, low hut that served as the airfield's reception centre was thronged with servicemen from several nations and the strip's apron was filled with an assortment of aircraft waiting for the weather to clear before taking off. Tiller reported to the reception desk and showed his movement order to the clerk, who ran her pencil down a long list.

'Tiller, Sergeant Colin, Royal Marines?'

'That's me.'

'Special Boat Squadron.' The clerk looked up and flashed him a friendly smile. 'Is that as special as it sounds?' she asked. 'I think it must be, as Special

Operations Group have sent a jeep to take you to the railway station. It'll be parked opposite. It'll have a red and white shield on the front.'

She stretched out a slim, bronzed arm and pointed with her pencil. Tiller noticed how the finest of fine down on her forearm glistened in the heat.

He swallowed his lust and said: 'Thanks. Tell me, what's this place Hyatt's Ferry like?'

She had unusual hazel-coloured eyes. They rested on him noncommittally. 'Wonderful beaches. I often go there when I've got a weekend off duty.'

'Might see you there, then,' said Tiller, picking up his kitbag and swinging it over his shoulder.

'You might,' she said. 'The best beach has a snack bar called Sam's. Everyone goes there.'

He found the jeep, tossed his kitbag into the back, and climbed in beside the driver. She wore trousers, a lance-corporal's single stripe on her khaki shirt, and dark glasses, and she drove the seventeen miles to Kandy with an expertise that Tiller found by turns unnerving and exhilarating.

Being suddenly thrown into contact with female company after months of operational duty – the hospital at Cox's Bazar had been staffed entirely by male nurses – made Tiller feel reticent, and it was the driver who did most of the talking. She chattered on about Ceylon, while Tiller looked at the passing scenery.

'There seem to be almost as many women here as there are men,' he said.

'Almost,' said the driver, 'Supremo likes having plenty of women around. It helps make for a happy ship. That's what he says.'

'I believe him,' said Tiller fervently.

'And a happy ship is an efficient ship,' said the driver. 'It's one of his sayings.'

'And is it efficient?'

The driver laughed derisively. 'You must be joking. It's one vast bureaucracy.'

'Ah,' said Tiller. 'It's rife here, too, is it?'

She looked at him sharply. 'How do you mean?'

'One of the fighting man's biggest enemies,' Tiller explained. 'Disease, the monsoon, mother nature and bureaucracy. The Japs don't get a look in.'

She laughed. 'You could be right.'

She drove Tiller past Kandy's Botanical Gardens, where the new supreme commander's headquarters had been set up in a magnificent white palace, before dropping him at the station. He took a train to Jaffna, at the northern end of the island, where he was met by another jeep – but no female driver – and arrived at the camp soon after dark. He was shown to his quarters and then taken to Blondie Tasler's office.

Tasler pumped his hand enthusiastically and interrogated him closely on SBS operations in the Arakan. He soon detected Tiller's liking for what the SBS were doing and said: 'I know you want to return to Burma as soon as possible, Tiger. But I think Danforth's right about putting you out of reach of the local bureaucracy for the time being. Besides, you're needed more here right now.'

Tiller's heart sank. Here it came.

Tasler grinned at the sergeant's glum expression. 'No, it's not the instructor's job. The Welmans have arrived at Trincomalee, but they're still sitting on the docks. So you're safe for the moment.' He paused to light a cigarette, and then said: 'You know all about Z SBS, of course?'

Tiller nodded.

'And Force 136 and what it does?'

Again Tiller nodded.

'So much for SEAC security,' said Tasler wryly. 'But at least you're now allowed to know officially, as you were given security clearance in London.'

'I was?' Tiller said, astonished. It was the first he had heard about it.

'Yes. By those two gentlemen who were in my office at Combined Operations that day you came to see me.' Tasler paused and then went on so that Tiller knew there must be a connection between the two subjects. 'Incidentally, Tiger, and I know you won't like me raising this again, but it would be much easier all round if you would take a commission.'

Tiller groaned inwardly. Tasler had raised the matter of him becoming an officer several times over the past few years and each time he had become more insistent. Each time Tiller had refused.

'I couldn't do it, sir. I just wouldn't feel comfortable.'

Tasler blew a ring of cigarette smoke into the air and watched it disintegrate. 'You mean you know you can get away with doing what you want by staying a senior non-com, isn't that right?'

Tiller grinned at him. 'I didn't say that, sir.'

'But it's what you mean.' Tasler shook his head in frustration. 'You're right, of course. Look what's happened to us. After Bordeaux I get promoted and become a staff officer pushing a pen; you get promoted, seconded to the SBS, and are involved in just about every small boat operation going. However, there is one recommendation I insist you abide by.'

Tiller looked at Tasler warily.

'Your promotion to colour sergeant has just come through. I assume,' the major added with heavy irony, 'that that won't conflict with your own personal arrangements for fighting this war in any way?'

Once he was involved in the war, promotion had meant very little to Tiller. You were as dead as a corporal as you were as a sergeant and in the SBS, where every man was trained to act independently, rank counted for very little. But he felt strangely pleased that he was now the same rank that his father had reached nearly thirty years before.

'Thank you, sir.'

'Don't thank me,' said Tasler tersely. 'Supremo has ruled that all non-commissioned SEAC instructors should be a sergeant-major or its equivalent.'

'I thought, sir . . .' Tiller began.

'Look, Tiger, I don't run SEAC any more than you do,' Hasler cut him off wearily. 'Special Operations Group have you on strength as an instructor and if SEAC decide they want you as an instructor there is nothing much I can do about it. Luckily for you, at the moment they're so stuffed up with bumf that they don't know where the Welmans are or who should be trained for them when they find them. Tomorrow's another day. At this moment I need you for a Z SBS operation.'

'I'm on for that, sir,' said Tiller eagerly. 'When do I start?'

'You'll be on your own with this one,' Tasler warned him. 'But I want you fully rested for it. Take tomorrow and the weekend off. And that's an order. Report here at 0730 on Monday morning. And get those crowns sewn on above your stripes as quickly as possible. Supremo won't abide anyone improperly dressed.'

The next evening Tiller found Hazel-eyes sitting in Sam's snack bar as he somehow knew she would be. Later that night, much later, she suggested they were just ships that passed in the night, that was all, and on Monday morning Tasler said that he hoped Tiller was rested because he was not going to get much from then on.

'Not rested, sir,' Tiller said with a straight face, 'but relaxed.'

'See that Catalina?' Tasler pointed to a high-winged, two-engined flying boat. It was moored to a large buoy in the strait between the sand spit where the camp was situated and a small island on which stood an old Dutch colonial fort – Fort Hammenhiel – where the SBS kept their stores. Either side of the Catalina's fuselage were large Perspex blisters which held heavy machine-guns. A fuel boat was moored alongside it, pumping fuel into the wing tanks. 'That's your transport.'

'American, isn't it?' Tiller asked.

'The Yanks let us have quite a few,' Tasler explained. 'They're reliable, you'll be pleased to know. Very reliable.'

'Where's it going to take me?'

Tasler turned away from the window. 'You'll know all about that in good time, Tiger. First things first. One of the techniques we've been trying to develop here is to parachute canoeists and their canoes into the water from a Catalina. You'll understand that the vast distances out here don't always make it possible to deliver canoeists to their operational areas by submarine.'

'Sounds interesting, sir.'

Jumping at night was part of a parachute course; jumping into water was not.

'As long as you keep your legs together and release your parachute quickly, there's no problem,' said Tasler. 'The problem is the canoes. They tend to get damaged or distorted by the air pressure if they're slung under the Catalina and they're too long to be launched through the fuselage door. And parachuting them in in pieces has proved a non-starter.'

'Can't the Catalina land on the water and the canoe then be assembled on the wing?' Tiller asked.

Tasler shook his head. 'The fly boys don't like that, though they'll do it if they have to. But the sea is often too rough to land, which means they will have flown a long way for nothing. Also, the Catalina's far too vulnerable to attack when it's on the surface. We're going to have to think of something else. Any ideas?'

Tiller rubbed his chin thoughtfully. 'We had a visit from a Yank a month or so back. Member of the OSS, apparently.'

Tasler looked up sharply. 'And?'

'He had various useful stores. He gave us a number of what he called Pin-Up Girls. You know them?'

Tasler nodded. 'I've heard about them. What else did he have?'

'He said OSS's Maritime Unit had developed a fast rigid inflatable which is powered by a silenced outboard engine. Major Danforth asked me to make notes about it as he thought it could be of interest to the SBS.'

'That chap who holds the land speed record has been trying to develop a silent outboard,' said Hasler. 'He's here. Name of Malcolm Campbell. Hasn't had much luck so far. Last one he made sounded like a waterborne air-raid siren.'

'The one this bloke described is a 9.7hp Evinrude. They've made an effective silencer for the carburettor intake and for the exhaust.'

'That won't silence it completely.'

'No, but they've managed to make an acoustic felt cover for the rest of the motor which muffles the sound.'

'How the hell did they manage that when the engine gets so hot?'

'They've developed some kind of heatproof aluminium lining for the cover apparently. He said you can get within 1400 feet of the shore without anyone on land hearing anything. And at slow speed you can apparently get to within 280 feet.'

Tasler whistled. 'You might just have solved the biggest problem, Tiger. The other one is using an inflatable instead of a canoe. Our parachute expert is wrestling with that. Deflated, it'll go through the fuselage door without any problem, of course. But somehow he's got to find a way that allows the dinghy to inflate automatically once it hits the water. It would be too tricky for the operator to inflate it himself when he's in the water.'

'We'll find a way somehow, sir,' said Tiller forcefully. He knew he would have to if the operation was to be mounted before the powers that be realized that the Welmans had arrived. 'You get an Evinrude and the OSS inflatable, and I'll see to the rest.'

In fact it did not take long to find the solution in theory once Tiller had talked to the Group's expert on parachutes, but in practice it was far more difficult. By the Friday evening – when Tiller again met Hazel-eyes at the snack bar – they had lost quite a few inflatables and had still not solved the problem. By Sunday night Hazel-eyes had decided that she and Tiller weren't ships which passed in the night at all, but were the helpless victims of a collision at sea and that she, for one, was sinking fast.

On the Tuesday the parachute expert managed to adapt the inflatable's carbon-dioxide bottle mechanism successfully so that it inflated the dinghy when it hit the water. On the Wednesday Tiller made his first jump into the sea, and landed reassuringly close to the inflated dinghy. Then, on the Thursday, the OSS dinghy and engine arrived from Kunming.

On the Friday morning Tiller and the Chinese agent Tiller was to ferry ashore were briefed by Tasler before taking off in the Catalina; and that evening – just as an expectant Hazel-eyes was stepping on the train for Jaffna – a staff officer in Kandy called Tasler and officially requested Colour Sergeant Tiller's presence at the beautiful white palace to discuss his posting as a Welman instructor.

But by that time the Catalina, its specially fitted extra fuel tanks brimming, had just waddled off the water on the strait and was beginning to weave its way through a lower layer of monsoon cloud.

13

A hand touched Tiller's shoulder and he opened his eyes immediately. The dispatcher crouched down beside him so that Tiller could hear him above the steady roar of the Catalina's engine.

'Sinapore's dead ahead to the north of us. Half an hour to go. Thought I'd give you plenty of warning.'

Tiller glanced at the luminous dial of his watch. 'When's dawn?'

'Any minute now.'

Tiller looked across at the joe. The man was wide awake but his almond eyes stared straight ahead as if focused on something in his mind. Poor bugger, Tiller thought, rather him than me. What was that quote he had heard somewhere? 'Nothing concentrates a man's mind so much as knowing he's to be hanged in a fortnight.' Something like that.

He wondered what it was the joe had to do in Japanese-occupied Singapore. He hadn't asked him, of course, and Tiller certainly hadn't been told anything except where he was to land the Force 136 agent, what he could expect there, and where he was to rendezvous with the submarine which was to pick him up. The 'need to know' policy which governed all clandestine operations confined his knowledge to these few basic facts. The joe would know what he had to do, so would his handler in Colombo, who would be listening in for his signals. But only the bigwigs in Force 136, whose headquarters were at Meerut near Delhi, would know what the operation was really all about.

However, Tiller at least knew that the joe was not on a sabotage mission, for there were no explosives or limpets in the supply container. There was just the wireless, rations, water, medical kit and a .45 pistol with only one spare clip of ammunition.

The dispatcher handed Tiller a mug of steaming coffee, which Tiller accepted eagerly, wrapping his hands around its cheap china surface. It was surprisingly cold in the unpressurized Catalina, which had had to climb high to avoid the worst of the monsoon cloud. The dispatcher offered coffee to the joe, but he just shook his head without taking his eyes off whatever it was he was looking at inside himself.

The Catalina droned on, and then Tiller heard the engines change pitch slightly and felt the aircraft gradually start to descend. He stood up, put on his parachute and dragged the container with its inflatable and outboard engine closer to the door. The dispatcher did the same with Tiller's supply container, which had a spare wireless, extra clothing, food, water, fuel for the outboard, Sten gun and extra ammunition – everything that was needed for Tiller to survive for several days among the maze of islands that lay to the south of Singapore and its great harbour.

Tiller looked at the joe and then glanced at the dispatcher and raised his eyebrows. The man had not moved. His parachute lay by his side with his helmet on top of it. The dispatcher went over to him and crouched down, but still the joe remained motionless and deep in thought.

The dispatcher began talking to him – Tiller could not hear what he was saying above the roar of the engines – but he could tell something was wrong. Eventually the joe stood up and allowed the dispatcher to buckle on his parachute and adjust the helmet on his head.

'I don't think he's going to jump,' said the dispatcher in Tiller's ear.

'Shit.'

'He might follow you if you jumped first.'

'Don't be fucking stupid,' Tiller exploded. 'Me down there and him up here? What good's that going to do?'

The dispatcher shrugged. 'Up to you, mate.'

He opened the fuselage door and a blast of air buffeted Tiller as he tugged at the wire that ran at head height the length of the fuselage, to make sure it was secure. If the wire came away from its fastenings the static line would not open the parachute and the result would be what was known as a 'roman candle'. Satisfied, Tiller indicated that the joe should snap his static line on in front of his. Obediently, the man did so and Tiller thought the crisis was past. The joe's eyes were even moving now and he acknowledged Tiller's look with a nod.

Then Tiller snapped on his static line and waited for the dispatcher to call the joe forward. The dispatcher kept glancing at his watch and then out of the door, where the monsoon cloud still swirled and eddied in the half light.

Tiller could feel the Catalina sinking further and

the engines took on a different note. Down and down the aircraft went, circling now, until the clouds thinned, thickened again, then parted to reveal below a confusing pattern of islands and ocean, alarmingly close, all half shrouded in an early morning mist.

They would jump at only 700 feet to ensure accuracy. Water glittered below them.

The dispatcher signalled the joe forward and rested his hand on his back between his shoulder blades. The joe took up his position correctly at the door, his hands holding on to the fuselage on either side, his knees slightly bent, his feet on the edge of the aircraft so that the toes of his boots were in space.

Tiller thought then that he should have told the dispatcher to make sure the joe kept his head raised, but it was too late now. He saw the joe look down and his whole body seemed to stiffen. The light above the dispatcher turned from red to green indicating that the pilot was over the drop zone. The dispatcher struck the joe firmly on his back: the signal for him to jump. But the joe didn't move and when the dispatcher hit him again, harder this time, the joe humped his body and straightened his arms.

The dispatcher yelled something, but the joe wouldn't move. Tiller slid his static line forward along the wire and grasped the joe's upper arm. The man turned and looked at him and Tiller could see the sheer, frozen terror in his face and the blankness of his unfocused eyes.

Tiller dropped his hand, turned to the dispatcher and shook his head.

The co-pilot came out of the cabin. 'The skipper wants to know what the fuck's going on?' he yelled above the roar of the Catalina's engines. A pilot could instantly tell from his aircraft's trim if its cargo was still on board.

'You're going to have to land,' Tiller yelled at him.

He had only once before seen a parachutist refuse to jump.

In his panic, the parachutist had resisted all persuasion with the strength of a madman and it had ended with the dispatcher having his jaw broken. So it was pointless trying to lever the joe out of the aircraft. Even if they managed to do it without injury to anyone – including the joe – they would not be able to eject him at the right moment: split-second timing was needed to ensure the parachutist landed on the right stretch of water and not on one of the jungle-covered islands.

The co-pilot did not argue but disappeared back into the cabin. Tiller wondered if the pilot would abort the operation, as he had every right to do, but after a few moments the Catalina began to swing round and drop towards the water.

Tiller tapped the joe on the arm.

'We're not going to jump,' he yelled at him. 'We're going to land.'

He reinforced his words by taking off his helmet. The joe understood the action if not the words, for he relaxed and backed away from the door. Tiller unclipped his static line and unstrapped his parachute, and the joe followed suit.

The dispatcher said to Tiller: 'We never had this trouble when I was in Liberators. They all went down a chute together. Went out like peas in a pod.' His tone was dispassionate and matter-of-fact. It had been just another technical hitch. There was no hint of criticism of the joe, who, the dispatcher knew – they all knew

– was about to embark on a mission from which he could easily fail to return.

The Catalina throttled back.

'Hold tight,' yelled the dispatcher.

The Catalina seemed to go tail down, then almost stall, the engines revved hard and then cut, and moments later the flying boat was bouncing across the water. A wall of spray swept through the open door, soaking the dispatcher. Tiller grinned at him. He found he was infinitely relieved he didn't have to jump. Though they had been given cans of shark repellent no one had seemed sure how effective the stuff was and he still had a vivid picture in his mind of the sharks feeding on the dead Japanese in Kyaukpyu harbour.

The Catalina slowed and then squatted down into the water until it came to a halt, its engine idling.

The co-pilot stuck his head out of the cabin and nodded.

'Let's go,' said the dispatcher.

The co-pilot handed Tiller a chart and pointed to a cross on it. Tiller nodded his thanks and stuffed the chart in a pocket. He swung out of the door and on to the lower strut of the wing while the dispatcher bundled the container with the inflatable into the water, yanking its static line as he did so. The container opened and Tiller heard the hiss of the carbon-dioxide bottle filling the inflatable. The dispatcher handed him the static line and began breaking open the supply containers.

When the rubber dinghy was fully inflated Tiller fitted the wooden duckboards into its bottom to make it rigid, tied it to the wing strut and then jumped into it. He checked that all the dinghy's gear was present and undamaged before rigging the Evinrude outboard. He lowered it through a metal aperture in the inflatable's stern which looked in size and shape rather like a bucket without a bottom. When Tiller had screwed it firmly in place the dispatcher began passing him the supplies.

The inflatable – the Americans called it a Nylon Pneumatic Boat – was eight feet long and three and a half feet wide and had a pointed and upturned bow and stern. For stability it had twelve plastic air-filled sausage-shaped 'bladders', each of which could be replaced if punctured. There had been no time to test it before the operation but Tiller was instantly reassured by its stability and rugged construction, so much better than the British Y-type rubber dinghies, whose three-ply fabric could not take much wear and tear.

The joe climbed on to the wing strut and then lowered himself into the dinghy. Tiller watched him carefully and was pleased to see that he moved slowly and cautiously: it showed he had been in an inflatable before and knew how easy it was to overturn them.

When the joe was settled in the bows, Tiller undid the static line and began paddling the inflatable away from the Catalina, which immediately began revving its engines in preparation for taking off. The dispatcher gave the thumbs up through the door before shutting it.

The Catalina seemed to move across the surface of the water for an age, spray blossoming from its floats. As the engines reached a climax it slowly left the water and climbed away into the mist. The sound of the engines dwindled quickly and then faded completely.

Tiller thrust his Sten gun at the joe.

'Don't use it unless I say so,' he said. The man nodded calmly.

Tiller took out the chart and a pocket compass. He wondered if the aircraft had been heard or seen. He had been told in the briefing that the area was not garrisoned by the Japanese but the loyalties of the natives who lived on the islands were unknown, and he needed to find shelter quickly. The sun, which appeared temporarily from the monsoon cloud, was burning the mist quickly off the water and visibility was improving all the time.

Tiller studied the chart and decided to make for the nearest land, Bulat Island, so that they could lie low until nightfall. The engine started first time and proved as silent as the Texan had predicted. The inflatable bounced across the smooth, oily water.

Bulat rose out of the water reassuringly quickly and within an hour they were ashore and the inflatable was under cover. They rested all that day without exchanging a word and as dusk arrived they ate a meal from their self-heating cans. In the last of the light Tiller called over the joe and traced with his finger where they would be going: through the Bulan Strait, which separated the islands of Batam and Bulan, then through a maze of smaller islands before crossing Main Strait to Bukum Island, which lay close to Singapore. There Tiller's responsibilities ended, and the joe was on his own from then on. On the chart it did not seem far, not more than thirty miles, but Tiller had been warned that the Bulan Strait was narrow and treacherous and that Main Strait was the principal route for Japanese shipping in the area. The joe followed Tiller's finger and nodded.

'Not far,' he said. He was quite calm and collected now, almost cheerful.

'Far enough,' Tiller replied and the joe flashed him a smile.

'I know about the SBS,' he said, pointing at Tiller's shoulder flash. 'You'll get me there.'

They launched the dinghy, and Tiller paddled out a little way and then started the engine. Navigation was easy, for once night had fallen they headed straight for the great loom of light to the north of them: Singapore was at the extreme range of American bombers stationed in India and the Japanese still did not bother to take proper blackout precautions.

They reached Bukum just after midnight and Tiller even found the short, rickety pier he had been told to expect at its western extremity. The joe clambered on to it and Tiller handed him up his wireless and his haversack.

The joe bent down and stretched out his hand. 'Very sorry about jump. Bad coward, yes?'

Tiller took his hand and wrung it warmly. 'No, not coward at all,' he said, and meant it. 'You're a very brave man. Good luck.' He swung the inflatable away from the pier. He would have to hurry if he was to get back in time.

As the inflatable moved away Tiller looked back and saw the joe watching him go, a lonely figure, his arm raised in farewell. Tiller waved back, and realized then that he had not even known the man's name.

14

The Supreme Commander, immaculately turned out in the tropical undress uniform of a full admiral, stopped in front of Tiller. 'I know you, don't I? Tiller, isn't it?'

'Malta, sir,' Tiller replied. 'Nineteen thirty-eight. Tug-of-war team from *Ramillies*.'

'That's right. We beat you, didn't we? Glad to see so many Marines in the Group. Good luck to you, Colour Sergeant,' and he moved on to inspect the rest of the Special Operations Group, which had been paraded before him. When he had finished he sprang lightly on to the bonnet of the jeep in which he had driven to the camp, and waved the parade forward.

'Gather round, everyone.'

Officers and men broke ranks and clustered round the vehicle. Supremo, his hands characteristically on his hips, watched them assemble around him. He delilberately wore his cap at the same rakish angle that Noel Coward had worn his when Coward had played him in the film *In Which We Serve*, then being seen by packed service audiences all over Ceylon.

'You know what the Special Operations Group is called by everyone in SEAC?' he said when they had settled down to listen. 'You're called Mountbatten's private navy.'

Loud laughter and cheering greeted this information, drowning out a wag at the back who pronounced it 'better than being called 'is private parts, any road'.

Supremo held up his hand and silence returned.

'I'm very proud to be so closely associated with you because you are doing a magnificent job of work. But the job has only just begun. The enemy are on the run in Burma. They have suffered a crushing defeat there, at Imphal. But they are far from beaten and now that the monsoon is coming to an end the fighting there will intensify.'

His audience murmured among themselves. Supremo waited until this news had been absorbed and then continued.

'The Japanese high command have ordered their generals in Burma to plan what the Japanese call *jikatsu jisen*. That is, they must subsist on their own and fight on their own. That means they will fight to the death. They are not going to surrender.'

Someone next to Tiller muttered something obscene about Japanese tactics. Tiller thought *jikatsu jisen* sounded very much like the motto Major Jarrett had thought up for the Special Boat Squadron: 'Sink or Swim'. In other words each canoe team, ultimately each individual, was on his own. It had summed up how the SBS had operated.

'And our American allies are having a tough time clearing them from the Pacific and the Philippines. There is a lot to do. I can't go into details, but I can tell you that part of the Japanese Mobile Fleet has sailed from its Pacific base.'

A murmur of interest rippled through the audience. The speaker waited until it had died down and then added: 'The Japanese have a habit of doing the unexpected. So we must be on our toes, for we are fighting a brave and resourceful foe.'

The men were quiet now, watchful. They waited expectantly.

'We have, of course, our own strategic plans for the area and the part you men of Special Operations Group have to play in these are vital. Possible landing beaches reconnoitred, intelligence gathered and the enemy harassed at every possible opportunity. Each of you is expert in one or more of these forms of warfare. I say to you: "Well done. Keep up the good work."

'But today I also want to tell you the part I am playing in all this. I call it the three Ms: Morale, Monsoon and Malaria.'

As the Supreme Commander explained in his clipped English how he was raising morale, how advantageous it had been for his forces to fight through the monsoon and how he had cut the incidence of malaria, Tiller's mind wandered back to the man he had left on that rickety wooden pier in the middle of the night. It took all sorts, he thought philosophically, to fight a war and wondered if there was any connection between the delivery of the joe to Singapore and the movement of part of the Japanese Mobile Fleet. His instinct told him that somehow there must be.

Supremo finished his pep talk, stepped lightly from the bonnet of the jeep into the driving seat, and then drove slowly down the avenue of cheering men.

'He's some showman, isn't he?' said Tasler when everyone had returned to their normal duties. He threw some papers into his pending file and indicated that Tiller should draw up a chair.

'He's got a memory any elephant would envy,' said Tiller.

Tasler retrieved one of the pieces of paper from the pending file and studied it. 'Talking of elephants, Tiger, B Group SBS have just been given the task of supporting an Indian division which is poised to cross the River Chindwin in upper Burma. I want you to go with them. You'll be using the new Mk VI canoes.'

'Not the Welmans then, sir?'

It was meant to be a joke, but Tasler looked unusually grim. 'No, not the Welmans, Tiger. Not yet.'

'They found another instructor then, sir?'

'They did. I told them you were away on business and that you might not return, as it was very risky. That shut them up.'

'Away on business' was an expression Tasler always used for anyone going on a clandestine operation.

'Not for me it wasn't risky,' Tiller said meaningfully.

'Anyway, they flew someone out from Scotland last week. So you're in the clear.' Tasler pressed a switch on his intercom. 'I want to introduce you to your new CO. Name of Grayson. Good chap.'

Ian Grayson was a captain in the Royal Scots who soon made it known to Tasler, in the nicest possible way, that he did not like Supremo's decision ultimately to transfer SOG's work – and those SOG personnel who would agree to it – to the Royal Marines.

'You must understand, sir,' he said in his soft Lowland burr, 'my regiment is the army's senior regiment. We're fast of foot and right on the line.'

Tasler made the soothing sounds he always employed to smooth ruffled feathers. He pointed out that the change was bound to be a postwar one and that for the moment all that mattered was the closest co-operation between army and navy. He realized Grayson's B Group was entirely an army unit, but reassured the captain that Tiller was no Trojan horse. 'I'm sure you'll find him useful,' he said. 'And I promise you he isn't going to start a recruitment drive.'

The captain seemed mollified and at dawn three days later Tasler was up to see off the small group of men, their supplies and their Mk VI canoes, which had all been dismantled and packed in containers. The journey took them by air, road, rail and sea to Calcutta. Dimapur, Imphal and Kalewa, and finally by Dakota to a forward airstrip near the Chindwin at Mawlaik, where they were greeted by the divisional commander himself.

Major-General Dai Llewellyn, late of the Rajputana Rifles, was a short man. But his diminutive stature was the only aspect of him that was undersize, for his personality, as B Group soon found out, was larger than life. He had men of many races under his command and he seemed to be able to speak all their languages, whether it was Ghurkali, Hindi or Urdu. A firebrand who did not drink, smoke or swear, Llewellyn spoke with a soft Welsh accent that could turn to sandpaper when he was annoyed. Which was often. It was said that he fired his staff almost as often as he fired his divisional artillery. He wore a broad-brimmed Gurkha hat on the front of which was pinned a large gold general's badge. On its right side he had had sewn his divisional flash, a hand holding a dagger. Round his neck he always wore a bright red silk scarf so that he was easily identifiable to his troops. He flew a large red divisional pennant on his jeep for the same reason – a fact the Japanese had long ago discovered but had so far been unable to exploit.

Llewellyn drove his men ruthlessly, for he knew he could not afford to pause for even a day. If he did the Japanese would use that time to dig in, to set booby-traps and to fell trees across the jungle tracks, so that it would be harder to force them on to the back foot again, and that to do so would cost lives that might have been saved by pushing on ruthlessly. His men, who worshipped him, knew this. They grumbled a lot but they kept going. Now they were close to the mighty Chindwin, one of the three great waterways of Burma, and the momentum had to be maintained.

'The Chindwin, gentlemen, is not the Thames,' Llewellyn stated bluntly to the officers and NCOs of B Group, who had been gathered for his briefing. 'At the point where we will approach it it is nearly five hundred miles from its source in the Pathai and Kumon ranges, and some two hundred miles from where it joins the Irrawaddy. It is several hundred yards wide in some places and at this time of the year it is full of water, sandbanks – and crocodiles. There will be a nasty current. On the near shore there will still be Japanese stragglers trying to escape across the river, while on the far shore there are Burmese refugees trying to join us to escape the clutches of the Japanese. In short, once the division closes up to the river, you can expect two-way traffic. I want the maximum number of my men across the Chindwin in the minimum time. Speed is what counts, gentlemen.

212

My G1 will now go over the details of the operation. Thank you.'

The division's Grade One General Staff Officer, Operations, his G1, stood up and rolled out a large-scale map of the area, which he hung on the blackboard. He was a full colonel, astonishingly young, who spoke with the accomplished ease of someone who knows his brief backwards.

B Group, he told them, were to make a report to him immediately on the suitability of the crossing point, and would then help secure the division's flanks by patrolling the Chindwin above and below the crossing. They were to let no Japanese escape across the river; nor were they to allow those who had already managed to cross to establish defences on its far bank.

Above all, they were to prevent any Japanese riverborne attack while the division was being ferried across.

'They are known to have some local native boats upstream from here,' he said. 'I don't care how you stop them using them to pester us while we are crossing, but stop them you must.'

He paused when Grayson caught his eye to ask him why the RAF didn't deal with them.

'I thought you might ask that,' said the G1. 'But our Japanese friends are too wily to be caught out by daylight attacks from the air. We have discovered that what they do is every morning take out the bungs of their craft and sink them in the shallows, where they can't be seen by aircraft. Then every evening they put the bungs back in and bail the water out.'

'Cunning bastards,' said Grayson admiringly.

'I dare say they have a lot more tricks up their

sleeves,' said the G1. 'And I don't need to tell you how vulnerable our troops, artillery and transport are going to be while they're being ferried across. We will, of course, establish a defensive perimeter on the far bank first, but that won't be able to cover any attacks coming up or down river. From what I've heard about the SBS you're a resourceful lot. You're going to need to be because we won't be in any position to help, though I can spare you one regiment of artillery standing by for an emergency. Apart from that, gentlemen, you'll be on your own. Good luck.'

'*Jikatsu jisen*,' Tiller repeated to himself. 'Sink or Swim.' That's how it was and that was exactly how he liked it.

The following night, under cover of darkness, B Group moved up to the river in lorries, established a temporary base at the mouth of a *chaung*, and began assembling the Mk VI canoes, which only a few of them had tried out in Ceylon.

'Now that looks like a proper war canoe,' Tiller said to his new partner, a lugubrious Liverpudlian corporal who, because his name was Wood, was naturally nicknamed Timber.

The Mk VI was a rigid canoe made of fabric-covered plywood which had been treated with a sealant. It was assembled by bolting its three sections together and was lined with a rubberized material which kept the hull watertight if the wood skin was punctured. On either side of the canoe outriggers were attached to the hull on alloy arms and between the two canoeists was an engine whose exhaust pipe stuck up vertically into the air.

214

Fitted in the bows on a traversing mount was a type of machine-gun Tiller had never seen before. It looked something like a Bren gun without a butt but had a circular metal magazine like a cake tin on top of it instead of the Bren's curved one.

'It's a Vickers K-gun,' Timber informed him. 'Originally they were fitted to RAF fighters with open cock- pits and so have a very fast rate of fire. The magazine takes a hundred rounds of ordinary .303 ammo.'

Tiller then took off the wooden engine cover, which had a wire-stiffened skirt to protect the engine from spray.

'Is the engine going to be able to cope with the current?' he asked.

Timber nodded. 'It's four horsepower, which pushes it through calm water at seven knots or so. Should be more than enough, as they reckon the current at the moment is only about three or four knots.'

Tiller peered into the engine compartment and saw that there was an aluminium sleeve through the bottom of the canoe into which the engine was clamped. Timber showed him how the sleeve rotated so that the propeller was lowered into the water. He said the only thing to watch was that the engine's water-cooling system didn't get choked with sand.

'It's silenced, I hope.'

'Very effectively,' said Timber. 'In fact there are two silencers. The main one is on the water-cooling system but another can be added to the exhaust when extra-silent running is needed. When both are working you can't hear the engine further than a couple of hundred yards.'

'It's going to need a good range,' grunted Tiller, looking out across the river. 'Looks more like the English Channel than a fucking river to me.'

Timber explained that though the main tank didn't hold much there were a number of supplementary tanks which gave the canoe a maximum range of 110 kilometres at full throttle and 145 kilometres at half throttle.

The next evening at dusk they went out on their first patrol. Grayson sent three of the canoes upstream and three downstream with orders to reconnoitre the river so that they could familiarize themselves with every yard of it. The other members of the group would work, right under the noses of the Japanese, on assessing the area where the crossing would take place, measuring the depth of the water, the firmness of the shelving beach and its gradient.

As his canoe forged steadily upstream against the current, Tiller noticed immediately that central Burma had a different landscape to the Arakan: the jungle was sparse and the forests – many of them of teak – were much larger and more dense. The humidity was lower and with the monsoon coming to an end the rains had almost petered out.

The canoes were as silent as Timber had said, but in mid-stream, despite the alleged strength of the engine, it was difficult to make any headway against the current, so Tiller took his tiny flotilla of three canoes as close to the shore as he dared.

Timber sat in the forward position and kept the K-gun trained on the bank while Tiller steered with the twin metal rods that were connected to the rudder. These ran the length of the boat so that, in an emergency, either crewman could steer. They motored upstream for about five miles as darkness closed in on them, and then in line abreast the three canoes turned and drifted with the current, listening and watching, noting the whereabouts of the sandbanks and the contours of the river, testing the depth of water and gauging the strength of the current.

They repeated this twice more until they were familiar with every twist and bend in the river, and every likely ambush position on its banks. They also carefully noted the position of every sandbank – though these, they knew, constantly shifted and changed according to the amount of water flowing down the Chindwin.

By the time they had returned to the base that had now been established for the group up the small *chaung*, the first glimmer of dawn was showing above the teak trees.

The next evening, as the division began to close up to the river ready for crossing it the following night, Tiller allotted his three canoes their own stretch of water to patrol. He and Timber took the upstream stretch, knowing they could quickly come to the aid of the others should they need it.

Llewellyn's advancing division had already driven most of the Japanese across the Chindwin, but there were still plenty of stragglers who were trying to rejoin their units. Every night there had been reports of small groups trying to get across with vehicles or guns, or with just their personal weapons.

Tiller decided that the best tactic to intercept these stragglers was to lie in wait for them in the dead water under the near bank. They did not have long to wait.

The first group – Timber counted that there were five of them – arrived soon after midnight. They arrived upstream of the canoe and stood chattering quietly about what they should do. They were out of range of Tiller's silenced Mk V Sten gun and he did not want to use the K-gun unless he had to, as firing it would alert any other Japanese in the area to their presence.

Eventually the Japanese decided to make a raft and spent an hour binding three large logs together. When it was completed they began poling it across, but the current caught it and swept it towards the waiting canoe.

When it came level with the canoe Tiller raised his Sten and opened fire. As it was fitted with a silencer he could fire only single shots. They sounded like champagne corks. Three of the Japanese toppled into the river. The fourth dived in, but the fifth swung up his rifle and was about to fire when Tiller shot him too. The raft drifted past with one Japanese still draped across it. Then they heard a splash and the arm of the Japanese, which was trailing in the water, was seized. The raft tipped up and the Japanese rolled over and hit the water with a splash, before vanishing in a swirl of spray and mud. It happened so quickly that Tiller hardly realized what had occurred.

'Hope the poor bugger was already dead,' said Timber, swivelling the K-gun back to the shore. 'I wouldn't wish anyone a death like that.'

'What about the others?'

'If they weren't dead when you hit them, they will be now.'

They moved further upstream, scanning the bank for movement, but if there were any other Japanese in the area they stayed hidden, and after an hour they turned and drifted with the current.

It was then that they saw movement on the near bank and cautiously circled wide of the area. There were more Japanese this time, perhaps as many as a dozen. One group was manhandling a pontoon into the water while a second was pulling a field gun of some kind out of the bushes. Boxes of shells for it were piled on the bank.

Timber flicked up the sights of the K-gun, but Tiller laid a restraining hand on his shoulder. It was too big a prize not to use the K-gun but the field gun was better at the bottom of the river.

'Wait till they get it afloat,' he whispered.

Timber nodded and they waited in dead water downstream from where the Japanese were planning to cross. Eventually the pontoon, with the field gun aboard, left the shore, but its outboard engine was too weak to counter the current. The pontoon took a crablike course across the river so that by the time it was parallel with the canoe it was only a couple of hundred yards away. Timber crouched over the K-gun and took a bead on the pontoon.

One in five of the cartridges in the gun's magazine was tracer and as Timber opened fire it arced across the water and on to the pontoon. Tiller, who had looked away so that the tracer would not impair his night vision, could hear the Japanese screaming and cursing and the pontoon swung erratically towards the canoe.

A second burst from the K-gun hit the boxes of

ammunition and the pontoon detonated with a blinding flash and a muffled roar. The canoe rocked from the force of the explosion. The pontoon went down stern first and the field gun slipped quickly into the water.

Tiller could not resist looking round.

'Good shooting,' he shouted, thumping Timber on the shoulder. 'Let's see what else we can find.'

They prowled the river for the rest of the night, but no other Japanese attempted to cross it in their sector. At dawn they returned to their base in the *chaung* and found that the other canoes had been equally busy.

The SBS teams ate and then slept for most of the day, but were woken in late afternoon by the divisional artillery opening up. It was a preliminary bombardment to clear the way for the troops who were to form the initial bridgehead on the far side of the river. At five o'clock Captain Grayson received his orders from the G1 by wireless. The crossing would start at midnight that night and would continue until it was completed, even if that meant crossing in daylight. The RAF had supremacy in the air and it was highly unlikely that the Japanese air force would try to attack.

The G1 confirmed that the greatest threat to the Division were the native craft hidden upstream. For V Force, the intelligence scouts used by the Fourteenth Army, had managed to capture a Japanese who had said an all-out attack was being planned for that night in an attempt to throw the crossing into confusion. Most of the boats would attack downstream though it was known that a few might try to attack against the current. Grayson therefore sent four of the canoes upstream under Tiller and kept the other two for any Japanese who might attempt to come up the river.

Tiller decided the best tactic would be to force any Japanese boat that came downstream to run the gauntlet of the four canoes. So he spaced them out at one-mile intervals and positioned himself in the upstream spot. As the senior NCO he felt he had the privilege of taking the first crack at anything that came down the river.

They kedged the canoe in slack water and settled down expectantly. They did not have long to wait, for gliding out of the mist that hung above the water came two long, low boats. Both were quite close to the near bank, out of the main current. If they kept their present course, it looked to Tiller as if they would pass very close to the SBS canoe.

At first, in the dark, it was difficult to judge how big they were, though they could soon hear they were powered by outboard engines. As they came closer Tiller recognized them from the sketches aboard Davy's ML as being *lundwins*: thirty-foot, canoe-type native craft which shifted agricultural produce up and down the largest Burmese rivers. Their central 'doghouse' made of matting and their very high counters on which the helmsman sat made them easily identifiable.

As the *lundwins* moved nearer, Tiller could see they were filled with Japanese troops and that in the bows of the leading one a large mortar was mounted. To Tiller it looked like an 81mm, a fearsome weapon in the right hands.

'Get that leading boat,' Tiller told Timber urgently. 'If they get that mortar firing they could fuck up the whole crossing.'

He had abandoned his silenced Sten for a tommy-gun. Now he dragged it out of the canoe and cocked it.

By now the *lundwins* were about 200 yards from the SBS canoe and bearing down on them rapidly. Tiller could even hear the Japanese chattering among themselves. They must have thought they were a long way from any danger.

'Wait till you see the whites of their eyes,' he urged, and heard Timber chuckle at the cliché. 'At all costs that first boat mustn't get past us.'

As Timber corrected his position he rocked the canoe and the glitter of phosphorescence this caused caught the eye of a Japanese lookout in the leading *lundwin*, who cried out a warning to the one behind. The second boat sheered away into mid-stream while the helmsman on the first one laboriously turned it towards the canoe, miminizing the target that Timber had to fire at. He pressed the trigger of the K-gun and Tiller could see the bullets ploughing into the boat's thin planking. Splinters of wood flew everywhere and someone in the *lundwin* began shouting – orders perhaps, or just words of encouragement or fright.

Tiller let the boat approach as close as possible and then, disregarding the rifle fire that was beginning to come from it, lobbed a 36 grenade with great accuracy on to its crowded deck. The grenade exploded with a shattering crunch that slewed the vessel round and Tiller shot the soldier in the stern who was steering it.

Without anyone at its helm the *lundwin* started to spin in the current and the high chatter of the K-gun almost drowned out the screaming of its occupants. It was over in seconds as the current bore the *lundwin* on past the canoe and Timber could not traverse the K-gun quickly enough.

Tiller swore out loud.

'The others will get it,' said Timber coolly, deftly changing the K-gun's magazine. 'One of the bursts I got off must have riddled it below the water-line.'

Tiller turned away and fumbled for his walkie-talkie.

He was warning the next canoe down what to expect when he heard Timber shout: 'Watch it, Tiger', and the K-gun started chattering again. Tiller looked up and dropped the walkie-talkie into the bottom of the canoe and grabbed his tommy-gun just as a hail of fire spattered into the water around them.

They had forgotten the second *lundwin*, which had sheered off towards the middle of the river. It was now heading directly for them, obviously intent on ramming them. To increase its speed, or perhaps its manoeuvrability, some of the Japanese were using large sweeps.

'I've never engaged a fucking rowing boat before,' muttered Timber. 'They must be fucking crazy.'

With one swift movement Tiller extracted his commando knife from its sheath and severed the kedge rope. For an agonizing moment the canoe hung motionless in the water. Then the current sluggishly caught its bows and swung it round towards the oncoming *lundwin*.

'Grenades!' Tiller shouted at Timber. Timber stopped firing and reached down into the canoe.

Bullets sang overhead and one pinged loudly off the engine's vertical exhaust. The engine came to life with a heart-stopping cough and then spluttered quietly into action. Tiller pulled the rudder hard over so that the canoe began to swing downstream just as the *lundwin* was upon them. It hit the port outrigger, swinging the canoe hard round and one of the *lundwin's* sweeps snapped in two. Tiller looked up and saw a Japanese leaning over its side. As the man brought his rifle up to his shoulder to shoot Timber, who was busy extracting a grenade's safety-pin with his teeth, Tiller, still holding his knife, instinctively reversed it and threw it at the man. It hit him in the face and bounced off.

Surprised, the Japanese dropped his rifle and clapped his hand to his face, and Tiller swung up his tommy-gun and shot him. The soldier toppled over and fell into the water, just missing the canoe, which was still grating along the *lundwin's* side. The soldier went under and Tiller did not see him come up. Then, as Timber threw one grenade and then a second, the canoe scraped free. The *lundwin's* high counter loomed for a second above the canoe. The grenades curved through the air and at the same time Tiller turned and fired a burst at the Japanese perched high on the stern, steering the *lundwin* with a sweep. He saw him fall and moments later the *lundwin* was rocked by one explosion and then a second. Out of control now, the boat slewed round, hit the bank and came to a stop. Then it burst into flames as a third explosion rocked it from stem to stern. Shadowy figures, outlined by the flames, leapt from its bows on to the bank; others jumped into the water.

'Bring her round, Tiger,' Timber yelled as he fitted a new magazine to the K-gun. 'Bring her round, for Christ's sake.'

But the port outrigger had been almost torn off by the collision with the *lundwin* and try as he might Tiller could not get the canoe to turn into the current. Instead, he turned it downstream and was relieved when it began to answer to the helm. He bent down and opened the engine throttle and the bows of the canoe began to swing towards the bank.

Timber opened fire in short, conservative bursts, neatly picking off the figures outlined by the fire that now raged aboard the *lundwin*. Tiller let the canoe drift downstream slightly and then forged back up, trying to keep as steady a platform as possible for Timber, who continued to fire until there were no more shadows to fire at. By the time he had stopped, the *lundwin* had burned down to the water-line, and the flames flickered and spluttered and died.

For a moment they relaxed and Tiller thumped his number one on the shoulder.

'Good shooting, Timber,' he said.

Instinctively, they looked away from the dying embers of the burnt-out boat to preserve their night vision and it was then that they saw it upstream of them, emerging out of the mist that still hung over the river.

'Jesus, look at that,' said Timber. 'Fucking Japs must have got hold of the fucking *Queen Mary*.'

Coming from Liverpool, Timber knew his ocean liners.

15

They watched in awe and some trepidation as the apparition emerged slowly out of the mist. It took Tiller some moments to realize that much of the boat's sheer bulk was created by a huge square sail rigged on its single mast, above which were set two smaller, square topsails. Even so, he calculated it must be twice the size of the *lundwins*.

'A *laung-zat*,' he murmured to Timber. 'The Burmese use them on the Irrawaddy.'

'But why the fucking sails?' hissed Timber.

'Makes sense,' whispered Tiller. 'Surprise attack. They'll want to get downstream as quietly as possible.'

He shook his head at the amazing persistence of the enemy. Those aboard the *laung-zat* must have heard the previous exchange of fire and must have known they were sailing into an ambush. Yet they were making no effort to avoid it.

'And what about getting back up river again?'

'Japs don't think like that,' said Tiller, realizing that he was at last coming to grips with the enemy's psychology.

'Kind of one-way ticket, is that it?' Schooled in the backstreets of Liverpool, Timber did not disguise his disdain for an enemy who failed to follow the elementary rules for survival.

The *laung-zat* was still some distance from them.

'Exactly. You can't retreat across the bridge if you burn it behind you.'

'Christ, I hope we haven't burnt ours,' Timber muttered. 'What do you reckon we do to stop that bastard?'

Tiller wondered how the crew could manage such a huge area of sail even in the soft breeze that was presently carrying it so sedately downstream.

'We don't,' he replied quietly. 'We've lost our port outrigger, so there's not much we can do. I'm going to call down a stonk.'

Timber nodded his agreement and Tiller picked up his walkie-talkie.

The SBS canoe teams had been specifically given permission to call on the division's regiment of artillery in such an emergency and a stonk – gunners' slang for a block of concentrated fire on a prearranged grid reference – was the only way to deal with such a large vessel.

Tiller spoke urgently into the walkie-talkie as the huge boat approached and then slowly and gracefully ghosted past them. Even though it was near the middle of the river, and the river was shrouded with thin wisps of mist, they could see it was packed with soldiers.

Tiller followed the *laung-zat's* stately progress for a couple of minutes and then started counting distances into the walkie-talkie. 'Three hundred . . . two hundred . . . one hundred . . . fifty . . . twenty-five . . . fire . . . fire . . . fire.'

Silence enfolded them as they watched the vessel continue to recede into the distance.

'Some . . .' Timber started to speak, and then stopped

as white spumes of water began spurting up all round the *laung-zat*. As thunder follows lightning, the crack of the guns came seconds after the shells began straddling the native craft.

The concentration was so great that the boat almost disappeared among the welter of water and smoke that rose around it. Then the mast toppled and seconds later they heard a muffled explosion. When the smoke cleared there was no sign of the *laung-zat*. It was as if it had never been.

'Check, check, check,' Tiller said into the walkie-talkie. 'Target destroyed. Many thanks. Over and out.'

He put down the walkie-talkie. 'There's nothing more we can do up here without a frigging outrigger. We'll go downstream and join the others.'

He put the canoe's engine into gear and steered it at slow speed as close as possible to the river's edge. Without its outrigger the canoe was unbalanced and they had to move with the greatest care. They passed through the area where the *laung-zat* had sunk and saw chunks of it floating in the water. Bodies were scattered everywhere, some of them already dismembered by the crocodiles which churned up the water around them.

The two SBS men averted their faces from the gruesome sight and minutes later the next canoe down came through on the walkie-talkie to guide them to where it lay.

The crew of the second canoe were elated, for they had attacked the *lundwin* with the mortar and had driven it ashore, but they said the third and fourth canoes wanted some action. Tiller had planned to rotate them anyway, so he contacted them by walkie-talkie and sent them both upstream.

Still the Japanese kept trying, this time in motorized sampans, but they, too, were driven ashore or sunk by the SBS canoes and most of the soldiers in them were either killed or drowned. A few very determined soldiers even tried to float down on logs but were spotted and eliminated. None got anywhere near the crossing zone and by the following evening the fighting elements of the Indian division were across the Chindwin and fanning out eastwards towards Mandalay.

Their task accomplished, the SBS teams returned to their base and the following day began dismantling their canoes to load them into the trucks that would transport them back to the forward air strip. They were just about to leave when they saw a jeep flying a large red pennant approaching. It screeched to a halt and out jumped Llewellyn. Grayson called them all to attention and saluted smartly, but Llewellyn asked him to get them to stand easy.

'I just wanted to say,' he said in his soft Welsh accent, 'that you've done a fine job and we're all very grateful to you. But if you think you're going back to Ceylon to lie on the beach you've got another think coming. You'll be pleased to hear that on my recommendation you're going to be moved down to the Irrawaddy. It's even bigger than the Chindwin and a lot muddier. Too many Japs are escaping across it for our liking. You're going to have to stop that. And you'll probably be helping another division to cross when the time comes. For these operations you'll be reinforced by two sections of SRU. Good luck to you.'

'Who are the SRU?' Timber asked Tiller when Llewellyn had driven off.

'Sea Reconnaissance Unit.'

Timber laughed in disbelief. 'You mean that crowd with paddleboards that hung around Hyatt's Ferry for a while? Rather them than me. At least we've got a canoe between us and the crocs.'

It was one of the first questions that Tiller put to a member of the SRU when, the following week, the two units met up at Pakokku, some twenty miles below where the Chindwin joined the Irrawaddy.

'They're like sharks, we reckon,' said the Marine corporal Tiller had questioned. 'We won't attract them if we're moving quietly and smoothly. It's panic movements and blood that draw them.'

Grayson asked the unit's CO, a Canadian naval commander, to explain the SRU's origins and its present functions to his assembled B Group. The commander explained that his idea for a special unit to attack enemy shipping in harbour had come from an illustrated article he had read about the abalone divers of California, who used paddleboards, diving masks and swim fins. He had put up a proposal to form a force using this equipment which had ended up on the desk of Mountbatten, who was Chief of Combined Operations at the time. Mountbatten backed the formation of the SRU, but it was only when he became Supreme Commander in the Far East, and decided to form the Special Operations Group, that the SRU became operational – not as a force to attack enemy shipping but for reconnaissance purposes. The commander then showed B Group the twelve-foot paddleboard the SRU used.

'Notice the pointed stern, very different to the square ones of the boards used for riding the surf in California. And unlike surfboards, the paddleboard is hollow, not solid. So it draws hardly any water and is fast and manoeuvrable across it. It is propelled entirely by hand and special scoops are fitted to the hands for this purpose. We use our fins only when we are swimming in through surf to land on a beach. We call ourselves frogmen.'

Tiller knew of the naval commander and his ideas as he had worked with the Royal Marine Boom Patrol Detachment at Portsmouth just before Tiller had joined it. In those days the commander's unit had been called 'operational swimmers'. Tiller had never heard the word 'frogman' before. It seemed an appropriate enough description.

'I can tell you one useful thing about this method of approach to an enemy-held position,' the commander said. 'A swimmer emerging from the sea gives off no scent at all, so guard dogs cannot detect him. The swimmer can retain this advantage by coating himself in dry sand by rolling in it while still wet.'

Below the point of the Irrawaddy where the SBS and the SRU sections set up their base, both banks were still held by the Japanese. To attack the Japanese crossing points the SBS therefore had to adopt methods similar to those the Japanese had used on the Chindwin: they had to float down on their targets, unheard and unseen, until they chose to attack. But unlike the Japanese, they had also to give thought to the best method of escape.

After some experimentation Tiller and Timber developed a new type of attack craft from an abandoned

Japanese motor boat that had been found by a patrol. It had been badly damaged below the water-line and the engine wrecked. Once the boat was repaired, and the engine replaced by a powerful 22hp outboard, the two SBS men built a platform across the bows on which they mounted two Bren guns. Bamboo poles were then rigged either side of the boat amidships to which were attached smoke generators to cover their retreat.

This new floating war machine was manned by five SBS men: the two Bren gunners in the bows, who also acted as lookouts on the way downstream and activated the smokescreen on the way back; the CO and his observer, who were both armed with hand-grenades with shortened four-second fuses; and the helmsman, who operated the outboard clamped to the boat's counter.

Tiller, not happy with the accuracy of his weapons at night, decided to experiment. He removed the stock of his tommy-gun and taped a torch to the top of its barrel so that he could depress its signalling button with the forefinger of his left hand while squeezing the tommy-gun's trigger with the forefinger of his right. Zeroing the beam on a target ensured the accuracy of the tommy-gun when he fired it. To maintain rapid fire, two of the weapon's magazines were taped together so that when one magazine was exhausted he had only to unclip it, turn the magazine around and insert the full one.

When intelligence was received by the SBS that the Japanese were crossing the Irrawaddy in increasing numbers some miles downstream, it was decided to see how efficient the boat was. So instead of sending the normal patrol of two Mk VI canoes, they launched the boat at dusk. The outboard could not be used, as it was not silenced; instead the boat was borne down on the current and was steadied when necessary by paddles wielded by Tiller and Timber, who acted as his observer.

Within an hour they had moved past the British-held west bank into no man's land and then to the part where both banks were known to be still held by the Japanese. As they approached the village of Nyaungu on the eastern bank, Tiller paddled the boat into dead water and waited for what might appear.

After an hour they saw headlights on the far side of the river and heard the rattling of empty oil drums being unloaded and rolled into the water. Then the headlights of the lorries were shone on the river's edge, where the SBS men could see a team of Japanese at work.

'They're building a raft of some kind,' Timber whispered to Tiller. 'A big one too.'

As they watched, they heard the rumble of moving vehicles on their side of the river just below where the boat was lying, but from their position they could not see how many there were or what they contained. When the raft was finished ropes were sent across by small boats and the raft was then pulled across the river with them.

At a whispered command from Tiller the boat was gradually eased forward until they could see the vehicles. There were six or seven of them, all drawn up nose to tail on a dirt road which ran parallel with the side of the river for about a quarter of a mile before curving away across the dry plain. One had an anti-tank gun in tow, another had a searchlight, while a third was crowded with soldiers.

They watched as the Japanese ran the first vehicle on to the makeshift ferry, which was then hauled across the river by the ropes. Then the ferry was hauled back and the process repeated, while all the time additional lorries were arriving at the river to await their turn to cross.

'We'll sink the ferry first,' Tiller told his crew in an undertone. 'Once it's in mid-stream all we have to do is perforate the oil drums.'

'What about all those lorries?' Timber objected.

'We'll shoot those up on the way back.'

They waited until the cumbrous ferry had been loaded and was beginning its laborious journey back across the river, and then moved out from under cover of the bank. Tiller gripped his tommy-gun in anticipation when he saw that this time the ferry was loaded with the lorry towing the anti-tank gun.

As they approached they saw that several soldiers were in the open lorry and several others were riding on the gun. When the ferry was halfway across the river he told the helmsman to start the outboard engine and its throbbing roar cut through the quietness of the night. But it did not cause any immediate reaction among the soldiers aboard the ferry, for they were not alert and must have thought their enemy was many miles upstream of them.

Even when the boat appeared out of the shadows they did not immediately realize what was happening, and it was only when the two Brens opened up that they scrambled for their weapons. By then it was too late.

Two of them even tried to swing the anti-tank gun

in the boat's direction before they were cut down by the Bren guns. The Brens then punctured the oil drums nearest them while the helmsman guided the boat up to the ropes that connected the ferry with the west bank.

'Shove it in neutral,' Tiller shouted at him above the steady knocking of a 'woodpecker' that had opened up on them from the far bank. 'I'm going to cut them.'

The helmsman threw the outboard out of gear while Tiller grabbed the ropes trailing in the water and severed them with his commando knife. Then the helmsman revved up the engine and steered the boat so that the Brens could riddle the oil drums holding up the other side of the ferry.

By now water had begun to fill the upstream drums, making the ferry tilt, and suddenly both lorry and gun slid into the water with a tremendous splash, and the Bren gunners turned their attention to the men struggling in the water before lighting the smoke generators as the boat continued to surge downstream. Seconds later the river was covered by a pall of white smoke and the firing from the banks slackened and then stopped.

Tiller shouted for the helmsman to swing the boat round and, under the protection of the smoke, roared towards the west bank, where the remaining vehicles were lined up.

The boat roared through the smoke and when it emerged on the other side, both Bren gunners emptied their magazines into the lorries. One exploded with a tremendous blast which for a moment lit up the whole area as if it was daylight. It revealed Japanese soldiers running in all directions.

As the boat passed the lorries lining the bank, Tiller saw the mayhem they were causing and felt the adrenalin coursing through him. He shouted to the helmsman to maintain his course alongside the bank so that the Bren gunners could pick off some of the figures running along it. He brought up his tommy-gun and levelled it at the shore. His thumb found the torch's button and the powerful beam scoured the bank. One Japanese, crouching by the river's edge with his sub-machine-gun raised, was caught in its glare. Tiller pulled the trigger. The tommy-gun bucked in his hand as he emptied his magazine at the Japanese, who staggered under the impact of the heavy .45 bullets and then fell into the water.

'There's another,' shouted Timber, raising his carbine and aiming over Tiller's shoulder.

Tiller took his thumb off the torch button, wrenched out the empty magazine, flicked it around and inserted the full one.

Timber's carbine cracked by Tiller's ear.

'To the right, Tiger, to the right! Where's the bugger gone?'

Suddenly, and unexpectedly, bullets from an automatic weapon began whipping above the boat and several smacked into the makeshift platform.

Tiller raised his tommy-gun, the stress in Timber's voice giving him a surge of urgency, but the strapping holding the torch had been loosened by the vibration of the tommy-gun and his thumb could not find the torch button.

'For Christ's sake.' It was Timber's hoarse voice beside him.

The machine-gunner on the bank had found his

range now and bullets began splintering the boat. Out of the corner of his eye Tiller saw one of the Bren gunners slump over his weapon. Then his thumb found the button and the torch beam probed the darkness. It wavered along the bank and zeroed in on a Japanese lying on the ground frantically working to clear the cartridge feed of his light machine-gun.

Tiller let his tommy-gun rip, emptying his magazine in one vengeful burst. But as he fired, the boat bucked and rolled and, miraculously, the soldier seemed unscathed. But, instead of rolling to one side to avoid the cricle of light on him, the Japanese stood up and attempted to throw a hand-grenade at the boat as it surged past him. He had just got the grenade in his hand when he was cut down by the hail of bullets from the uninjured Bren gunner. But even on the ground he continued to try to prime the grenade – until Timber's carbine barked again.

'Silly bastard,' said Timber with some satisfaction. 'Teach him to be heroic.'

'Get the fuck out of here,' Tiller shouted at the helmsman, who swerved the boat towards the middle of the river and opened the throttle as far as it would go.

For a few long, agonizing moments bullets continued to hit the water around them and to fly over their heads, and then from the further bank a parachute flare was fired and lit the water with an eerie pink glow. But instead of it being fired ahead of the retreating boat the flare just illuminated the carnage the SBS had wreaked. It swung in the air before descending slowly into the river and spluttering out. Wrapped in darkness, the boat sped upstream.

'I'll run out of fuel if we keep going at this speed,' the helmsman shouted to Tiller above the roar of the outboard.

'Keep going,' Tiller ordered as he moved forward to look at the fallen Bren gunner.

'He's dead,' said the other one flatly. 'We were just too fucking slow.'

Tiller accepted the criticism with a nod. He felt the adrenalin ebb from him and despair and exhaustion edge in. He dragged the gunner into the bottom of the boat and looked down at the young face. Either he was getting too old to fight, he thought bitterly, or the SBS were recruiting underage volunteers. He covered the body with a tarpaulin.

'It wasn't your fault,' Timber said.

'Then whose fucking fault was it?' growled Tiller, and Timber shrugged and looked away.

'It wasn't your fault, Tiger,' Grayson said when they reported in after the operation. 'That Jap must have been just plain suicidal. Anyone with a grain of self-preservation would have kept his head down. He must have ignored the incoming fire completely.'

'He even stood up after he had been peppered and tried to chuck a grenade,' Timber said in some awe.

'Fanatics,' said Grayson in disgust.

Tiller kept his own counsel. He had heard that word so often since he had been in Burma, mostly on the lips of those who did not actually encounter the Japanese in battle. At first he had thought the same: that the enemy were just simple peasants who had been indoctrinated to die for their Emperor.

But he knew now it wasn't as simple as that. The

same went for the earlier widespread belief that the British had been defeated in Burma – one hell of a beating, as one American general had described it – because the Japanese had been used to the jungle and knew instinctively how to fight in it. The truth was that the Japanese had not known any more about fighting in the jungle than the British: they had just trained better and had employed better tactics. Some called them fanatical. He called them brave, very brave.

Courage wasn't the preserve of one side in any war. Yet once again he had underestimated the bravery of his opponents. That was why the death of the young Bren gunner was down to him. He should have known that they would be lying in wait for the boat upstream, and that whatever fire-power the SBS could have laid down would not have diverted the ambushers from their task. He knew he should have broken off the attack while he had been ahead of the game. And he hadn't.

Well, he intended to return that night and, using different tactics and different weapons – a two-inch mortar properly mounted might be very effective – he was going to avenge the death of that gunner many times over.

Grayson took him to one side.

'I had a signal while you were out. You're wanted back in Ceylon instanter.'

'What, now?'

'Now, Tiger. A Dakota's being diverted to pick you up.'

When the Group had been moved from Ceylon to the Chindwin they had had a signal from India saying: 'Hours count.' Yet when they had arrived at Calcutta no one had known who they were or where they were meant to be going. One wag had even asked what ship they were the survivors from. 'Immediately' to Tiller meant next week, next month – certainly not today or tomorrow. He had other business to complete.

'I've got a different plan for tomorrow night, skipper,' Tiller said. 'Ceylon can go fly a kite for a few days.'

Grayson studied Tiller discreetly. As one of the first officers to be trained by Roger Pountney, Grayson had seen enough action in the Mediterranean to know that when an NCO or junior officer was bent on getting his own back his judgement was impaired. That was dangerous. Grayson knew the accuracy of the Spanish saying: 'If you want revenge then first dig two graves.'

But Grayson was also a skilled officer; he knew there were times to lay down the law and there were times when it was best ignored. He just told Tiller to get some breakfast and then to get his head down, and when Tiller had left he sent a signal saying the colour sergeant was delayed. An hour later he received a reply which simply said: 'Undelay. Hasler.'

During the morning Grayson was told by the air controller at the forward airstrip that the diverted aircraft was expected in three hours. The airstrip was an hour away by jeep.

Grayson groaned and went to Tiller's tent and shook him awake. 'Sorry, Tiger,' he said. 'Orders are orders.'

Tiller simply nodded, dressed, packed his kitbag, shook Grayson's hand and climbed aboard the waiting jeep. He didn't feel like saying goodbye to Timber or anyone else. They would understand.

16

'You were quick,' said Tasler, waving Tiller to a seat. 'Grayson said you were going to be delayed.'

Good for Grayson, Tiller thought, he'd done his best. What now?

'What now, sir?'

'What do you think, Tiger?'

'Those effing Welmans, sir, if you'll excuse the expression. That's my guess.'

Tasler's normally cheerful face was grim.

'You've got it in one, Tiger.'

Tiller felt resignation overtake him, but perhaps his time had come. He had had a good run, a remarkable one, really, when he came to think of it. He knew he shouldn't have been so angry at losing that young gunner. It was an infallible sign that when a man reacted like that it was time he was rested. Perhaps a stint as an instructor was just what was required. Like hell it was, he thought, irritably.

'And am I going to be an instructor here in Ceylon or somewhere else, sir?' he asked in a subdued voice.

Tasler looked at him sharply. 'Sorry. I thought you understood. I went you for an operation.'

The weight lifted off Tiller and he leant forward eagerly. 'That's different, sir.'

'Very different,' Tasler agreed. He hesitated, and

then went on: 'You understand, don't you, that only volunteers are required? You are under no obligation whatsoever – to me or anyone else – to volunteer. Your position as an instructor is open to you at any time.'

Even as he was speaking, Tasler knew his words were falling on deaf ears, but it was a rigmarole he had to go through.

'You understand, Tiger?'

Tiller nodded, finding it hard to hide his impatience. 'What's the job, sir?'

Tasler leant forward and pressed his intercom button, which connected him with his WRNS secretary. 'Daisy, send in Lieutenant Commander Davidson, please.'

Tasler rose from behind his desk and paced his office. 'I'm not sure how to phrase this, Tiger, but there comes a time when – well – when a man has seen too much action. Everyone has their limits. You've been on the go ever since Bordeaux. Don't you think . . . ?'

Tiller was relieved that Tasler was interrupted by an abrupt knock on the office door. Had the major gone troppo or something? Perhaps staff-officer duties had finally sent him round the bend. They knew each other so well it would have been difficult for Tiller to hide his doubts about the major's sanity if Tasler had persisted.

'Ah, Harry. Thanks for coming along. This is Colour Sergeant Tiller. I mentioned him to you.'

Davidson smiled and nodded at Tiller. He was tall and studious-looking, with courtly manners. In peacetime he had been an Oxford don, a lecturer in Oriental Studies. Now he was one of the best intelligence officers SEAC had. He knew this, but he wasn't yet sure if everyone else did. Under his arm he carried, like a telescope, a huge rolled-up map of South-East Asia and the western Pacific. He dropped it on Tasler's table and spread it out.

'Our problem is the enormous distances involved,' he said. 'If we are to pre-empt any attacks by the Japs . . .'

'Hold on, Harry,' Tasler raised his hand. 'Before we get down to the nitty-gritty, I think you should fill the picture in a little more fully for Tiller.'

'Of course. As I am sure you are aware, Colour Sergeant, General MacArthur's forces are beginning to work their way up the Philippines while the Pacific advance has reached the Palau Islands here.' The lieutenant commander's finger pointed to a number of tiny dots in the Philippine Sea. 'You can see that both advances are still a long way from Japan itself, but logically the Japanese should now be massing all their forces, particularly their naval ones, to prevent any further advance on their homeland. However,' – and here Davidson glanced up at both the men listening to him – 'Western logic does not appeal to the Japanese. Our logic is intellectual, theirs is intuitive. In short, we find it hard to know which way they're going to jump.'

'Know thine enemy,' said Tasler.

'Exactly, Blondie. But that's easier said than done. I once asked an English colleague of mine who was married to a Western-educated Japanese academic if she really understood her husband. She smiled and said: "We get on extremely well together except that every now and then his mind slips back a thousand years." I find it is the same with the Japanese high command.'

Davidson paused, mustering his thoughts. Tiller said

helpfully: 'You mean the Japs have moved their Mobile Fleet away from the Yanks?'

'Exactly. It sounds absurd to us, I know – rather like resurrecting William the Conqueror's tactics at the Battle of Hastings – but in AD 975 the Japanese beat an invading Korean force not by defeating them on the ground but by a counter invasion. I believe the high command is thinking along the same lines now. By striking south-west into the Bay of Bengal instead of south-east as we would anticipate, they would create two simultaneous situations. They would catch us on the hop and they would sever our supply lines into Burma and China. Frankly, they still have the naval resources to get to Ceylon and beyond, just as their fleet did in 1942. Given the strength of our naval forces in Ceylon it would be like a hot knife through butter.'

'They might get there, but they'd never get back,' said Tasler. 'Not without massive air cover.'

Tiller remembered the *laung-zat* floating gracefully down the Chindwin and said: 'I don't think that would enter their minds, sir.'

Davidson smiled appreciatively. 'Spot on, Colour Sergeant.'

'So you think they're going to strike in this direction?' Tasler asked.

'We simply don't know. It could just be a bluff. But Supremo thinks we can't afford to be wrong on this one. Hence a pre-emptive strike.'

'Against what and where, sir?' Tiller asked Tasler eagerly.

The two officers exchanged glances. 'He's got the highest security clearance,' said Tasler. 'He's got to know sometime.'

Davidson nodded. 'I agree.'

Tiller's mind flashed back to his last interview with the commanding officer of the Welman course. 'It must be one of the Jap battleships,' he said. 'They have the world's biggest, don't they?'

'There's only one left after Leyte Gulf,' Davidson said. 'The *Kamato*. We know she's reached Singapore along with other units of the Mobile Fleet.'

Singapore! So that was it!

'Do you know anything about her?' Tasler asked. 'She's over 800 feet long and displaces 64,000 tons.'

Tiller gave a low whistle. 'She'd make something like the *Ramillies* look like a motor boat, sir.'

'Her main armament is nine eighteen-inch guns. They can outrange any major Allied warship afloat and at twenty-seven knots she's faster than most of them. Her secondary armament is almost the equivalent of two of our latest cruisers.'

'Her main belt armour?' Tiller asked. He wasn't concerned with her deck or turret armour, but the main belt armour protected the ship's most vulnerable parts just above and below the water-line.

'We're not sure. At least sixteen inches.'

'Not even a Welman charge could penetrate that.'

'Quite. But that only protects her engines and magazines. Like all warships, it must be thinner towards the bow and stern. By how much we don't know.'

'And it can't extend down to her keel.'

'Exactly, Tiger. That's where she's vulnerable.'

'And from the air, sir, surely?'

Tasler looked across at Davidson.

'Yes, of course from the air,' Davidson agreed. 'But the Japs have amassed a huge concentration of naval

fighters – mostly the latest Zeros – in southern Malaya.
Presumably, they're there to protect her. That's what
first alerted us to something unusual. But there's
something else, too. Intelligence sources say she has
a new anti-aircraft shell which can be used by her
main armament.'

'Her *main* armament?' Tasler queried. 'Surely not.
You mean her eighteen-inch guns can fire at aircraft?'

'Incredible, I know,' Davidson said. 'But true.'

He turned to Tiller. 'As an explosives expert, it'll
interest you. It's called a *San-shiki* shell. It has a time
fuse in its nose – not unlike our proximity fuse – which
explodes the shell in front of an approaching formation
of aircraft. It's packed with tiers of incendiary-filled
shot. Six thousand rounds to be exact. These tiers
rest on a base of explosive which is connected to the
time fuse by a central column of explosive. As the
flash passes down the column it ignites each tier in
turn before reaching the explosive in the shell's base
which breaks it apart. Its effect is similar to some giant
shotgun blasting a flight of birds.'

Outside Tiller could hear members of 385 Detachment being put through their daily paces on the makeshift parade ground. He could see that the Catalina was
back on its mooring in the channel.

'No air attack, then,' he said.

'Super-fortresses could reach Singapore from India,'
Tasler said. 'But the Yanks don't have many of them
and they're all committed to pounding Japan from the
Marianas. Under the circumstances, the Yanks don't
feel inclined to withdraw any of them except in a
real emergency. You can't blame them.' Tasler's voice
trailed off. He obviously did blame them.

'Singapore is SEAC territory,' Davidson added by way of explanation. 'Our pigeon really.'

'But SEAC's a joint Allied command, isn't it, sir?' Tiller said.

'Yes, well . . .'

Davidson's sentence remained hanging in the air, but Tiller knew what had been left unsaid. SEAC was a joint command when it suited the Americans, a British one when it didn't. The Japanese were threatening British lines of communication and British colonies. So it was a British problem.

'And the intelligence source, sir?' Tiller asked Davidson.

Davidson smiled. 'Now you know perfectly well, Colour Sergeant, I am in no position to reveal that.'

There was a pause and Tasler said: 'I think under the circumstances you can, Harry.'

Davidson looked across at him, surprised. 'Really?'

'Tiller delivered him,' Tasler said.

'Is that right?' remarked Davidson. 'Well, you did a good job. Congratulations.'

'Is he still there?' Tiller asked. 'Or have you brought him out?'

Davidson looked uncomfortable.

'I'm afraid we've lost touch with him,' Tasler explained. 'Frankly, it doesn't look good. But before he went off the air he gave us invaluable intelligence about the *San-shiki* shell. He also smuggled out a plan of the harbour which shows where your principal target is lying.'

'The *Kamato* you mean?'

Tasler shook his head. 'She's not your principal target.'

Tiller looked puzzled. 'She's not?'

'The *Hoko* is.'

'The largest aircraft carrier in the world,' Davidson explained. 'The Japs have only just launched her. If the *Kamato* and her escorts are going to move into the Bay of Bengal – probably using the Andaman Islands as their base – they're going to need air cover and lots of it. The land-based Zeros will cover her up to the Andamans but not much further. No air cover, no advance. We will, of course, ask you and your team to have a go at the *Kamato*, but it's the *Hoko* we want out of the way.'

'In Pan Kon's last message he said he didn't think either of them are ready to sail yet,' said Tasler.

At least he knew the name of the joe now, Tiller thought.

'There's another thing, Tiger.'

'Sir?'

'You're going to have to assess very quickly what you're going to use to attack these Jap ships.'

Tiller looked puzzled. 'I assumed we'd be using Welmans.'

'Probably. But we've also recently received some Sleeping Beauties. They have certain advantages over the Welman, but you'll have to make up your own mind about which to use. Sergeant Whitaker's the man who's been trying out the SBs.'

'My team's been chosen, then?'

Tasler nodded. 'There are four of you altogether, plus two reserves in case of illness or accident.'

'And how do we get within striking distance of Singapore?'

'The navy has pulled out all the stops,' said Davidson.

'They've converted two subs to carry either the SBs or the Welmans on their decks.'

'You seem to have thought of everything, sir,' Tiller said with a grin.

'It's my business to,' said Davidson. 'We've been reckoning for over a year that if the tide turned against the Japs they might try something desperate. We had to have something up our sleeve. That's why we got the Welmans here. And you.'

Tiller looked across at Tasler, who shrugged. So Blondie had known all along, Tiller thought. He might have guessed as much. 'How big is this *Hoko*?' he asked Tasler when Davidson had left.

'She started life as a sister ship for the *Kamato*, but when the Japs realized the war at sea would be won or lost with carriers they converted her hull into an aircraft carrier. She won't have much armour under water but she's shielded by torpedo nets – that much we know. She won't be easy to get at.'

Tasler studied the pencil he was spinning between his thumbs and forefingers.

'There's another thing, Tiger.'

Tiller know there would be. He waited.

'It will mean a night attack.'

Jesus. A Welman couldn't be used at night. Everyone had said it was impossible.

'That's impossible.'

Tasler continued as if he hadn't heard. 'The full-moon period begins in ten days' time.' He looked up at Tiller. 'It's the best we can do, Tiger.'

Tiller found Sergeant Whitaker studying a Sleeping Beauty with the other members of the team.

'What's it like under water?' Tiller asked him.

'Trouble is keeping it under,' said one member of the team. 'It behaves like a fucking porpoise.'

'Just a matter of practice,' said Whitaker calmly. He was a calm, dogged man, unflappable. 'The good thing about it is its versatility. You can paddle it, sail it or motor it.'

'We're not going to want to do the first two where we're going,' said Tiller. 'How powerful is the motor?'

'Just under a half horsepower. It's driven by four six-volt batteries in this watertight compartment here. Flat out, it can cover twelve miles at four and a half knots on the surface.'

'Sounds reasonable. And under water?'

'About half that.'

The same as the Welman, Tiller thought.

'Maximum depth?'

'Fifty feet.'

The same depth as the Welman was allowed to operate, but Tiller knew the SB was equipped with wire-cutters so that its pilot could slice through any anti-torpedo nets he encountered. A Welman had no alternative but to go under them. Whitaker pointed out the instruments to Tiller – a magnetic compass, a depth gauge and a clock – which enabled the pilot to keep a check on the SB's submerged running time, depth and direction. He then ran through the procedure for trimming down, diving and finally returning the SB to the surface. Like the Welman, the craft was submerged by flooding two ballast tanks which were vented by high-pressure air from two bottles when the pilot wanted to return to the surface.

Unlike the Welman, which used a compensating

balance weight screwed fore or aft by the operator, there was, Whitaker explained, a third tank fitted in the bows. This was used for trimming the SB to keep it on an even keel at any depth up to fifty feet. He also pointed out a plug in the keel which flooded the SB until it was awash and a mechanism which expelled the water when the SB was to be used on the surface. Once awash, the pilot could trim down the SB until only his head was above water, or he could flood the ballast tanks and dive by using the hydroplane and then use the trimming tank to bring it level.

'Looks simple enough,' said Tiller.

'Even the Sardine Men prefer them,' said Whitaker.

'That doesn't surprise me, Billy,' said Tiller drily.

They launched the SB and Tiller watched Whitaker, dressed in a Mk V parachute water suit and oxygen breathing apparatus, manoeuvre it round the harbour, first in the surface position, then in the trimmed-down position, and finally under water. Then Tiller borrowed the suit and the oxygen apparatus and tried himself. The SB was much more difficult to control than the Welman and it porpoised too easily, but there was no doubt that the SB was a more advanced design.

'But what can it carry in the way of explosives?' Tiller asked after the trial.

'Six limpets,' said Whitaker. 'Sink anything afloat.'

But Whitaker did not know what their targets were.

The next morning Tasler rang Tiller to say that naval Intelligence were certain the *Hoko*'s anti-torpedo nets would extend more than fifty feet below the water.

'I guessed they would,' said Tiller quietly. 'But

there's no way we can use the SBs. They can't carry enough explosives.'

'The Welmans it is, then,' Tasler said briskly.

Tasler didn't mention what they both already knew: it had proved impossible to modify the Welmans to increase the strength of the rectangular viewing window.

The following evening the two submarines left the harbour of Hyatt's Ferry and headed east.

17

With the first signs of dawn the submarine made ready to dive. With a roar the air tanks were blown and it then slid slowly down to sixty fathoms on its electric motors. In the dimmed light the captain, a lieutenant commander in the regular navy, studied his charts. The Japanese had laid two minefields to protect the Straits of Singapore and the course he took had to be carefully plotted. Clocks ticked. The soft whirr of the electric engines buzzed, slackened, buzzed again.

Tiller lay on his bunk in the tiny petty officers' mess in the submarine, flicking through a magazine. He thought idly of Hazel-eyes. He and his team of five had been kept in strict isolation from the time they had been given their briefing, and he had never had a chance to find out if he would find her sitting in Sam's bar on a weekend evening. If she was, she was almost certainly not waiting for him. Not any more.

'How much longer, Tiger?'

Tiller turned to the opposite bunk, where Whitaker was composing a letter to his wife. Married men should not be allowed to volunteer for operations like this, Tiller thought. But Whitaker was a skilled and experienced operator, a solid rock of a man, as tough mentally as he was physically. Besides, they needed the best men available.

'The skipper reckoned if we get through the mine-fields without a hitch we should be in position by late afternoon.'

They lay in silence for a while, their ears alert for any scraping, metallic sound along the hull that would indicate they had snared a mine. But all they heard was the intermittent buzz of the electric engines, and the captain and his navigator talking in undertones. The submarine was rock-steady; there was no feeling of movement at all. It was as if they were suspended in time and space.

At midday a seaman brought them both steaming mugs of ki, the navy's thick, syrupy, sweet cocoa. In looks and consistency it reminded Tiller of the Irrawaddy – and probably tasted like it, too, he thought. The thought didn't stop him draining it to the last muddy dregs as he consumed the huge sandwiches which came with it. Whitaker, however, refused both ki and sandwich. Not a good sign, Tiller reflected, but he refrained from saying anything. Every man faced a hazardous operation in his own way.

They both slept until they were shaken awake by the same rating who had brought them their meal. He said to Tiller: 'The captain asks if you would join him, Sarge.'

The sound of the engines was different. It immediately told Tiller that the submarine was back under diesel power, obtaining its oxygen and exhausting its diesel fumes through its *Schnorkel*, or 'snort' as the navy called this invaluable Dutch invention that stuck above the surface like a periscope. It enabled a submarine to run just below the surface for indefinite periods of time.

The captain beckoned Tiller to join him by the periscope. 'I thought you'd like a dekko at the area before it gets too dark,' he said, stepping back. Tiller put his hands on the periscope's handle and his eyes to its lenses. At first he found it difficult to make out anything. But as his eyes became accustomed to focusing beyond the periscope's numbered graticules – which enabled the captain to gauge the distances and angles of convergence of his targets – Tiller picked out several vessels on the surface. He swivelled the periscope and saw the thin, continuous line of land to his left and a broken one to his right. He then swivelled it aft and instinctively flinched as the seemingly huge hull of a merchant ship flying the Japanese flag filled the lenses.

He heard the captain laugh behind him. 'Don't worry, he won't run us down. He's a lot further off than he looks.'

The captain stepped forward, snapped up the periscope's arms and pulled the periscope back down into its housing. 'It will be dark in half an hour and we'll be in position off Tekukor island about half an hour after that.'

To avoid the anti-submarine patrols in the strait the submarine dived once more and its interior was again filled with the somnolent, uneven buzz of its electric engines. Supper of sausages, baked beans and mashed potatoes was served with a tot of rum. Tiller polished off the food but handed his tot to Whitaker, who pushed aside his untouched meal and downed it gratefully.

Then both of them, for the umpteenth time, spread out a copy of the agent's sketch of Singapore harbour and compared it with vertical photo-reconnaissance shots which had been taken the previous week by a US Lightning fighter whose long-range tanks and stripped interior had given it the necessary extra range to get to Singapore and back from India.

The photographs, taken at a height that avoided the exploding anti-aircraft shells that were blotched all over them, showed the area where the sketch indicated that both the battleship and the aircraft carrier lay. But somehow the Japanese had camouflaged the two massive vessels so well by breaking up their outlines that even the expert PR interpreters had not been able to say for sure whether the two ships were there or not.

Something was there all right, but it looked like two or three or more smaller vessels, and as many times as the two SBS men had studied the photographs they could not be sure either.

'They could have moved them,' Whitaker said.

'They could have,' Tiller agreed. 'But surely ships that size couldn't get far without being spotted by recce flights or submarine patrols?'

'Don't you believe it, Tiger,' Whitaker said sourly. 'The open sea's a bloody big place. I was aboard the *Rodney* when the Home Fleet was after the *Bismarck*. It was like hunting a needle in a haystack. The Home Fleet went in the wrong direction, and as for the *Ark Royal* coming up from Gib, none of her aircraft even got within cooee of her. It was a right shambles, I can tell you, whatever the bloody newspapers said. It was a sheer fluke that that Catalina pilot saw her. The heavy cruiser with her slipped through our fingers as easy as pie. No, a bloody big place is an ocean, whether it's the Atlantic, the Indian or the Pacific.'

'We must have coast watchers in the area. They'd report back if they'd seen them.'

'Not if they slipped out at night before the moon rose, they wouldn't,' Whitaker retorted. 'And anyway, how long do you think it takes for intelligence to get fed back from Singapore?'

Tiller shrugged. When a radio wasn't, or couldn't be, used, he didn't know how it was done.

'Weeks, mate. Has to go through Kunming, most of it. This sketch would be at least five weeks old.'

Tiller didn't let Whitaker's doubts unsettle him. In his mind the *Hoko* and the *Kamato* were in Singapore all right and would be right where Pan Kon had said they would be. In his experience it was never any use dwelling on the uncertainties of an operation.

Instead, he again went through the details of the plan with Whitaker. They were to attack the *Hoko*, the other pair of Welmans were to attack the *Kamato*. There could be no co-ordination between the two attacks, or even between the two Welmans attacking the same target, for there was no means of communicating between the four operators. Each man had his own appointed task and after performing it each would return to the same spot from which he had been launched – where, with any luck, the submarine would still be waiting.

Whitaker was to place his charge by the *Hoko*'s engine rooms while Tiller was to put his next to the aircraft carrier's propellers and rudder. Even two charges as powerful as the ones the Welmans carried would not necessarily sink such large ships, but Hasler had been completely confident that they would certainly damage them enough to make them inoperable.

After a while they could feel that the submarine was

climbing at a gradual angle towards the surface and then they were again taken aft, where the captain was peering through the periscope.

'All clear,' he said to his number one. 'Prepare to surface.'

The submarine levelled out and came to a halt. A rating opened the hatch and warm, damp but refreshingly fresh air – richly perfumed with unidentified aromas from the nearby island – flooded into the submarine.

The captain was first up the ladder, followed by his number one, then by Tiller and Whitaker, and finally by the two ratings who were to unfasten the Welmans from their cradles.

The island loomed close by on their port side and Tiller thought how skilled the captain must be to bring his submerged submarine into such shallow waters. Second nature made him note the bearings of two prominent features – a conspicuous bald hill inland and a derelict beach house on the shore – so that he would know the exact position to return to for the rendezvous with the submarine.

The captain shook Tiller and Whitaker by the hand and wished them luck. The two SBS men then shook hands before moving off in opposite directions down the submarine's casing. The two ratings had each brought up with them from below a short wooden ladder to enable the SBS men to clamber into their Welmans.

Once the SBS men were in the Welmans and had secured the hatches above them the ratings freed the miniature submarines from their cradles and returned to the interior of the mother submarine with their ladders.

The Welman seemed even more cramped than usual and Tiller could feel its steel sides touching his shoulders while the top of the hatch almost brushed the comforter he had on his head. It reminded him why the members of the SBS who had been trained with Welmans had been called Sardine Men. He strapped on his oxygen mask and while he waited for the submarine to go under he polished the oblong porthole in front of him and the two circular ones on either side.

Without warning, the Welman bumped against its cradle and then floated free. Though the submarine sank gradually, the suction it caused when submerging dragged the Welman down too. They had not been able to practise this part of the operation, so it came as something of a surprise to Tiller to find the Welman being sucked under the water. But the Welman had a strong positive buoyancy and it soon bobbed to the surface again.

Tiller started the electric motor and edged slowly along the line of the island. At the end was a long promontory. Once he reached the end of it Tiller turned on his luminous direction indicator and lined it up with the harbour entrance, which he knew was directly ahead of him some six miles from the island. Then he submerged to a depth of fifty feet.

They had practised covering long distances submerged and found that though the Welman went slowly – only two knots – it was quite steady. However, since it was vulnerable to tides and could easily be swept off course, the direction Tiller had set on his indicator allowed for some tide to take him to the east.

But the submarine captain had timed his arrival at

the island with great accuracy so that the Welmans were able to cross to their destination when the tide was almost slack. The minutes turned into an hour, then two hours, and all Tiller saw through the portholes was swirling mud and the occasional fish. It was like swimming blind and if he had not practised it so often he would have had little confidence in arriving at the right place.

After two hours and forty minutes he eased the Welman towards the surface. It was now nearly midnight and he calculated he should have passed under the first anti-submarine net guarding one of the harbour's main exits.

Very slowly, he managed to manoeuvre the Welman so that its conning tower just broke the surface. This was also a manoeuvre he had practised time and again, and in the smooth waters of the harbour he had little difficulty keeping the tiny vessel on an even keel so that the reinforced glass window in front of him was just above the surface.

The full moon had risen now. He had been warned that the harbour would be patrolled, but he could see nothing moving on it. He could not see the Hoko either, for although the lights of the city were ablaze the harbour itself was full of dark corners which even the moon could not penetrate.

Tiller checked his direction indicator and sent the Welman down to twenty feet. He ran it at one knot for twenty minutes and then rose slowly to the surface again. Now he was among anchored shipping and close to the docks.

He cursed the vessel's restricted vision. Sweat poured from him. It was crazy bobbing up and down in a vulnerable little submarine in the middle of an enemy-occupied harbour. Yet he could see that the surrounding water, shimmering in the light of the moon, was as quiet and as flat and as deserted as it had been twenty minutes before.

He glanced at the gauge on the oxygen cylinder to see how many atmospheres there were left in it and was glad to see that he had used less than half the cylinder. He certainly did not want to launch his attack and then have to change the cylinder halfway through. He told himself he must remember to change to the spare cylinder before he started the long trip back to the island.

He kept the Welman stationary on the surface, the water just lapping below the front window of the conning tower, while he again scanned the shipping and the wharves that he could see ahead of him.

As his eyes became accustomed to the light and shadow of the moonlit harbour they began to distinguish the anchored ships from those moored alongside the wharves and could see, too, what were dock cranes and what were either masts or derricks aboard the larger ships.

But still he could not see the *Hoko* and he remembered Whitaker's sober warning that she could have sailed or simply moved to another part of the vast harbour where it could take days to find her.

Tiller inched the Welman round to improve his restricted view of a particularly crowded part of the docks. As he did so his eyes, well attuned now to the scene around him, registered that the shape and continuity of what looked like a large quay with some structures on top of it, was not quite right. He began edging the submarine closer, never taking his eyes off the shape ahead of him. Slowly, he began to discern that the quay was not a quay at all but a large, continuous shape that, he became increasingly certain as he moved towards it, was his target.

He halted the Welman and for a moment closed his eyes to clear his vision. He recalled then a camouflage lecture he had attended at Hyatt's Ferry. The lecturer, an American naval officer, gave an illustration of how clever the Japanese were at illusion by recounting how they had camouflaged one of their airfields on New Georgia. Instead of felling trees to clear the jungle for the airstrip, they had severed them but had kept the top half of the trees upright off the ground by a series of cables. They had then completed the strip under cover of the canopy of suspended trees. From the air the jungle had looked undisturbed. When the airstrip was finished the Japanese had simply removed the trees and flown in their aircraft, by which time it had been too late for the Americans to make it inoperable.

He opened his eyes and looked again. Was he imagining it or was it really there? Was his brain playing tricks with his eyes, so that he was seeing the *Hoko* because he wanted so desperately for it to be there? Was it, as it were, ordinary trees he was looking at or were they cleverly suspended tops?

The more he looked the less he saw. He was concentrating so hard that it was just sheer luck that out of the corner of his eye he saw a movement in the starboard porthole. He turned and saw the outline of a launch heading in his direction, a small searchlight in its bows scanning the water around it. He felt the clamminess of his hands on the joystick. Any movement would

262

be bound to catch the attention of those aboard the launch, yet part of him wanted to push the joystick forward to escape the probing light. But he knew from his canoe operations that lying still was the best chance he had of escaping the patrol's notice. He kept the electric motor in neutral and waited.

The launch moved nearer, its searchlight stabbing the dark waters in an even sweep. The beam first played on the water beyond the Welman. Then the launch altered direction slightly away from the tiny submarine, with the result that the next sweep of light fell short of it.

The launch passed within fifty yards and Tiller could see the silhouette of the man operating the searchlight and of another two men in the boat's cockpit. They were not even looking in the Welman's direction. The launch's engines throbbed briefly and then it was past. The Welman bobbled slightly in its wake, and when the beam of light next played on the water it was no more than a dim flicker in the port porthole.

Tiller wiped the palms of his hands on his jungle greens before engaging the electric motor and easing the Welman forward. The fear of seeing the launch had galvanized him. His eyes were sharper now and as he approached the huge mass in front of him he discerned the flare of the aircraft carrier's bow and the hawse-pipe underneath it and the anchor chain running almost vertically from it into the water. Further aft the carrier's sides were shrouded in a patterned and shaped material that in the darkness made it difficult to distinguish anything. And the huge superstructure of the bridge and funnel, which reared up from the deck on the side nearest to him, was also covered by a material which was kept in place by two huge cranes.

Tiller again brought the Welman to a halt and scanned the immediate area. Beyond the bulk of the carrier was the dockside to which its stern was moored. There seemed to be some activity there, for he could see the lights of vehicles and one or two figures moving around. Probably just a routine motorized patrol, but it seemed to him no place to loiter. He worked the main vent lever to flood the ballast tanks and then eased forward the joystick. The water rose slowly up the front window and then covered it.

Tiller let the depth indicator tick round to fifty feet and then brought the submarine on to an even keel by turning the small wheel in front of the joystick that altered the position of the trim weight control. With any luck, he told himself, the torpedo nets might not extend downwards for much more than fifty feet. But he knew that was wishful thinking.

It seemed that the light of the moon could not penetrate so far down and the water in front of him was pitch-black. He was tempted to switch on the small searchlight the craft carried in a recess in front of the conning tower, but decided it was too risky. He would just have to probe his way through the murky water.

The Welman inched forward through the blackness. A large ray swam lazily towards the window before lifting itself with the flip of a long tail over the hull, the white underside of its wings and belly looming large in the front viewing glass before disappearing. Tiller felt sweat trickling down his face, but did not dare lift his hands from the joystick. If he hit the netting he was going to have to react very quickly to avoid becoming entangled in it. He kept his eyes strained into the murk.

The seconds ticked by. Bits of seaweed and a jellyfish drifted towards the Welman's front window, before vanishing. Tiller's eyes pricked with the effort of concentration.

Then suddenly it was there like a blanket towering over him, and he felt the familiar surge of adrenalin as he put the Welman into reverse.

The netting moved to and fro in the water like a huge, leisurely frond. Carried by its own momentum, the Welman bumped gently against it, but almost immediately the electric motor took effect and the craft backed off. The netting receded into the gloom.

Gradually, Tiller moved the Welman forward again and then manoeuvred it sideways until the side of the hull was scraping gently along the netting. It was the only way, in the pitch-blackness of the water, to keep contact with the netting without fouling it.

For the first time he registered that the depth indicator was at more than fifty feet and the nightmare of the fractured window and the spurt of water hitting him returned.

Saliva refused to come into his mouth and he quickly took a swig from his water bottle and dabbed at the sweat pouring off him. Then deliberately, slowly, he eased down the joystick, allowing the mesh to rub along the Welman's side.

The needle of the depth gauge crept round to sixty feet, and still he could hear the net scraping the hull. He swore under his breath and then out loud. Anxiously, he watched the dimly lit dial as the needle flickered up to sixty-five and then crept round to seventy. The sweat was pouring off him now. Seventy-five.

He had to force himself by sheer will-power to keep the joystick forward so that the Welman continued to dive gently. Seventy-six, seventy-seven. Any moment now the front window must crack and the black water cascade in . . .

The scraping stopped.

Gingerly, Tiller levelled the Welman off with the trim weight control, turned under the net and drew the joystick gently towards him. The submarine started to rise.

At forty feet the water became lighter and the change in the texture of the murk ahead warned Tiller he was approaching the aircraft carrier's bottom. Using the trim weight control, he brought the Welman on to an even keel and suddenly the vast acreage of steel was above his head. Much of it was covered in weed and some other kind of growth which blotched the hull. It looked to him, as he craned his eyes upwards, rather like some huge inverted soccer field.

For the first time since he had left the island Tiller wondered if Whitaker had found his way successfully. He might have been and gone. Or, for all Tiller knew, he could be right next to him at that very moment without knowing it.

Tiller glanced at the depth gauge. It was at forty feet exactly. He eased the Welman down slightly more before adjusting the trim weight control again. Then he turned the midget craft carefully so that he could begin moving along the length of the carrier's hull towards its stern.

The visibility was better now. The water seemed

clearer than it had been and the steel bottom of the carrier appeared to reflect and magnify what light there was.

After a minute or so the configuration of the carrier's bottom changed. First it became flatter and then the four propeller shafts that protruded from its hull gave it an irregular shape. He followed the port centre shaft aft towards its propeller, passing the massive rudder on the way, and then stopped the Welman and peered upwards, trying to find a patch of hull that was clear of any obstructions on to which he could attach the charge. He reversed the Welman gently and then decided on the gap between the rudder and the inner two shafts.

Judging the distance so that he did not make contact too hard with the carrier's hull was going to be difficult, and he decided he would have to risk turning on the Welman's searchlight. With infinite care he brought the craft round and pointed its bows at the spot just aft of the rudder. To make contact he decided he would have to blow some water from the ballast tanks. He hoped that any bubbles which rose to the surface would either not be seen or would be thought to come from the carrier.

He turned the valve screw of the compressed-air cylinder and heard the hiss as the air expelled some of the water from the ballast tanks. The Welman drifted upwards towards the hull. Quickly Tiller turned down the valve screw and then spun the wheel of the trim weight control to allow the Welman's bow to rise and bring the bulbous charge right up to the carrier's hull.

The contact made the Welman rock and shudder,

but in the glare of the small searchlight Tiller could see it was now held fast by the two magnets on the charge.

Tiller switched off the searchlight and wiped the sweat from his eyes. So far as he was concerned, the trickiest part of the operation had now been accomplished. Provided the Welman's mechanism for releasing the craft from the charge worked, he had only the return journey and the rendezvous with the submarine to worry about.

He began turning the wheel that released the Welman from the 560lb charge and automatically started the five-hour time-delay fuse. The wheel seemed very reluctant to turn but after Tiller had wrenched it hard it spun easily enough and eventually he felt the Welman float free.

Hastily, he turned his attention to the trim weight control wheel to ensure that the trim weight compensated for the loss of the weight of the explosive charge. At first the Welman continued to hang bows up. But then slowly, gradually, as he wound the weight towards the bow it came on to an even keel, and Tiller turned it and headed for the carrier's bows.

Away from the carrier's bottom the water became black and impenetrable again. The needle of the depth gauge quivered at forty-five feet but it began to swing erratically and he knew there must be something wrong with it. To his relief there was no netting around the carrier's bows. Either that or he was deeper than he thought. With the depth gauge playing up, there was no way of telling.

He calculated when he was well clear of the ship, and turned the Welman hard to starboard, knowing he needed to gain open water as quickly as possible in order to surface and get his bearings for the return trip.

But as the Welman tilted and turned it struck something, surged forward, was thrown back, and came to a halt, its electric motor whirring. Cursing, Tiller put the motor full ahead and tried to correct the Welman's tilt. But the submarine refused to budge.

He knew immediately what had happened: he had forgotten the carrier's anchor chain and had run into it. He remembered his instructor's advice: if you get into trouble take your hands and feet off the controls and think the problem through. There's always an answer.

He removed his feet from the rudder bars and took his hands off the joystick, and turned off the electric motor. Then he sat on his hands and forced himself to think calmly. He had plenty of oxygen and now was the time to change the cylinder before he started the long trip back.

He found the routine movements of changing the cylinders soothing. They came automatically to him. When he had finished he tucked his hands underneath him again and tried to reason out what was the best way of escaping. He could look back through the rear porthole but he could not see how the Welman was snagged.

He started the motor and worked the Welman backwards and then forwards, but it would not move. He tried diving and then surfacing, but still it would not budge.

Think it through, he reminded himself.

If he jettisoned the keel the upward force of the

Welman being relieved of so much weight might break it free from the anchor chain. But he would then give away the whole operation and, almost as bad, would be a prisoner in Japanese hands. No, he wasn't going to jettison the keel.

Think it through.

He tried to visualize exactly how the huge metal links of the anchor chain could have snared the Welman. The hydroplane, rudder and propeller were protected by an iron bar. This ran in a curve from the Welman's stern to the aft end of the drop keel. It was designed, as were the two wires that ran forward and aft from the conning tower on to the deck, to divert anything that might snare the craft. No, it couldn't be the bar or the parts of the Welman it was designed to protect.

But above the bar, sticking out on either side of the hull, were two small stabilizing fins. Somehow, one of these must have become jammed into a link as he had turned.

Even the links of the anchor chain of a ship the size of the *Hoko* were not wide enough for this to happen. But lengthways it might be possible. And as the anchor chain at this depth would not be almost vertical, as it was near the surface, but almost parallel with the harbour bed, then he could visualize how it had happened.

It followed that he must be closer to the seabed – and to the anchor – than the depth indicator had showed, and the tilted Welman must be held by its fin at the same angle as the chain. He tapped the depth gauge and the needle shuddered back to zero. Great. That was all he needed.

He turned his attention to the inclinometer on the

dashboard and saw that the needle was showing that the Welman had retained the fifteen-degree list that it always took when it was turned to port or starboard.

Despite the loss of the depth indicator he felt a lot better now.

The Welman was listing to starboard. That meant it was between the chain and the carrier, not between the chain and the sea. It also meant that it was pointless trying to go straight forwards or backwards, or up or down. He was going to have to try to move the Welman's fin *sideways*. The only way he could do that was to put the rudder hard to port and move the motor to full power while keeping the craft at the same depth. This would drive the Welman anticlockwise round the chain, like a dog chasing its tail, which would swing the ensnared fin away from the link that was holding it. It wouldn't work immediately because the chain would twist, but if the pressure was strong enough the link and the fin must part company.

He rehearsed the scene once more in his mind's eye to make sure he had it right and then repeated to himself what he had to do. What he did not know was if the rudder would be effective with the Welman tilted at its present angle. Well, he just had to find out.

He started the motor and gave it full thrust, at the same time putting the rudder hard to port. The Welman jerked forward, taking up the slack of the twisting chain, and Tiller could feel the craft beginning to swing. But then it stopped, the motor whirring. Tiller, afraid he might overtax it, cut the motor back, and he could feel the Welman being moved by the untwisting chain.

The inclinometer's needle showed that its angle of

list had altered slightly and he repeated the manoeuvre. This time the Welman surged forward faster. Tiller swore and shouted at it. The craft twisted, tilted and suddenly came free with a jerk that, if there had been room, would have thrown Tiller from his seat.

The inclinometer needle was on nought now. He pulled the joystick towards him and the needle of the depth indicator suddenly moved round to thirty feet. Jerking the Welman back on to an even keel must have made it operable again. He ran at two knots for ten minutes and then surfaced, keeping the front window just clear of the water. The brightness of the moon made him blink. He scanned the harbour in all directions but there was no movement anywhere. Ahead of him was the harbour exit he had come in by. He set the reverse course to the island on his luminous direction indicator, and dived to forty feet.

As he levelled the Welman off he thought that he had been a mite pessimistic. Perhaps, after all, Hazel-eyes would be waiting for him at Sam's snack bar.

18

The commander-in-chief of the Eastern Fleet propped
his elbows on his large teak desk, placed the tips of
his fingers together as if in prayer and pursed his
lips in displeasure. Around him was gathered his
immediate staff.

'You mean only one of the four returned?'

Davidson nodded. 'It seems so, sir.'

Admiral James Manderville sighed.

'Of course, the others could have been captured,
sir,' Davidson added hopefully. 'We mustn't give up
hope.'

'No, we mustn't,' Manderville said. The irony in his
voice escaped no one in the room. 'We mustn't ever
give up that, Commander. But, as you and I know,
the chances of anyone surviving our Japanese friends
in those circumstances must be about nil. The Japanese
don't think highly of anyone allowing themselves to be
captured, especially if caught in the act of blowing up
their ships.'

Davidson could hear the large ceiling fan above him
swishing steadily round, stirring the hot, dank air of
Kandy into a tepid coolness.

Manderville leant back, bunched his fingers and
banged his fists lightly on the desk. 'So the carrier is
out of action?'

Davidson nodded. 'No doubt about it, sir. She's down by the stern. Intercepted signals indicate that her rudder and propellers are very heavily damaged.'

Manderville flicked open a folder in front of him. 'And your assessment was that without air cover the *Kamato* would be unable to operate?'

'Yes, sir. But . . .'

'No buts about it, Commander. Now we find the *Kamato* is no longer in Singapore. She has sailed through the Straits of Malacca and is heading, you have deduced, for the Nicobars or the Andamans.'

Davidson nodded.

'Why there, Commander?'

'She could operate against our convoys from there, sir, while protected by air cover from Malaya.'

'And your assessment is that she won't move beyond that air cover?'

'She'd be crazy if she did, sir.'

A reddish hue began to suffuse Manderville's cherubic face, and his ADC, who knew the signs, inwardly blanched. Academics might be clever fellows but sometimes they were incredibly stupid.

'Crazy, Commander, crazy? Is that the best assessment I can receive from my naval intelligence division: that the enemy's crazy?'

Manderville, in his ADC's terminology, was now spitting chips.

Davidson swallowed hard and said nothing. Manderville fiddled with the folder on his desk. The telephone rang. Manderville picked it up and said: 'I see. Thank you. Keep me informed,' then put down the receiver.

'Well, gentlemen, air reconnaissance has just reported that the *Kamato*, escorted by six destroyers, has been sighted south-west of the Nicobars. She's heading west, not north, at twenty-seven knots. Now why should she do that?'

Everyone looked at Davidson. The Intelligence Officer wound up his courage. 'Kamikaze tactics, sir. She's going to attack Kandy if she can get near enough. Her main armament has a range of nearly twenty miles.'

Manderville looked puzzled. 'But why Kandy?'

'The centre of SEAC. The Supreme Commander is here. It would be a grand final gesture. Who knows, they might even hit his headquarters. They might even kill him. They might even kill you, sir.'

Manderville rubbed his chin. 'You know, I think you could be right, Commander. By our standards they are crazy. By theirs it is a logical thing to do.'

He picked up the telephone. 'Manderville here. Get me the Supreme Commander, please . . . Dickie? Manderville. I thought you should know that the *Kamato* has sailed from Singapore and has been spotted heading this way. Yes? Yes. I agree. Suicidal. Without air support, she hasn't a chance. But I think you'll agree we should put Kandy on red alert.'

He replaced the receiver and nodded to his secretary, a commander in the Supply Branch, who said: 'I'll see to that at once, sir.'

'So what precautions have we taken so far besides air reconnaissance flights?' Manderville asked when his secretary had closed the door behind him.

'We've diverted convoy ME-CA, sir,' said his Chief Operations Officer, 'and have put a submarine screen in place. Also, there are four squadrons of torpedo bombers standing by. Two on the *Tenacious*, sir, which sailed at dawn, and another two at Trincomalee.'

'Anything else?'

The Chief Operations Officer hesitated. 'And the Americans have put a squadron of Super-fortresses at our disposal, sir.'

Manderville rose from his chair as if he had been hydraulically jacked from it. 'The Americans. We can't even defend ourselves without the Americans.'

He swung round, put his hands behind his back and looked out of the huge window that overlooked the Botanical Gardens. Then he turned back and said: 'And the fleet?'

The vice-admiral in operational command of the Far East Fleet said gently: 'The cruisers and destroyers are escorting the *Tenacious*, sir. The battleships have sailed, too, but we're keeping them out of harm's way. They would just get massacred.'

'Massacred,' muttered Manderville. 'My God, Jack, I never thought I would live to see the day when the greatest navy in the world has to be rescued by a squadron of American bombers and has to keep its battleships "out of harm's way", as you so tactfully put it.'

'We don't need them, sir,' the vice-admiral said firmly. 'And they're too old to be of any use. The fly boys will do what's necessary.'

The leonine head was shaken as a great animal shakes its head in its death throes. 'I know we don't need them, Jack. I know that. That's just my point. Well, gentlemen, all we can do is wait. I suggest we go to the operations room, where we can follow the course of the battle.'

The operations room was below ground in another building. As the small group crossed to it the sirens started up, their melancholy, uneven wail piercing the late-afternoon lethargy of Kandy.

The room was new and still smelt of the green and white paint with which it had been decorated. A vast table, whose top was a map of the whole SEAC area, dominated the room. Around it were several groups of naval officers, male and female, and along one wall were a number of radio and radar operators with their equipment. The officers around the table snapped to attention.

'At ease, everyone, at ease. What's the situation, Harry?'

A naval captain stepped forward and with a billiard cue pointed to a number of wooden blocks on the table. As he began to speak several blocks were moved around by two WRNS officers with what looked like wooden rakes used by croupiers.

'*Kamato* is maintaining her course and speed, sir. Visibility is excellent and sea conditions calm, so air reconnaissance is having no difficulty in keeping track of her. Our battle group is here, sir, ready to intercept immediately *Kamato* is beyond the range of any land-based air support. She is approaching the submarine screen now.'

'Hmm. How many have we got out there?'

'The whole flotilla, sir.'

A loudspeaker connected to one of the radios crackled and a voice resonated from the ether. 'Mabel One, Mabel One calling Ace Jack Two. How do you read me, Ace Jack Two?'

A clearer, crisper voice replied. 'Ace Jack Two. I hear you loud and clear, Mabel One. Pass your message. Over.'

'Mabel One's the Catalina over the target, sir,' the captain said in a hushed voice. Manderville nodded.

'This is Mabel One. One-tenth cloud, visibility excellent, am at cruising altitude of 10,000 feet, repeat 10,000 feet. No hostile flak. Hostile destroyers are peeling off from the main target. Over.'

'They must have picked up a sub on their asdics,' said the captain. They waited. Half an hour later a naval rating took a slip of paper from one of the radio operators and brought it to the captain. The captain scanned it and passed it to Manderville. 'One of the screen has sighted the target, sir, and is making its first run.'

Silence descended on the operations room. The officers waited as the radio operators kept track of the messages flying through the ether, both Japanese and English. Within an hour it was known that the battleship had been hit by two torpedoes, but she was now beyond the submarine screen and was still travelling at close to her top speed.

An hour after that the *Tenacious* launched her first strike of twelve torpedo bombers. Only two of these penetrated the battleship's fierce anti-aircraft barrage and only one hit its target. Its torpedo struck near the battleship's rudder and jammed it.

Excited voices from the ether filled the operations room. 'Target veering to starboard, repeat starboard . . . oil slick on port side . . . speed reduced to approximate one-fife knots, repeat one-fife knots . . . we've got her . . . congratulations, Charlie Dog . . .'

Those in the operations room now heard orders for the carrier's second strike to be launched, and the impersonal, measured voice of the air controller marshalling his forces in the air.

The minutes ticked by, then the silence was broken by the leader of the second strike: 'Target dead ahead . . . estimated speed one-fife knots . . . movement erratic but still moving in a westward direction. Am going in now.'

'They attack at thirty-five feet above the surface, sir,' said the captain, referring to the torpedo bombers. Manderville nodded impatiently. He might be a battleship man, but he knew the necessarily suicidal tactics used by his pilots.

The second strike left the battleship dead in the water and listing heavily to starboard. Then the bombers from the *Tenacious* swarmed in and forty minutes later the Catalina pilot reported laconically: 'She's going . . . she's going . . . she's gone.'

Manderville stepped out into the bright sun, paused and breathed in deeply. At least they hadn't needed to call on the bloody Yanks to finish the job for them. Otherwise he felt no particular pleasure or relief – only a sense of weariness at the futility of it all.

TITLES IN SERIES FROM 22 BOOKS

Available now at newsagents and booksellers or use the order form provided

continued overleaf . . .

SOLDIER OF FORTUNE 1:   Valin's Raiders
SOLDIER OF FORTUNE 2:   The Korean Contract
SOLDIER OF FORTUNE 3:   The Vatican Assignment
SOLDIER OF FORTUNE 4:   Operation Nicaragua
SOLDIER OF FORTUNE 5:   Action in the Arctic
SOLDIER OF FORTUNE 6:   The Khmer Hit
SOLDIER OF FORTUNE 7:   Blue on Blue
SOLDIER OF FORTUNE 8:   Target the Death-dealer
SOLDIER OF FORTUNE 9:   The Berlin Alternative
MERCENARY 10:   The Blue-eyed Boy
MERCENARY 11:   Oliver's Army

*   *   *   *   *

MARINE A SBS: Terrorism on the North Sea
MARINE B SBS: The Aegean Campaign
MARINE C SBS: The Florida Run
MARINE D SBS: Windswept
MARINE E SBS: The Hong Kong Gambit
MARINE F SBS: Royal Target
MARINE G SBS: China Seas

*   *   *   *   *

WINGS 1:   Typhoon Strike
WINGS 2:   The MiG Lover
WINGS 3:   The Invisible Warrior

All at £4.99

All 22 Books are available at your bookshop, or can be ordered from:

22 Books
Mail Order Department
Little, Brown and Company
Brettenham House
Lancaster Place
London WC2E 7EN

Alternatively, you may fax your order to the above address. Fax number: 0171 911 8100.

Payments can be made by cheque or postal order, payable to Little, Brown and Company (UK), or by credit card (Visa/Access). Do not send cash or currency. UK, BFPO and Eire customers, please allow 75p per item for postage and packing, to a maximum of £7.50. Overseas customers, please allow £1 per item.

While every effort is made to keep prices low, it is sometimes necessary to increase cover prices at short notice. 22 Books reserves the right to show new retail prices on covers which may differ from those previously advertised in the books or elsewhere.

NAME ....

ADDRESS...

....

....

☐ I enclose my remittance for £_____
☐ I wish to pay by Access/Visa

Card number
☐☐☐☐ ☐☐☐☐ ☐☐☐☐ ☐☐☐☐

Card expiry date
☐☐ ☐☐